TEACH ME

SOUTHERN NIGHTS

ELLA SHERIDAN

PRAISE FOR TEACH ME

"Teach Me has very frightening suspense, a beautiful love story and makes your pulse race for both these reasons. I couldn't put this book down." – Tea and Book

"A cat and mouse game in between a sweet naïve woman and a psychopath with all the right connections... It really grabbed my attention." – Ramblings from This Chick

"I stayed up past my bedtime just to see what would happen. Readers who love romantic suspense will devour this book." – So Many Reads

"The perfect blend of suspense and romance." – Guilty Pleasures Book Reviews

"Chock full of violence, suspense, sex, and romance. Teach Me never stops moving forward, which makes it very difficult to put down, each chapter leaving you ready for the next." – Hines & Bigham's Literary Tryst

ALSO BY ELLA SHERIDAN

Silver Foxes of Black Wolf's Bluff

40 and (Tired of) Faking It

40 and (No Longer) Fighting It

40 and (So Over) Fixing It

Assassins

Assassin's Mark

Assassin's Prey

Assassin's Heart

Assassin's Game

Southern Nights

Teach Me

Trust Me

Take Me

Southern Nights: Enigma

Come for Me

Deceive Me

Destroy Me

Deny Me

Desire Me

Archai Warriors

Griffin Undone

Phoenix Falling

If Only

Only for the Weekend

Only for the Night

Only for the Moment

Only If You Stay

Secrets

Unavailable

Undisclosed

Unshakable

———

For news on Ella's new releases, free book opportunities, and more, sign up for her monthly newsletter at ellasheridanauthor.com.

You can also join Ella's Escape Room on Facebook for daily fun, games, and first dibs on all the news!

Southern Nights: Teach Me

Cover Art Design by Sweet 'n' Spicy Designs

Editing by Rory Olsen

Published in the United States.

To Conlan.

The minute you edged into my consciousness, I knew you were special. Thanks for making me a writer.

1

What the hell are you doing here?

    This wasn't the first time in the last five minutes that Conlan had asked himself the same question. Maybe if he had an answer, the revolving door in his brain would stop spinning, but that didn't seem likely. Not anytime soon. Not with the beautiful brunette he'd come to see sitting close enough that, if he let himself look, he could detect the light dusting of freckles across her nose. But he wasn't looking, and he shouldn't be here, so how had he ended up standing in line behind the thirtysomething latte league? It sure as hell wasn't for the coffee.

    Legs braced wide, he shifted from one hip to the other, the creak of his motorcycle chaps reminding him he could be enjoying a few extra minutes on the Harley before work instead of spending that precious time here, mooning over a woman. Doe Eyes. The first time he'd seen her all those months ago, he'd thought her eyes reminded him of sweet Georgia pecans and skittish does. The name stuck, as had the memory of her eyes—and a hundred other glimpses he shouldn't have taken.

Another name called, another latte dispensed, another shuffle forward.

He hadn't seen those eyes in eight weeks, and yet still he'd shown up every Monday, like clockwork, hoping for one more glimpse and calling himself an idiot. Wasn't like he planned on asking her out. So why the hell did he torture himself with these weekly forays into enemy territory?

Sex. Or sex appeal, at least.

Another step closer to the counter. The move didn't ease the constriction behind the zipper of his jeans. This was what she did to him, thinking about her. Especially now, after so long apart.

The thought had a snort escaping. Ahead of him, Mr. Suit and Tie startled and glanced over a shoulder, but Conlan ignored the look. He was too busy figuring out when "this" had become enough like a relationship in his head that he would think things like "after so long apart." Doe Eyes might appear prominently in his thoughts from time to time—especially *certain* times—but he'd never seen her outside of this coffee shop. And he wouldn't. A quick roll in the hay was one thing, but Doe Eyes wasn't the kind of woman who had one-night stands. He could tell that much just by looking at her. She was a relationship kind of woman, and he was a relationship-phobic kind of guy. Which meant he seriously needed to get a grip—and not on the part of him growing even harder at the idea.

He should be at work. Southern summer heat brought out the crazies almost as well as full moons did, and JCL Security was feeling the impact, juggling cases like they had eight arms, which they didn't. Too many sleepless nights had been spent at his office, especially with the Bennett case coming up. Just a couple more weeks before Thea Bennett had her bastard of a husband before a judge and hopefully out of her life, but the paper- and prep work to get the high-profile bastard there had been a bitch. He seriously needed to—

"Conlan, hey!"

For a passing moment he was convinced the voice belonged to the woman filling his thoughts. But when the high, candied voice called again, he realized it was coming from the counter. The cashier. Tonya, Tammy? Tracy? He couldn't remember. She was blonde with a deep tan he would've deemed impossible in a landlocked city like Atlanta, the shade a stark contrast to her white smile. Stepping up, he threw her a grin. "Hey."

She batted long lashes, almost hiding the way her glance slid down to the crotch of his jeans, framed in his leather chaps. "Long time, no see."

He winked automatically. "It's a long wait between Mondays."

The woman giggled. "Your usual?"

"That's right. Thanks," he said, passing over a ten-dollar bill.

She made change, certain to caress his hand as she laid the money in his palm. Conlan was more interested in the dark Colombian roast another employee was walking toward them. High-octane all the way. The sight of the near-black brew had him salivating for something other than Doe Eyes for the first time that morning.

He reached the condiment counter just as his phone buzzed in his back pocket. Probably Jack. Retrieving the cell confirmed his suspicion.

Where the hell are you? his partner had texted.

Piss off, Con replied, a grin tugging at his lips. The irony that he'd spent too much time asking himself the very same question didn't escape him. In a half hour he'd be at the office and they could both stop wondering.

With a little back-and-forth he managed to cram the phone back into his tight jeans. He glanced around absently, and his gaze snagged on a pair of amber-brown eyes that suddenly met his.

He froze.

Doe Eyes dropped her chin and shifted over the slightest bit, enough that her friend's position blocked her from view, but not before he caught the blush coloring her creamy cheeks.

His cock banged against his zipper as if begging to be let out. The bite of pain caught his breath in his throat. Jesus, what the hell was he—

Don't! Ask. Again. He knew what the hell he was doing here, and he needed to go; he really did. He needed to stop letting his dick run this show, grab his coffee, and get back to reality.

He was restless, that was all. He was a man who needed action. Needed to be doing something, anything, not sitting behind a desk like he'd been for weeks while prepping Thea's case. Usually he worked off his frustration in a way that involved cool sheets and bare skin and satisfaction on both sides, but there'd been no damn time. Just his hand and the additional chafing it provided, which wasn't near as effective—or satisfying. That had to be the reason he couldn't stop thinking about his mystery woman.

Of course. That had to be it.

Popping the lid off his cardboard cup released the rich aroma of ground coffee beans into the air. He lifted his cup and blew across the hot liquid, the sound almost a sigh of relief. He was already reaching for the packets of sugar when black squiggles caught his eye. There. On the part of the paper sleeve now facing him, he could see a name and number were clearly written:

Tiffany. A 470 area-code phone number.

So that was her name. A glance over his shoulder found the cashier leaning across the bar where drinks were picked up, her mounded breasts shelved there, on display. *Come back soon,* she mouthed, her shoulders doing a little wiggle. On reflex, he threw her a grin, but her seemingly seductive move couldn't pull his glance downward. His dick didn't even twitch. Apparently only one thing could trigger his runaway libido this morning.

He added the sugar, trying to ignore the panic in his gut and his one-track mind. The latter was impossible. He wanted to know Doe Eyes' name, *her* phone number. Were her breasts as full as they looked beneath that starched white button-down? Was her hair as soft as he swore it would be when he fisted it between his fingers?

He stirred a bit too vigorously, and coffee sloshed over the side of the cup.

Don't look. Don't. He realized he'd closed his eyes. A sigh escaped as he rubbed a thumb and finger against them, but as soon as the lids popped open, he searched for her. Had to see her. Felt his heartbeat pick up knowing she might meet his eyes.

He was so screwed—and smart enough to admit it. He let go, let the conflict and the churning in his gut and the tension cramping his muscles go. And then he looked toward her table.

It was empty.

"Well shit."

He stood for a moment, cursing himself, the coffee, and everything else he could think of. When another customer stepped up behind him and cleared his throat, wanting access to the counter, Con grabbed his cup and headed out the door. On his way, he chucked the coffee in the trash without a single sip.

2

————

"He's watching you," Cristina teased. Jess ducked her head, but the hot tide spreading across her cheeks was impossible to hide.

It wasn't mere embarrassment. She was mortified. If she could've started her first day back at work anywhere else, she would have, but Cris had insisted. Since Jess began her job right around the corner at Ex Libris Media straight out of college, she and Cris had met here for coffee on Monday mornings. It was their girl time, and Cris would be damned if she'd let what had happened to Jess take that away from them.

Jess, on the other hand, thought sometimes change was good.

That wasn't her lying down and giving up. Yes, she'd been attacked by her boyfriend two months ago, but she'd survived. There were things she was determined to make happen—like standing on her own two slightly wobbly feet. It was just...seeing the man she'd fantasized about for months wasn't one of them. Not now, while she still felt the imprint of every bruise, every cracked bone, every foolish dream across her healed skin. She felt ugly because what had happened was ugly, and no matter how hard she scrubbed, all these weeks later, she couldn't get the ugly gone.

"I love watching bikers," Cris mused, seeming oblivious to Jess's discomfort. "If only I could get Steven to wear leather, I'd be a very happy wife."

Sneaky woman. Who could resist laughing at the image of Steven, all five-feet-eleven lanky inches of him, being swallowed whole by a leather jacket and pants? Not that he wasn't cute; he was just more Mr. Rogers than Mr. Hell's Angels. "Sounds like a good setup for chafing."

Cris choked on a sip of tea. Spluttering, laughing, she finally managed, "Why do you think it has the cutout right there in the middle, huh?"

"For convenience."

"Pffttt." A flick of Cris's hand brushed the idea aside.

"Display purposes?"

Cris tilted her head, considering. "Okay, that too, but..."

Jess shook a finger at her friend. "Uh—"

"But—"

"Uh-uh."

"Je—"

Only one thing had ever stopped Cris when she got on a roll: The Look. Jess used it now.

"Party pooper." Cris's bottom lip poked out.

"Am not."

"Are too."

They both laughed. To Jess's horror, she felt mirth give way to the burn of tears at the backs of her eyes.

"Oh, Jess..."

Shit shit shit.

"That's it. I'm calling Saul."

Jess jerked her head up. "You're not calling my boss. I'm fine. I was cleared to work, and I'm going to work."

"You're not ready."

Closing her eyes, Jess counted impatiently to ten. Cris meant well, but Jess had won this fight repeatedly in the past week—both with Cris and herself. She didn't want to have to do it again.

She opened her eyes and stared straight into Cris's. Love and concern radiated from her friend. So did fear. Jess was intimately familiar with the feeling. And with her decision. No way in hell would Brit take over her life. Saying no to him could very well have led to her death. If she could say it then, she could say it now, when only his memory was here to stop her.

She didn't speak; she didn't have to. Instead she gathered her purse and her coffee and stood. Cris tightened her lips but didn't argue as she got to her feet. Together they made their way to the door, dumping their trash along the way.

Ignoring the slap of summer heat as she stepped outside, Jess scanned the parking lot. Cris would be doing the same, she knew. The fact that both of them worried, wherever they went, about Brit showing up pissed her off. After producing a convenient alibi for the night of her attack, Brit had walked out of the Atlanta Police Department and onto an airplane. Work, or so Detective King had informed Jess. Brit's position as vice president of his father's tech company—and his family's prominent position in city politics—lent legitimacy to the story, for everyone but Jess. Cat and mouse was Brit's favorite game, and what better way to keep the mouse on edge than for the cat to disappear? Two months after she'd last seen him, she couldn't stop searching the streets for his face.

The not knowing had been Cris's primary argument

against Jess's return to work. Jess had acquiesced far longer than she should've, far past the time it took for her injuries to heal. But she had a life to live. She couldn't sit on her rear in a locked apartment, waiting. Wondering. Driving herself closer and closer to insane.

No. No matter what happened, she would face it on her feet, not cowering in a corner.

They came to Cris's car first. When her friend would've kept walking, Jess cleared her throat.

Cris heaved a sigh. "Really?"

"Really."

Cris faced her, looking ready to argue, but Jess wasn't having it. "Move it before you make me late for work," she said, her tone softened by the knowledge that Cris only wanted her safe.

Her friend's goodbye was a warm bear hug that avoided Jess's still-sore ribs. "Call me when you get home tonight."

"Yes, Mom."

Cris's chuckle was watered down a bit by the tears glazing her eyes, but it was there nonetheless. "Hey, I'm not the one you want spanking you."

Jess didn't encourage her by replying. Besides, Cris didn't need to know the idea of a man spanking her turned her stomach. She didn't think she'd be considering erotic games like that for a long while, even in fantasy. She stepped to the side, waiting while Cris started her sporty yellow Nissan. When the car didn't back out, Jess jerked her phone out of her pocket.

Would you go already! she texted.

A smiley face sticking its tongue out popped up on the screen, and then Cris reversed, blew Jess an apologetic kiss, and drove toward the exit. Jess walked a few spaces down to her car, still shaking her head as she fingered the Open button on her key fob.

"Well well well, look what the cat finally dragged out."

Jess whipped around, pain shooting through her hip as it collided with the side-view mirror of the car next to hers. Speak of the freakin' devil. Clearing her heart from her suddenly tight throat, she forced out, "Where did you come from?"

Did it matter? For God's sake, the man who'd tried to kill her—and gotten away with it—was standing between her and freedom. But the thought was all her adrenaline-addled brain could produce.

Brit pushed his blond curls back off his forehead. That was how he'd taken her in, those innocent curls and bright blue eyes. Something Dr. Jekyll-ish would've been more accurate.

"Come on, Jess. Didn't you miss me?" His perfectly polished John Lobb's clicked on the pavement as he stepped closer. Jess backed up, wishing she was anywhere but stuck between two cars and an asshole. When said asshole's eyes lit up, she winced. *Never run from the cat,* she reminded herself, but her legs weren't listening. They took her backward again and again until the thick bushes lining the parking lot poked through her thin summer skirt.

Brit flashed that bright white smile she'd come to hate. "I'm just checking on you, Jess. Making sure you're all right. Come here and give your fiancé a proper greeting."

Like a kick in the balls? "You were not my fiancé. I would never marry you. Stay away from me." She fumbled with her cell. "I'm calling the police right now."

The smile went wide, but Brit's eyes went dark. He clucked in mocking disappointment. "Go ahead, love."

The sound of a car slowing behind her, readying to enter

the parking lot, drew her attention. She glanced over her shoulder as an APD cruiser crawled by. Hope flared for the tiniest second in her knotted stomach. She nearly sagged in relief...until she faced Brit.

He was waving at the squad car. Unconcerned. Smiling that smile.

And why shouldn't he be? They'd let him go before, right? It was his well-backed word against hers, and no one had believed hers. She doubted they'd even bothered to investigate his alibi. Her grip on the phone tightened until she could hear the plastic creak.

Brit took another small step forward. "Come here, Jess."

The words were low, aroused. He wet his lips, and Jess shuddered.

It was broad daylight, for Christ's sake. Why wasn't anyone helping? "No way in hell. Leave me alone."

The last word rose beyond her control as she watched Brit's muscles tense, watched him prepare to lunge. She drew a breath, ready to scream.

"Jess, com—"

"Everything all right over here?"

The words were rough, hard. Strong. Standing at the opposite side of her bumper from Brit, facing the other man down like they were gunfighters at the OK Corral, was her biker. Her fantasy. She blinked, told herself she was crazy, but when her eyes opened, he still stood there. For one second she wanted badly, hysterically, to do something completely girlie like swoon. Too bad there wasn't room in the tiny space between cars for her to fall flat out, but getting on her knees to thank God wasn't beyond possibility.

"I think I asked you a question," the man said.

Brit's eyes narrowed, his hands balling into fists. "Mind your own business, you pr—"

"No," Jess said, amazed her voice could sound so steady when her insides were shaking apart. "No, everything isn't all right. Please..."

The man didn't hesitate to push his way into Brit's space. Part of her fell a little bit in love on the spot.

"I think you should go," he said. Without taking his eyes off Brit, he extended his hand to her. Jess forced herself forward, gaze stuck on that hand as if it held all the hope in the world—and at that moment, maybe it did. She laid her hand in his. Felt his calloused fingers wrap hers up tight. And fell the rest of the way in love.

From one corner of her eye she saw Brit reach for her. Skittering away, she tightened her hold on her savior's hand.

She needn't have bothered. The man was faster than Brit, catching her ex's hand before it ever came close. Brit's skin went white around the man's grip. The air between them sizzled with tension. Jess held her breath.

"Let go," Brit warned, "or you will regret it."

"I don't think so. Leave. Now."

Like a mask falling over his face, the convivial Brit Holbrooke returned. He chuckled, stepped back, calm and cool. Only his eyes revealed the truth. "Of course." Those eyes centered on Jess. "Perhaps we'll run into each other again, Jess, catch up on things."

Her heart leaped to bullet-train speed. "No."

Her savior didn't look down, didn't take his eyes off Brit, but she felt the rough trace of his thumb across the back of her hand. The touch gave her courage. It soothed her rattled edges.

Brit lifted a brow, telling her exactly what he thought of her response, met her savior's eyes for one long moment, then turned away. It wasn't until he'd climbed into a black SUV, backed out, and exited the parking lot that what she'd done hit Jess. She bent forward, her free hand going to her stomach to still the nausea churning inside.

"Just breathe," the man said. He switched hands, one regripping hers, the other sliding along her spine, up and down, hypnotizing her with his touch. When she felt like she wouldn't rattle apart, she straightened, meeting the man's dark gray gaze head-on.

"Thank you."

The words weren't anywhere near adequate, but they were all she had. Her savior didn't seem to mind. He smiled, and a teasing glint lit his eyes. "Anytime. So...what's your name?"

"Jess." A laugh, tinged slightly with hysteria, escaped. "Jess Kingston, damsel in distress."

"Conlan James." He shook the hand he still held. "Knight in shining armor."

"A trait I very much appreciate right now."

Her heart did a tap dance against her ribs, but for totally different reasons than it had five minutes ago. The reality of the moment hit hard. Here he was, her fantasy man, standing right next to her. Staring into her eyes. Touching her. A black bandanna covered his hair, baring his rugged face to her gaze. He wasn't playboy beautiful like Brit, but the sexual appeal that dripped off him didn't need refining. He was bigger than she'd expected, broader; the top of her head barely reached his stubble-darkened chin. His size, like his touch, soothed her, made her feel safe, protected. And wasn't that a stupid, *weak* thing to think. Stupid Jess.

She should step back, let go of the heavy fingers wrapped around hers, but God, she didn't want to. She could touch him forever.

The need was so intense that, for a moment, she couldn't

breathe. And then it passed and she realized she'd been holding her breath. He was still staring at her. "Sorry."

Conlan's hand slid away from hers, almost as if he was as reluctant to let her go as she was him. He cleared his throat. "Is this a regular problem?"

"Brit?" Was twice a problem? Did she really want this man to know how big a problem this was? "Oh, um, no. Not recently, no." Her cheeks flashed hot. "No."

Yeah, I think he's got the "no" part.

He wasn't looking at her like she'd sprouted wings, though, so hopefully she hadn't made too much a fool of herself. "I should...probably go." She gestured over her shoulder toward her car. "Don't want to be late for work."

She turned, but as she moved between her car and the next, that moment when Brit had spoken behind her flashed in her mind. Her steps faltered.

"You know..."

She turned back to Conlan.

He was digging in his back pocket. He pulled out a black leather wallet and flipped it open. From inside he retrieved a business card. He held it between his fingers, hesitating, then squared his shoulders. "Listen, I don't know what your circumstances are, what's going on, but I know when to listen to my instincts. Here."

She took the card. *JCL Security.* The name and a local phone number were all that was listed. She glanced up at him.

"This company does private security here in Atlanta."

So, not his phone number. "Oh, I don't..."

He held up a hand. "Maybe you don't. That's okay. But I happen to know the owner, and they have some kick-ass self-defense instructors who are used to working with women in tough situations. If you need help, call them. Please."

She frowned. "You sound like you're pretty familiar with 'tough situations.'"

"A few." He stuffed his wallet back into his pocket, then offered her his hand. "And even if I'm wrong, it's good knowledge for any woman to have. You should check them out."

"Okay." Stuffing her disappointment at his lack of personal interest down deep, she took his hand. "Thank you, Conlan."

Their palms met, and a punch of heat shot up her arm, tightened her lower belly until she wanted to whimper. She'd harbored so many fantasies about this man. So many desires. And here he was, walking away. Longing tightened her throat, almost choking her as he released her hand.

"My pleasure, Jess." Her name in that rough voice made her heart ache. He nodded toward the business card. "Think about it, okay? These guys are good at what they do."

Unable to speak, she nodded. She didn't want to see him walk away, so she turned first, moving toward her car without hesitation this time. She started the engine, glanced over her shoulder, and backed out. Somewhere to her right, the motorcycle she knew belonged to Conlan roared to life. She didn't try for one last look; she kept her gaze on the road ahead, her mind on getting to work, and tried to forget the man with the power to make her want more.

3

She was gathering her purse at the end of the day when Saul Parker appeared at the doorway to her office.

"Heading out?" he asked.

Jess followed her boss through the door and turned to lock it, a little bubble of triumph bursting in her belly. She threw a grin his way. "Yes, sir."

Saul stuck his tongue out at her cocky *sir*, a move that somehow didn't come across as ridiculous despite his salt-and-pepper hair and the fine lines around his eyes. The courteous hand at her back guiding her down the hall? That fit him perfectly too.

"How was your first day back?"

Maternal tone alert. First Cris, now him. Jess hid her sigh by ducking to search for her keys in her purse. Saul was her godfather, of course, so at least he came by it honestly. Though he looked easily a decade younger than his late fifties, the vice president of Ex Libris Media had been her father's best friend since she was a girl. He'd spent her childhood mother henning her, unlike her parents.

"Aside from my neurotic need to lock all the doors so I can concentrate enough to work? It went great."

Saul's mouth formed a stern line as they turned the corner near the central staircase. "Neurotic? I don't think so. Besides, you're avoiding the question."

He knew her well—sometimes, unfortunately, too well. "Not really. Just clarifying." And more delaying than avoiding. She didn't want him to know about this morning; he'd only worry more. She'd caused the people she loved enough worry over the last few months. The truth was, if she could put aside the lingering nerves from her encounter with Brit... "It's been...good."

It had. Being busy, having her coworkers around and actually talking to someone instead of the four walls of her apartment had felt like unwrapping a cocoon she hadn't even realized she wore. It didn't hurt that security was strict here, either. From the moment she'd entered the doors downstairs and gone through the checkpoint, she'd felt the tension inside her decrease to a low simmer. She worked for Saul in the marketing department, the "public face" of the company, but a secure facility was necessary for some of the more sensitive research Ex Libris took on, especially the government-related projects. Knowing not just anyone could walk in had helped her focus on something other than her personal life for the first time in a long time. She'd been able to sit at her desk, pen in hand, and actually write instead of staring at a blank page. She'd missed that, and the feeling that she was needed more than she needed others.

Saul moved her toward the handrail along the big, curving staircase leading to the first-floor lobby. The sweeping entry would've looked right at home in a Southern mansion if not for the fact that glass and steel had replaced the more traditional wood and marble. She gripped the rail carefully, feeling an ache in her rib cage as they descended. Too much sitting in a computer chair today. She still got stiff sometimes, though the doctor had assured her everything had healed fine—physically, at least.

Saul slowed his steps, allowing her to do the same or stop if she needed to. The consideration had her throat tightening.

"I'm proud of you, Jess," Saul said, his voice gruff, a testament to the emotion also choking her up. "Your parents would be too."

Her parents? No, they wouldn't. They'd be mortified, maybe. Disappointed. Brit had been their choice, after all, a fantastic catch for their wallflower of a daughter. That, they'd been proud of. Not her education, not supporting herself or working at a job she loved. Only that the son of their most socially powerful friends had taken an interest in her. They had loved her in their own way, but distantly, always more concerned about money and position than their daughter's happiness. Jess had stopped worrying about meeting their expectations long before the car accident that had killed them both last year.

She stopped on the last step, hand gripping the rail to steady herself against the tide of memories. "I love you, ya know?"

Saul smiled, that same kind smile he'd given her all her life. "I know. And I mean it. I'm proud of the woman you've become. Your strength."

She couldn't hold back a snort at that. Strong and tired of being a doormat were two different things. The latter just kind of led to faking the former.

Saul ignored her doubt, simply blinking away the shine in his eyes as he returned his hand to the small of her back. "Let's get you home."

Thomas, the head of security's day shift, nodded to them as they passed. "Y'all have a good night, now."

"You too, Thomas," Saul said. Jess smiled at the man before stepping through the glass door leading to the employee parking lot.

She didn't freeze. Didn't panic. She was outside the doors, but she was okay. The thought gave a big boost to her flagging emotions. "I think I'm going to celebrate tonight."

"Oh really? Am I invited?" Saul winked at her.

"Normally, yes, but I think I'll celebrate on the couch." She could feel fatigue pulling at her limbs. Her favorite Mexican restaurant was on the way home, though. Fajitas sounded great.

She ignored Saul's fake pout and reached up on tiptoes to kiss his smooth-shaven cheek. "Thanks for walking me out." She hadn't even recognized the tactic until they'd arrived at her car—he was better at distracting her than Cris was.

"Anytime. Be careful. Oh, and Jess?" he called as she opened the driver-side door.

"Hmm?"

"Welcome back."

Under Saul's watchful eyes, she backed out of her space and drove toward the exit, her mind on salsa and guacamole and savory meat. She didn't notice the SUV until she stopped at the first red light. Big. Black. Vaguely familiar. She puzzled over it until the light turned green, then focused on rush-hour traffic. Twenty minutes later she was pulling into the Conquistadors parking lot. A twinge of unease, left over from this morning, probably, had her circling until she caught another car backing out of a space close to the door.

Jess felt sweat bead up as she stepped from the car, the

wall of heat that met her immediately suffocating—and it was only June. *Southern women glisten, my ass.* At this rate July and August would be truly hellish. Struggling to breathe the heavy air, she moved toward the front of the restaurant—

And pulled up short at the sight of a black SUV parking near the rear. Black, like Brit's vehicle this morning—an Explorer, maybe? Something more expensive? She couldn't remember, couldn't identify a car's make and model right now anyway; all she knew was that it had looked exactly like this one. That was why the vehicle behind her in traffic had looked familiar—because it was. It was Brit's.

Maybe. Or was it? Was she being paranoid? The panicked rush of blood in her ears convinced her she didn't care. She had to go, no matter how foolish it looked. She took one step back, two.

No one got out of the SUV.

Another step brought her to her bumper. She backed toward the door, fumbling in her purse for her phone, fumbling with the keys, fumbling the handle open to shove herself inside. The locks snicked into place.

Her last glimpse of the vehicle, nothing had moved.

She had 911 typed in and was ready to hit Enter when she came to her senses. What was she going to tell them, that she was being stalked by a strange vehicle? She could go over there, see if it was Brit...

No, God no. She needed to go home, where the locks worked and there was no glass to break that wasn't two stories off the ground, where...

She cranked the car.

Her route home was a straight shot, but Jess didn't take it. She circled and backtracked, feeling like one of those spies on late-night TV as she tried to figure out if anyone was following her. After the attack, she'd moved—or rather, Steven and Cris had moved her. They hadn't even put the apartment in her name, not yet. Nor her phone, utilities, anything of public record. It was all listed in Cris's maiden name until they could figure out whether Brit would come back, whether he'd harass her. Apparently the answer was yes, but she wouldn't make it easy. She wouldn't lead him to her only refuge if she could help it.

Even with the air on full blast, she was sweating an hour later as she pulled into her apartment complex. A quick glance confirmed no SUVs in sight, black or otherwise, so she circled around the back of her building and parked her car where it couldn't be seen from the road.

Get out.

Her fingers tightened on the door handle.

Get out.

Panicked breathing filled her ears. It took a moment to realize it was hers.

Come on, Jess. Get out.

A frantic scramble produced her key card. She held it stiff in her right hand, the jagged ends of her keys sticking out of her left, and tried to breathe.

Get out. Go!

The tendrils of hair stuck to her sweaty neck felt like her only covering as she yanked open the door and ran for her building, key card at the ready. She wanted a trench coat, a shroud, anything to take away the feeling of exposure, but all that would help were the solid brick walls in front of her.

She hit the door hard. Fumbled her card through the card reader. *Open the door. Run inside. Open, run; open, run; open, run!*

Only the heavy *clang* of the outer door relocking behind her kept her from collapsing to her knees. As it was, the wall made a good substitute for the floor, it's smooth, air-conditioned surface cool beneath her clammy palms. She rested a cheek against it and forced herself to breathe, to calm. Told herself she was safe. She'd almost managed to believe it when her phone rang.

Eyes on the heavy glass door, focus on her searing lungs, she swiped blindly and answered.

"Hello?"

Silence. She waited, a heartbeat, maybe two. "Hello?"

"You didn't think I couldn't find you, did you, mouse?"

Brit.

Jess sucked in a breath. That hated nickname. Just hearing it made her glance around frantically for the nearest garbage can. There wasn't one, and she swallowed back the nausea, determined not to give in to the control the man was trying to take over her body, her emotions.

"What do you want? Why are you doing this?"

She didn't bother with *How did you get this number?* He was Brit Holbrooke, heir to the Holbrooke technology empire, for goodness' sake! Why had she thought she could hide from him?

"You know what I want."

She did, and the thought made her feel even more sick. She'd never let him touch her again, not willingly.

A pause, filled only with Jess's wheezing breaths and what sounded like tires on pavement. Then, "Come on, Jess, no answer?" He chuckled, the sound scraping up her spine like razor blades. "That's okay. We'll play again soon."

The phone went dead, and as Jess watched, a big black SUV rolled slowly past the door to her apartment building. She didn't have to see beyond the heavily tinted windows to know Brit was inside. She just knew. She watched until the vehicle left the parking lot, heading down the street as if it was a normal car with a normal driver doing normal things. Only it wasn't; she felt it in her bones.

She swallowed hard and, with shaky fingers, dialed the detective who'd worked her case, all the while staring at the door as if Brit would come surging through it if she dared to look away.

"This is Detective King—"

"Detective, I—"

"I'm sorry I can't take your call, but I'm out of the office at the moment. Please leave..."

Jess pulled the phone from her ear. Stupid, stupid, stupid. Of course he wasn't there; it was almost seven o'clock. Clicking the Off button, she continued to stare at the screen, mind racing. A scan of her caller history showed that the number Brit had used was unfamiliar, not the one he'd had when they were together. Of course, neither was hers, but that hadn't stopped him from calling.

Probably one of those prepaid cells. No records. Would he even use it again?

No. Throwing away a phone after every phone call was a pittance compared to what Brit could afford. She briefly wondered if the police could do anything even if Detective King were available. Brit wasn't stupid; he'd know how to cover his tracks.

He seemed to know everything, including how to keep her under his thumb.

No way to track him. No way to retaliate. Was this going to be her life from here on out?

Glancing back down at the phone in her hand, Jess noticed a piece of paper on the floor: a business card. The one Conlan had given her this morning. JCL Security. Brit had all the money and time in the world to harass her, while hiring a bodyguard was far beyond her means. But maybe protecting herself wasn't. She wanted her freedom, and she wanted to feel safe again. Could this be an option?

Taking a deep breath, Jess reached down and picked up the card, the stiff paper feeling like a lifeline between her fingers. She dialed the number. When she brought the phone to her ear, a woman spoke. "JCL Security, how may I help you?"

4

He was supposed to be working on the Bennett case.

Yeah, right.

What was he doing instead? Mooning. It seemed to be a chronic condition, and he hadn't found the cure yet. Nothing seemed to be able to erase the image of a woman with innocent eyes and a fuck-me body. The memory of Jess wouldn't leave him alone, no matter how hard he tried to get away from it.

Jess and the man who'd cornered her. The jerk had been familiar. Did Conlan know him from somewhere?

Did it matter? He wasn't going to see her—or the jerk —again.

He wasn't.

Out of instinct, his fingers settled on his thigh and traced the ridge of scarring beneath his jeans, the only physical reminder of why he shouldn't allow himself to get so caught up in thoughts of a woman. Most of his scars were on the inside, the results of a fucked-up childhood and seeing too many other people's fucked-up childhoods, but the memories the thick scar on his leg evoked were a visceral kick to the gut every time they came up. Lee had been gone for almost five years now, and still his loss felt like a bomb had gone off in Con's chest mere hours before.

He closed his eyes and let the memory of Lee and that night overpower him. It felt like yesterday, like it had just happened—the pain of his wounds, the suffocating heat and choking sand of the Afghani desert, the life-altering sight of Lee being mowed down by enemy fire.

Because of a woman. Because Lee hadn't wanted to live without the one woman he thought he loved.

They'd been the three musketeers growing up, Conlan, Lee, and Jack. Roaming the woods around Lake Lanier, learning to fish and hunt from Con's dad, competing for girls and cars and beer in high school. Only Lee had stuck with one girl: Sarah. So sweet, so innocent. Until she got her claws into Lee. She'd dragged him around by the balls all through high school. Lee couldn't see it, wouldn't dig beyond the false image he'd built up in his mind. She would cheat, and he would break it off. She would beg, and he would forgive her. He'd say he'd had enough, but still he'd go back for more. It was like watching a yo-yo get yanked around for years and wondering just when the tiny string attaching it to its owner would finally break.

It had, in Afghanistan.

The bitch hadn't even given him the courtesy of a Dear John letter. No, a friend had mentioned Sarah's wedding announcement in a note sent with a care package from home. When Lee confronted his girlfriend over the phone, she'd told him their twisted relationship was finally, officially over, and hung up on him.

Lee believed her; when the wedding was held, he had no choice. He stopped caring—about anything.

Two tours in hell and terrorists' bullets hadn't killed Lee; one phone call had. Suicide by the enemy, in this case a boy barely old enough to shave but with adequate muscles to heft and fire an AKM. Lee had stepped in front of a bullet meant for Con, wounded and helpless in the dirt, but it was the relief in his friend's eyes as he turned to face his fate that woke Con night after night, screaming for Lee to stop, to bring up his weapon. It was as futile an act now as it had been then.

Growing up with a mom too much like Sarah for comfort had warped his view of relationships enough, but it was the memory of his friend, eyes blank, blood trailing past his opened lips, that reminded him again and again why he'd never, ever allow a woman that kind of power over him. He could lust after them, fuck them—and he did—even be friends with women, but they would never truly matter. He wouldn't let them in that deep.

Except Jess Kingston, with one sidelong glance from those soft brown eyes, had blown that resolution into as many pieces as the Frankensteined gun truck he'd been bombed out of that day.

Forget it—he wasn't going to get anything done here tonight. He threw a dirty look at the files scattered across his desk. Might as well try again at home, preferably after a long ride on the Harley and an ice-cold beer or two. He gathered everything he'd need and shoved it into his saddlebag. His chaps were lying over the arm of a chair by the window. He strapped them on, threw the saddlebag over his shoulder, and stalked toward the hall.

He could hear Lori on the phone before he reached the front desk. Their receptionist's short, curly hair covered her face as she leaned close to her computer monitor, flipping through screen after screen as she used her soothing voice on the person on the other end of the phone line. He and Jack teased her about that tone, how she could mesmerize anyone with a mere word or two, but given that they dealt with a lot of desperate women in dangerous situations, women who were often at the end of their rope before they found the safety JCL Security could provide, her talent came in more than handy.

"Yes. Right. I'm not seeing..." The *click* of her mouse provided a ticking clock for the long seconds of silence as Lori searched for an appointment. Finally she shook her head, curls bouncing, before seeming to notice Con on the other side of her desk. "Can you hold just one moment, please, Ms. Kingston?"

Kingston. Con's heart jumped from his chest to his throat at the realization that Jess had actually called. Lori didn't seem to notice as she put the call on hold and spun her chair to face him. Her frown spoke her displeasure before her words could get out.

"What's the problem?" he asked.

"Time, that's the problem." Lori's frown deepened. "I have a prospective client on the line needing private instruction and nowhere to put her."

He planted his fists on the edge of Lori's desk, leaning over to look at her computer screen. "Explain."

Lori ticked off on her fingers. "David's on paternity leave with the new baby. Regan is on vacation for the next two weeks, and you are off rotation until the Bennett trial is complete. We're short; all the instructor slots are full."

He turned the problem around and around, but no matter which way he looked at it, the only answer he found was the one he'd hoped to avoid. The reason he hadn't given her his name with the card was because he couldn't trust himself to teach her. Now it looked like he had no choice.

She needed this appointment—she needed help. The sheer pleading in her eyes when she'd looked to him this morning attested to just how desperately she needed it. And he was the only one who could make sure she got it.

He dropped his head, his eyes closing as the weight of inevitably settled on his shoulders. Fate was such a bitch.

When he raised his head, he could see his conclusion reflected in Lori's eyes. He nudged his chin toward the phone. "Put her in at the end of my schedule tomorrow night. Six o'clock."

The lines around Lori's mouth eased. "Sure." She reached for the phone but paused when he called her name. "Yes?"

He wavered, unsure for the first time in a very long time how best to handle the situation. "Don't...don't tell her my name, okay?" He should be the one to explain this.

"Okay, Boss." She picked up the handset. "Ms. Kingston?"

Con didn't stay to hear the rest. He headed for the elevators and the hot Atlanta night. The niggling feeling at the back of his neck, the one he hadn't felt since he'd come home for good, told him trouble was on the way. Even the rumble of his motorcycle's engine between his thighs and the searing wind scouring his body couldn't rid him of it. Nothing could take away what he already knew, way down deep in his gut: Jess threatened every decision he'd made for the last four years.

The question was, would he come out the other side unharmed? Would she? Or would they both carry scars— this time on their souls?

———

STEVEN TOOK her to work the next morning. She hated to ask, but despite his somewhat nerdy-engineer demeanor, he had a permit to carry, and she wasn't leaving the apartment building on her own. So she surrendered to the inevitable and let Steven drive her.

After a workday spent unsuccessfully trying to lose herself in the latest copy she needed to write, security called her a cab. It went directly to the parking garage connected to the downtown high-rise that housed JCL Security. There was not one sign of a black SUV the entire trip. After glancing warily at the dim recesses of the garage, Jess jogged to the elevator, through the open doors, and hit the button for level four with a shaky hand. When the doors slid closed with a near-silent *whoosh*, she sagged against the wall like a deflated balloon.

Jesus, it was starting all over again.

Eyeing the defeated figure in the polished steel of the closed elevator door, she thought back to the day she'd left the hospital after Brit's attack. Her injuries hadn't allowed her to stand upright, and she'd vowed then that she would stand up and face whatever was coming, no matter how scared she was. The memory stiffened her spine, her legs, her muscles, until she faced the soon-to-open doors with the same determination she'd felt walking into that coffee shop Monday morning.

One step at a time, Jess. And the first step would be through the elevator doors.

The *ding* announcing her arrival sent a flush of adrenaline through her body. Forcing her face into a calm mask, she stepped through the doors and into JCL.

The receptionist's desk sat in a tranquil cocoon of soft blue walls, leafy plants, and the soothing trickle of water from a fountain in the corner. More upscale spa than what

Jess had imagined a security company would be, but it certainly calmed the nerves, as did the smile on the receptionist's face. The woman was in her midforties, with short, curly hair and eyes that said she'd seen it all and could handle any of it. A return smile tugged at Jess's mouth as if afraid to disappoint the woman.

"Hello. You must be Ms. Kingston. I'm Lori; we spoke on the phone."

Jess relaxed even further under the lilting influence of Lori's sweet Southern twang. "Please, call me Jess."

"I will then." Lori gathered a clipboard and pen before ushering Jess toward the deep sofa sitting near the water feature. "Let's get your paperwork filled out, and we'll be ready to go."

By the time Jess had signed her name on the last page, the flowing water and calm surroundings had worked their magic. It wasn't hard to see now why the lobby was set up the way it was. Her muscles were loose and her mind free of tension as she handed Lori the papers and followed the woman down a long hall to the left.

"We'll meet your instructor and get you started right away," Lori told her. "You're in very good hands." She stopped at a door almost at the end of the hall and led Jess inside.

A complete workout room took up the massive space. The latest models of fitness equipment marched like sentinels along the inside wall, directly opposite a row of floor-to-ceiling windows allowing a view of the darkening Atlanta skyline.

"Wow. I don't think the gym I used to work out at is this well equipped," Jess said.

Lori nodded. "Our guys spend a lot of time sitting, waiting...seeing some pretty bad stuff. They need a place to blow off steam. Plus," she said, amusement boosting her accent a bit, "it's great for my waistline." Moving farther into the room, she pointed toward the opposite end. "You'll be down here."

The back half of the enormous room was wide open, the floor covered in large blue interconnecting mats. As Jess followed Lori, she noticed a pair of men wrestling on the mats, their sweat-slick bodies tangled into a seemingly inseparable pretzel. Grunts filled the air as the opponents jockeyed for a hold, shifting and reshaping but never gaining or losing an inch. Lori waited until she and Jess stood at the edge of the mat and then cleared her throat.

Both men glanced up, startled.

Jess gasped. *Conlan.*

5

A quick surge of butterflies broke loose in her belly. She didn't even glance at the other man, only had eyes for Conlan as he unfolded his long limbs and stood. How could she have forgotten how big, how utterly sexy he was? Tall, broad, wearing a thin T-shirt that hugged his sculpted body and black athletic shorts that revealed a lot—a whole lot—of heavy muscles and naked skin and a thick scar down one thigh. Her fingers itched to trace that scar.

What had to be a huge, totally sappy smile stretched her cheeks until they ached. She didn't bother hiding it. "Conlan!"

"Jess. It's good to see you again."

The solemn tone, broken only by his accelerated breathing, dimmed the flutter in her belly. Before she could question it, the second man stood...up and up and up. She'd thought Conlan was tall. This man topped him by a few good inches. Like Conlan, he added dark and handsome to his height: dark brown hair, tan skin, all muscle. A trimmed beard and mustache outlined his strong jaw and surprisingly full lips. Brown eyes narrowed on her, unreadable, intimidating. This was no one to fool around with.

"Jess, this is my best friend and co-owner of JCL, Jack Quinn. Jack, this is Jess."

Jack stepped forward to shake her hand, a quirked grin lighting his eyes and making him much more approachable. Jess met the smile with her own and prayed her growing nerves hadn't dampened her palms as their hands joined.

"Jack, it's nice to meet you. I'm eager to learn whatever you have to teach me." Very eager, given the last twenty-four hours.

Jack's grin faltered. He glanced at Conlan. "I'm not..." A deep V appeared between his dark eyebrows. "I'm not actually your teacher. Con is."

For a moment the words didn't register, and when they did, her heart stuttered. Conlan would be teaching her? Her body perked up with a silent *hallelujah!* but the sudden awkward feel to the air said this wasn't necessarily a good thing. At least, not for Conlan, if his frown was anything to go by. "Oh?"

She waited for someone to explain. No one did.

"So...um, why are you here, Conlan?" Maybe that string would lead to others.

Conlan sighed. Jess rubbed her aching forehead.

Jack flashed a smile that would've brought another woman—a woman not firmly entrenched in total fantasy-land over his best friend—to her knees. "Con and I own the security company."

Okay. "Do you normally teach private classes?" Wouldn't that be a bit below both their pay grades?

"No," Jack said. The hint of laughter in the word had her studying him more closely.

"We don't typically have time for one-on-one instruction

anymore," Con said, an edge to his tone she didn't under-stand, "but it turns out we're shorthanded, and I didn't want you waiting for one of our instructors to return from vacation."

That edge hurt. It shouldn't—the man obviously hadn't given her the card so he could see her again. Still, it had been nice to think a man wanted her, or hell, even just liked her. But to know he was irritated because he was being forced to do her a favor...

She squeezed down her panic at the thought of leaving and made herself say what she didn't want to say. "I can wait. It's no big deal."

Of course it was, but she wouldn't force him.

"Or I could teach her."

The teasing note in Jack's voice had her glancing over at him. Nope, she hadn't imagined that tone. The wink he shot her confirmed it.

Conlan crossed his arms over his chest, the thick muscles bulging against the cuffs of his T-shirt. "I don't think so, Jack."

"But—"

Lori giggled, the sound muffled but there. Jess couldn't pull her gaze from the two men long enough to look at her.

"No."

"But you're busy—"

"No, Jack. Don't you have that new case to get to?"

Lori giggled again, and Jack's full lips curved into a smile. "It can wait."

"No, it can't." Conlan's words came out in a low growl. Jess's confusion doubled.

Jack wasn't having the same problem. His blatant chuckle told her he was enjoying a joke she wasn't privy to. "If you're sure."

Conlan's answer was an impatient grunt.

Jack was still laughing when he turned to Jess and shrugged. "Okay. You're in the best of hands, Jess. Don't you worry." He stepped around her to lead Lori toward the door, fielding low-voiced questions Jess couldn't hear along the way. When the door clicked closed behind them, she turned back to Conlan.

He scowled at the door. Jess had a feeling Jack might need to watch his back later.

"Um, what was that about?"

"Jack being an ass."

The words shocked a laugh out of her. "Yeah, I can see that. I meant..." But she couldn't bring herself to say, *What's got your boxers in a twist?* Though that was kinda what she wanted to know.

Conlan shook his head, his look resigned. "Don't worry about it. We've got work to do. Ready to get started?"

Because he didn't sound like he was completely dreading it, and his frown lightened considerably when he held out his hand to her, Jess decided to let it all go and focus on what she'd come here for. "Yes," she said and put her hand in his.

He led her onto the mats. She took her shoes off where he indicated, and followed him on socked feet to the center of the blue landscape, all the while worrying about what was to come. She'd never taken self-defense classes before, but she did have some clue where this was going. There would be touching, she knew that, maybe even full-body contact. Her awareness of him hadn't died with the knowledge that he wasn't interested in her—how could it, with what those shorts did for his butt? The thought of trying to keep her physical reactions hidden while he taught her already had her sweating.

Pretend he's Steven or something, for goodness' sake. Don't embarrass yourself any more than you already have.

Steven. No embarrassment. Right. "Conlan, thank you for doing this."

His sexy black eyes met hers. "My pleasure."

I wish it was.

So not what she should be thinking right now.

Con indicated for her to sit, settling himself directly across from her. "Tell me about the bastard. He's why you're here, right?"

"Right." Hearing Brit called a bastard shouldn't make her feel good, but it did. Now if she could just figure out how to explain. Not that she didn't want to be truthful. There were just some truths that were too humiliating to share. "About eight weeks ago I broke things off with my boyfriend, Brit. He...wasn't happy about it."

"What did he do?"

Jess shrugged. "Hit me." *Basically.*

There was that growl again, the one he'd given Jack earlier, only this one sounded mean. Dangerous. It sent a shock jolting through her, that this man could feel that deeply about something that'd happened to her. Heck, after Brit's attack, no one but Cris and Steven and Saul had even seemed outraged on her behalf.

"And now he's back to sniffing around."

"Yes." She told him about Brit following her home yesterday. "He... I'm just scared. I'm not going to lay down and give up, but I don't really know how to take care of this myself."

"Well, you don't, not if you don't have to. Always go to the police first, get help, find someone nearby. Never face an opponent alone if you don't have to. But if you have to," Con said, his voice dropping into soft reassurance, "I'll show you what to do." He pushed into a crouch, obviously preparing to stand. "Any physical issues I need to be aware of?"

Jess followed Conlan up. "Um, ribs? They still aren't... They're healed, but they still hurt sometimes. I'm told that's normal."

Conlan froze, eyes unblinking. "He hurt your ribs?"

She nodded.

"How bad?"

Swallowing hard at the angry note in his voice, she barely managed a whisper. "Two broken, some bruising. Nothing too—"

"Don't," he barked, cutting her off, "say 'nothing too bad.'" He turned to stalk away from her, his hands rubbing hard over his face and into his hair, which he fisted. "He broke your ribs? You said he hit you; I assumed it was a slap. Not that that's any better, but it's not broken ribs."

Jess cringed. She didn't dare move, waiting instead until Conlan released a huge sigh and slowly faced her. One look at her face had him moving back to her. "Jess." When he got close enough, he cupped her jaw, his touch tender. "I'm sorry. The thought of him... Jesus." His hand tightened briefly, then let go. "Okay, be careful of the ribs. Anything else?"

Nothing that still hurts. Without speaking, she shook her head.

Conlan gripped her wrists. His thick fingers felt tighter than handcuffs but stayed gentle as he positioned her body, hands raised near her face, feet in a sort of elongated L shape. Her palms were sweaty again.

Here we go. Her breath got shorter.

"Jess."

She sucked in a gulp of air.

Conlan tipped her chin up until their eyes met. "It's scary. I know. I've worked with a lot of women who've been abused. Whether it was once or a hundred times, it doesn't matter. You'll be afraid. That's okay. It's part of working through it and getting your power back."

Was that what she was doing? All she'd really considered was trying to survive. But he was right.

The thought steadied her. "Okay." She nodded, not sure if she was trying to convince him or herself. "I can do this."

His fingers grazed her neck as he dropped his hand. "You can. He's already turned physical once; the odds that he'll do so again are high and going higher. You have to pay attention to your safety. I'm here to teach you how to do that."

Because he wanted her safe, not because he just wanted her. Who would, except, apparently, the maniac who refused to take the word *no* for an answer?

The thought made her angry. She tightened her spine. Con nodded his approval.

Folding her hands into fists, he said, "This is to block, both around your face"—his hands coasted down her forearms—"and your chest and rib area. The way your feet are positioned helps you keep your balance." He pushed against her forearms, and she felt her weight shift into the leg positioned a bit behind her. "Now stand up straight, feet together."

She did. This time when he pushed, it forced her to take a step back. There was no bracing if she stood upright.

"See what I mean?"

"Yeah, I do." She could get this. Something eased deep in her gut. She returned her feet to the braced position, one slightly back. "Okay, now what?"

"Now we practice some blocks."

Conlan took a similar stand a couple of feet in front of her. Hands up. Legs braced. The slight smile she'd given him disappeared. He looked a lot more intimidating than Brit ever had. Bigger. Jess felt small standing in front of him, a tiny David to his Goliath. She took a breath.

Suddenly Conlan's fist shot out, right at her face. The sight of the hit coming turned her body to ice. She froze, watching in morbid fascination as his fist opened, his fingers extended, and he delivered a light tap to her nose.

"Come on, Jess. Block. Open your hand and slap mine away." He reset, and Jess swallowed hard.

Another punch. Another tap.

She told herself to move. Think. Blink. Nothing; her feet stayed glued to the floor, her arms up, immovable. The only part of her that responded was her heart, which galloped so hard her chest felt close to exploding—if she could breathe that long.

A hurting grip. Bones ready to break. Screams burning her throat. That voice in her ear. "Mouse."

Conlan maneuvered around, trying to engage her, relentlessly patient with her lack of response. The standoff lasted for what seemed like forever but could've been minutes. Finally Conlan gripped her wrists, forcibly lowering them, and shook her arms out. Her fingers were numb. Con rubbed over them, his rough touch triggering the blood to flow again.

"Just breathe," he said, the deep slide of his voice obviously meant to be soothing.

"I can't." But she had to. She dropped her palms to her cotton-covered thighs, running them up and down her yoga pants in short, jerky strokes. "It's just—"

"Just what?"

A feeling of failure settled heavily on her shoulders. "I'm trying." She swallowed, the dry click grating on her nerves. "But when I see it coming, I just can't... It's like my brain and my body completely disconnect and I'm frozen so hard I can't even move to breathe. It's like I know I have to defend myself in here"—she tapped her temple—"but here"—she held up her hands—"nothing's happening."

"It will. You have to push past it."

"No kidding," she snapped. "You think I don't know that? You think I don't realize that the minute I walk out that door, any safety I might have is going out the window?" She snorted. The sane part of her brain wondered why she was jumping all over Conlan, assured her this wasn't his fault, but she simply couldn't get herself to stop.

"Jess—"

"Jesus, Conlan, I'm the one he attacked, remember? Every time you punch, all I see is his fist coming at me. I remember the pain and my body just...can't do anything." A massive shudder finally broke over her. "I can't... The thought of facing him, of anything... It's just—"

Con drew her trembling form to him. Some small part of her cried at the knowledge that she was too upset to enjoy it, but the soothing hush of his breath helped her own settle into an easier rhythm. Gradually, so gradually, the tension inside her drained away. The heat radiating from all that muscle filled her with an uneasy peace—and an aching sadness.

"This is normal, Jess." At her choked denial, he sighed. "It is. And I'm sorry. I know this is hard. I do. But we will get you through it." He leaned back, his gray eyes dark as they met hers. She wasn't sure what he was looking for, but he stared for several long minutes, searching, digging deep until she worried what he'd see. "Let's try something different, okay?"

Her body felt cold when he stepped back. "Okay."

Before she could comprehend what he was doing, Conlan spun her around so he stood behind her. Steely arms immobilized her instantly.

"No!"

6

Con thought his heart was going to break. As many women as he'd helped, he'd never wanted to give in, to stop teaching her to survive and just hold her and protect her and make sure nothing ever touched her again. Not until Jess. Forcing her to face her nightmares was killing him, no matter how necessary it was. Shuddering sobs echoed through the room, so loud they blotted out every other sound except his own ragged breathing, a rhythmic roar in his ears.

He closed his eyes, leaning his head toward her shoulder to avoid Jess accidentally head butting him. It would be okay. He could get her through this—they just had to get her adrenaline out, and then everything would be okay.

He kept repeating the words, trying to make himself believe them, to make her believe them as he whispered them in her ear and held her trembling body carefully, securely against him. She fit into him perfectly. And how much of a bastard did it make him that he couldn't ignore that fact? He'd fantasized about having her in his arms, but not like this. This shouldn't even register with his libido. But God forgive him, he couldn't ignore her.

Definitely a bastard.

Long moments later Jess's sobs finally quieted. Her breath was wet, clogged with tears, but the jagged edge of panic was gone.

After the last shiver shook her body, he felt Jess take a deep breath. "I'm—"

"Don't say you're sorry." There was only one person who should be sorry, and he wasn't in this room. Con wished he was, though. It would give Con something to focus on besides the pain he'd just witnessed.

Jess relaxed into his hold. The trust she showed shook him.

Get back to work. Back to a normal footing, for both of them.

"Are you ready?"

Jess's chest expanded once more. He could almost feel her rebuilding her defenses, putting herself back together, readying for the next round. She nodded. "Yes."

"Good." He adjusted his hold to just under her breasts. Gritting his teeth, reminding himself he couldn't grab her around the ribs for a reason, he ignored the soft mounds as best he could. "Believe it or not, panicking is an automatic response to an attack."

Jess's laugh cracked in the middle. "At least I did something right."

Without thought he dropped his forehead toward her shoulder again, pulling himself back sharply at the final second. *None of that!*

He teased her instead. "You did. And now you get to do the fun part."

"What's that?"

"Beating me up."

Her laugh was stronger this time. "Bring it on."

"You got it." He shifted his hips back ever so slightly, ignoring his cock's complaint. "So, panicking is normal. If you realize that, you can clear your head sooner. You might freeze, be shocked, disoriented. The first step is to recognize what's happening so you can move past it."

"Got it."

"An attacker expects you to freeze. What he doesn't expect is for you to fight back. Now, I want you to bend your knees. Feel as if all your body weight is settling into the lower half of your body."

Jess bent her knees, the rounded cheeks of her ass brushing his skin. His belly clenched.

Focus. "This is called dropping your weight. When someone is holding you tight, what do you need?" he asked.

Jess squirmed against him. "To be able to move?"

"Right. Now raise your elbows." She did. Immediately, strong as he was, the movement loosened his grip around her body. "See that? If you drop your weight and raise your elbows, you get room to maneuver." He had Jess straighten, and they practiced several times, allowing her to get the feel for the move.

"Good, Jess. Now, targets. Primary targets that are the easiest to go for—anything vulnerable, soft, anything that bends, especially if you can bend it the wrong way. Focus on the face, the ears, throat, ribs, feet, groin."

Jess tried to get her hand up to his face. "I can't reach you."

"Not right now. What can you reach?"

He felt her move, felt the brush of air across his thigh though she didn't actually touch his crotch. "Right. Vulnerability, that's the key. Whatever you can reach, you go for.

How about my fingers, bending them back? Twisting leg hair hurts. It's distracting. Or the top of my foot? All those tiny little bones—if I'm not wearing heavy boots, that would hurt like a mother."

Jess lifted her foot and settled her heel on his toes.

"Good girl. As for weapons, anything on your body that has a point or that you can fist is a weapon, so use it." When she didn't move, he bumped her back lightly with his chest. "Go on; try something."

"What if I hurt you?"

"Don't worry, Jess. I can handle it."

A sharp elbow drove back, headed for his ribs. He shifted quickly, allowing her strike to glance along the edge of his body. "Again."

He ran Jess through several moves, each one simple but giving her options depending on the circumstances and positions she found herself in. When he turned her to face him, he showed her how to ball up her fist, fingers curled, and strike at the face and throat with a hammer-like motion. "Never punch straight on like people do in the movies," he warned her. "That'll just get your fingers broken."

Con let himself fall into the rhythm of teaching, let Jess practice on him and then, full force, on the punching bag. An hour later they were both sweaty, but the bloom of confidence in Jess's eyes was worth it.

"I think that's enough for tonight," he finally said, letting loose a mock groan as he pushed the heavy bag back against the wall where they stored it. "I don't want to overload you too soon."

Or his libido, which was riding him hard. Thank God for the tight fit of his jockstrap. He turned away from the sight of Jess, head tipped back, throat working as she drank from a frosty water bottle, to walk over and grab a towel from the

ELLA SHERIDAN

edge of the mat. The rough terry cloth scraping over his skin couldn't erase the image in his head.

He ached, and not just from exertion, not just from the bruises Jess had given him. He ached from the tight rein he'd kept on himself all night. He shouldn't want her, but he did. Desperately. Maybe some time on the Harley on the way home would help.

Jess spoke, her voice so close behind him that he startled. "Conlan—"

He turned. Jess stood a few feet off, her bottom lip caught between her teeth. She looked shy and disheveled and utterly edible. He barely held back a groan as he stepped toward her, his cock throbbing like a son of a bitch. "Hmm?"

"Could you ask Lori to call me a cab? I took one here from work, and—"

"You came in a cab?"

"Yeah. After yesterday..."

"Right." He shook his head, hoping to dislodge the haze coating it. "I think Lori's probably gone already, but—"

"Oh." A slow flush crept up her neck. "Okay. I'll just grab my phone and call, then."

She walked past him, and before he could make himself think twice, he had her wrist in his grip and had tugged her around to face him. "Don't. I'll take you home."

"Really?"

"Sure." He might regret it, but he wasn't putting her in a cab and watching her drive away. "Let me run to my office and get a second helmet."

That adorable pink color brightened in her cheeks. "You brought your motorcycle?"

"I did." He eyed her. "And you've never ridden on one, have you?"

Excitement sparkled in her gaze. "No. But I'd love to."

He would be her first. Why the hell did that excite him so much?

Damn it, Con, get a grip.

He tried, he really did, but there was Jess, eyes shining, eager and willing and looking at him like he hung the moon. He couldn't resist teasing her. "Well, let's get going then."

He snagged a helmet and his leather jacket from his office. The material protected her but left him exposed, and just the thought of her hands on his T-shirt-covered body made it difficult to drag his jeans and chaps on over his workout shorts. He guided Jess ahead of him with a palm at the base of her spine, not daring to touch her anywhere else, and prayed she didn't catch him adjusting himself as they approached the elevator. By the time they reached the Harley, he had himself firmly under control.

Who knew a pretty brunette pressing her soft curves against his back would blow that control all to hell? And her hands. God, her hands flattened against his lower abs, way too close to his crotch for comfort. When they turned the corner and sped up the on-ramp, her fingernails dug into his muscles, tiny pinpricks of painful pleasure.

He just had to make it to her apartment, that was all. Just to her apartment, drop her off at the door, watch her go inside, and then he could gather his shredded resistance and put this craziness completely out of his mind. *Just a few more minutes.*

When he slowed to a stop at a red light, rocking a bit at the peak, her laughter spilled into his ear. Warm breath played along the sensitive skin of his neck. His booted feet hit the ground, and his eyes tried hard to roll back in his head.

Just a few more minutes.

Just a few more minutes might kill him.

At her apartment complex, Jess directed him around to the door closest to her second-story apartment. The lot was quiet, well lit, nothing suspicious. Con pulled up to the curb directly in front of the door, planting his feet solidly on the pavement on either side of his bike, and loosened his helmet. Telling himself it was a bad idea, he took his helmet off and shut down the bike.

The sudden silence screamed in his ears. Hooking Jess's arm through his, he glanced back. "Ready?"

"No," she said on a laugh. Her smile couldn't have been wider if she'd been a kid in her first candy store. But she leaned into him anyway and slid her leg over the back. Con steadied her as she got her land legs back under her.

Jess loosened her strap and slid her helmet off. "Thank you. I really enjoyed that."

He could tell. The view she provided as she shook her hair out, leaving it windblown and wild around her shining face, rivaled anything he'd ever seen—and made him antsier than being on guard duty in Afghanistan.

He had to get out of here.

"Glad you enjoyed it," he told her. "See you Thursday night?"

"Sure." She watched him stow her helmet in a saddle-bag. "Um, Conlan?"

He slid his attention from her helmet to his, avoiding looking Jess's way. "Hmm?"

"I was wondering...I know it's late, but...did you have plans for, um, dinner?"

The words barely made it to his ears, they were so soft, but they hit him like a lightning bolt. Everything in him shouted for him to say no, to take her up on the implicit invitation while he had the chance. But it wasn't a good idea. He knew it wasn't a good idea. And so he let the silence spin out, caught between should and want to.

From the corner of his eye, he caught the clench of Jess's fists.

"I'm sorry. That was...much too forward. You're my teacher..." Her voice trailed off, but not before he heard the faint wobble underlying it.

He shouldn't say anything. He should let her go inside, let her believe he wasn't interested, let her believe it was something about her that caused him to turn her down when the truth was, it was all about him.

It was the easy out. He couldn't do it.

"I'm the one who's sorry. I can't, Jess."

"Sure. I'm sure you have other plans. Maybe another night, right?"

She said it flippantly, but he wasn't bastard enough to leave her with any hope.

"I can't any other night either." His words caught in his throat, forcing him to clear it. "I can't because...because you're far too tempting."

She stared in his direction, her expression shadowed by the fading summer twilight, hiding her reaction from him. Her voice had lost its wobble when she spoke again. "That's a bad thing?"

He tried to smile, to ease the hit of his words, and failed miserably. "For me, yes. I'm unavailable."

"Married?" she asked sharply.

"No." He shook his head, lips tight. "Just...unavailable." *Emotionally, mentally.* How did he tell someone he was fucked up in the head and therefore not a good dinner/sex/anything prospect?

He lifted a hand to spear roughly through his hair. He

wished he could see her eyes, could make her believe it was him, not her, with the problem. Classic, huh? She wouldn't buy that line any more than she'd buy the truth—that she really was too tempting for his sanity.

"Sure, I get it. It's okay." Those fists tightened, the white of her skin visible even in the shadows.

"No, it's—"

"It is. I-it's fine." Jess turned toward the door hastily, tripping over her feet before finding her footing. He watched her rush the door. "Lesson Thursday night, same time?"

"Jess—"

She threw up a hand, dismissing him without looking back. "It's okay. I'll be there at six."

"Sure," he said softly even though she couldn't hear him as she opened the door and slipped inside. He watched her rigid back through the glass until she turned off, probably into the stairwell. Only then did he jam his helmet back on his head and turn the key.

Even the roar of the Harley couldn't drown out the memory of the so-small voice she'd spoken in. Reassuring him it was okay. Reassuring *him*.

"Con, you are a major fuckup."

His cock, sore from the constant rise and fall of his hunger and rubbing against his jeans, agreed—and it didn't let him forget it all the way home.

7

"How did Thursday night's lesson go?" Cris asked.

"Fine. Normal." Not embarrassing at all. Really.

They were at Brock's for Saturday morning brunch. A quiet rumble somewhere near Jess's belly button reminded her she hadn't eaten since lunch yesterday. Despite another session at JCL, she couldn't get past the feeling of being watched, even inside her apartment. She'd come home from work last night, crashed on the couch in sheer exhaustion, and woken in the middle of the night with Brit's voice in her ear, telling her they'd be together soon. And that was exactly why she couldn't stop seeing Conlan, despite the burn of humiliation every time she thought about Tuesday night.

Unavailable. Right. She only had to look in the mirror to figure out why he was unavailable.

Cris interrupted the morbid flow of Jess's thoughts. "You know what your mama said about frowning like that."

Jess raised an eyebrow. "That I'd never stop being a wall-flower if I didn't at least try to look more interesting?"

Cris stuck her tongue out at Jess. "That your face would freeze like that. Jeez! Whose mother doesn't tell them that?"

"Mine," Jess assured her but smiled at her friend as their waitress set glasses of ice water in front of them.

Cris knew how Jess's parents had acted; they'd been best friends since high school, when Cris had taken a front-row seat to Jess's parents' idiosyncrasies. Now that they'd been gone a year, it was easier for Jess to see them without the rose-colored glasses she'd worn right after their deaths. They'd raised her as they'd been raised, distantly loving and closely critical of anything that would be seen by others as "below their station." They'd given her stability and financial security, but they had not been easy people to live with, nor had they ever stopped mourning Jess's lack of societal awareness. Thank God for Cris's heretical influence or Jess might've wandered through her adult life, compliant but unhappy, never gathering the courage to step outside the box her parents had put her in.

"I still can't believe you're taking lessons from the yummy guy you've been gaga over for the last six months," Cris said as they joined the line for the buffet.

Jess rolled her eyes. "I told you, it's just some basic self-defense."

"Right, and I'm just a little talkative," Cris said, drawing a snort from Jess. Cris usually chattered as if there was a time limit and she had to get a set amount of words in before the cutoff. "Talkative" was more than a vast understatement; it was the quintessential mountain being labeled a molehill.

"There is that."

"Oh, shut up." Cris's amused tone belied her reprimand. "So spill. What happened? I told you I looked him up, right? The company site was very informative. That is one bad, bad boy."

The woman in line ahead of Cris turned for a frosty glance at the two of them from under her broad-brimmed hat. Cris glanced at Jess, the twinkle in her eye saying she enjoyed shocking the society matron. Jess hid a grin.

She couldn't argue. She'd thought Conlan was a "bad, bad boy" since the first time she'd seen him ride up on his Harley outside the coffee shop. She still thought he was the sexiest man she'd ever seen—and by far the sexiest man to ever shoot her down.

Scooping up a biscuit, Cris continued. "What? I'm married, not dead. You'd have to be dead not to notice that ass."

"Isn't that the truth?" Jess asked rhetorically. Cris winked at her.

Plates full, they headed back to their table. A couple of nibbles on her biscuit and Cris resumed her interrogation. "Now, tell me all about the hunk and what you did together while 'learning self-defense'"—she even added the air quotes—"and don't leave out the juicy details."

Since the juicy details were fairly embarrassing, there was every likelihood Jess would leave them out. "Well, he's everything I expected him to be." Including unavailable, much to her girl parts' dismay.

"Woot! I knew it! And he's tall—tall enough to tower over a woman in that perfectly panty-creaming way."

Denying that would be like denying the sky was blue. "Yep."

"Stop making me pull everything out of you, Jess! Tell me what he's teaching you. Do you get to hit him?"

Laughing a little at her friend's bloodthirsty tone, she proceeded to tell Cris about her lessons. Cris's eyes got rounder and her mouth got quieter as Jess described

Conlan's techniques and that yes, she did get to hit and punch and kick him.

"Wow! I think Steven needs to pay for some private lessons for me. I wanna hit on a pretty boy too," she said with a mock pout.

"Well, Jack, Conlan's co-owner, is fairly hot too."

"Great!" Cris smirked. "Did he ask you out?"

"Jack?"

"No! Conlan."

"N-no!" It wasn't a lie, just a little too close to the truth for her to not sputter. If she could get away with hiding what had happened between her and Conlan for, oh, a hundred years, maybe, then she might forget it herself. She certainly didn't want it living on in someone else's memory besides Conlan's; she'd erase it from his if she could.

"You've only been to two lessons. Maybe he's giving you time to warm up to him."

"He isn't."

"You don't know that."

"I do. He isn't." And she really didn't want to discuss this. Her search for a new direction for this conversation turned frantic.

Cris sipped her water, seeming oblivious to Jess's reticence. "That man is too good an opportunity to pass up." She brightened as if suddenly struck with an idea. Jess groaned. "If he won't ask you, maybe you should ask him."

"No, I shouldn't." Not *I already did*. That would lead to *he turned me down flat*.

"Come on, Jess. Take a chance. Put yourself out there. Don't let Brit turn you off dating. The guy's not worth it."

Why did every conversation about her love life have to revolve around Brit? The only person not thinking the man dominated her love life was Jess, and it pissed her off. "He didn't. He isn't. I did. I mean, well, I didn't— Not—" She groaned again.

"You did what?"

Jess toyed with a bite of omelet on her plate. "I did...ask him out."

"And?"

The bite went into her mouth, giving her time to think. Cris's demanding gaze made the food stick in her throat.

"Spill. What did he say?"

"He said no," Jess mumbled.

"No!"

Cris's shriek drew the attention of every table within a hundred-foot radius.

"Would you hush?" Jess hissed.

"Only if you don't." Despite her demand, Cris lowered her voice. "What happened?"

Jess explained, her face getting hotter by the minute. It was a bit like lancing a blister—something that hurt and that she'd prefer to do without an audience, but once she got all the bad stuff out, she didn't feel quite so wrecked over the whole thing.

Cris didn't laugh. That helped.

She wasn't daunted either. "If there's no ring on his finger, he might just be commitment-phobic. Or gay." She thought that over while she watched Jess dabble her fork in the syrup coating her pancakes. "Maybe he prefers the straight-to-bed approach. You should ask him."

"Absolutely not," Jess said hoarsely, but the response sounded weak even to her. Visions of being in bed with Conlan did that to her.

"You don't want to get laid?"

By him? Yes. "No."

Cris smacked Jess's unoccupied hand lightly. "Don't lie

to me." Her tone turned sly. "It would probably be good for you, you know. Very good. Although, from the look of him, good might be an understatement."

Restraining the urge to bang her head against something, Jess forced a playful—and patently false—note into her voice. "Hey, if I was gonna practice on someone, Conlan would surely be first choice. I think my dance card's full at the moment, though." She glanced down at her half-empty plate, then at Cris's still-full one. Her friend had barely touched more than a corner of her biscuit. "I thought you were starving."

"Hm? Oh...yeah, not so much."

This from the woman who ate like the proverbial horse. And was looking everywhere but at Jess. Jess wasn't the only one who knew how to prevaricate. "What's wrong?" she asked.

Cris folded her hands in front of her. "Just a bit nauseated. It comes and goes. That happens when you're pregnant."

Jess froze. Pregnant? "What?"

A sweet, dreamy smile curved Cris's lips. She actually blushed. "I'm pregnant."

"Cris...wha— I can't... You're pregnant?" Jess slid from the booth and swung to the other side to gather her friend into a fierce hug. "That's wonderful!"

Cris hugged her back. "It is."

Something about Cris's tone started a warning niggling at the back of Jess's brain. She leaned away to get a good look at her friend's face. "Is everything okay? Have you seen a doctor? What's going on?"

"Whoa!" Cris chuckled at the onslaught of questions. "You're the first person aside from my doctor to know. Let me enjoy it a minute."

So there was something wrong. Jess returned to her seat, darting a glance at the table as if she could see through it to Cris's stomach.

Once Jess was settled, Cris cleared her throat, then spoke, her tone soft but firm. "We're okay right now. We found out a couple of weeks ago—"

"A couple of weeks!"

"Yes." She sighed. "A couple of weeks. I'd done a test, but I was spotting... We didn't know for sure what would happen." She shrugged, but Jess could see the hint of worry in Cris's blue eyes. "The doctor's been keeping a close eye out. We got the call yesterday that things look good. Hopefully we're out of the woods."

Jess reached across the table, securing Cris's hand in a tight grip. "Okay...okay. What does he say?"

"That we obviously needed to use a different birth-control method." A grin played across Cris's lips and drew a mirroring one from Jess. "We were talking about it but still being careful, but obviously this little one didn't want to wait any longer. My hormone levels are going up steadily, just like they should. We're both fine—if you discount the way he or she is jerking around my appetite. I'm like a yo-yo, hungry one minute, barfing the next."

Jess struggled to smile through her worry. "How far along?"

"About six weeks. It's early days still. We wanted to tell you, but—"

Yeah, but. Things hadn't exactly been normal for her the past six weeks. She understood why Cris wouldn't want to give her something else to worry about.

She shoved that aside to focus on Cris. "That puts you due in..."

"April. No sultry Southern summer for this pregnancy, at

least at the end." She patted her still-flat tummy, ducking her chin to direct her words downward. "You sure timed that right, baby."

Jess listened for the next hour to baby plans and baby names, anything baby-related that filtered into Cris's stream of consciousness. It was as if holding back the news had bottled up a dam, and now the dam had broken and everything behind it just gushed out.

And if a little envy mixed in with Jess's worry for her friend, she ignored it. And the pictures that flashed through her mind of exactly what she would have to do to get pregnant. With Conlan. It was never going to happen. She had to get a grip on that reality before she went down a path that would only lead to heartache.

Cris finally swung from nauseated to hungry, and they talked a bit longer while she ate. Not until they were walking out to their cars did she return to the subject of Conlan.

Keys jingling, Cris shaded her eyes from the glaring sun. Her voice went low and serious. "Listen, Jess...don't wait, okay? If you want this guy, go get him." She pulled Jess into a hug, whispering in her ear. "Don't let Brit steal any more than he already has. You've started living your life again. Now you have to fight for what you want. 'No' isn't such a tough price to pay for taking a chance."

Jess watched Cris get into her car before walking toward her own, thoughts of Tuesday night spinning in her head. It had hurt, having Conlan tell her no. But not like having her ribs broken or her head bashed against the floor. She was tired of being afraid, and even more tired of being alone. Conlan was strong, safe, sexy. Perfect. And he made things tingle that had never tingled before. Her body begged to just share his airspace.

She didn't know what he meant when he said he was unavailable. Could she take one more chance if it led to the possibility of having him in her bed, for even one night? Maybe Cris was right—maybe he would be up for sex as long as commitment didn't come into it. It wasn't her ideal, but she'd take it with Conlan.

One more chance. As she slid into the heated interior of her car, she caught sight of herself in the rearview mirror and stared straight into her own eyes.

One more chance.

You never know. Maybe he'll say yes.

8

"Lie down."

Anticipation roughened the words more than Con would've liked, but damned if he could do anything about it. He'd been thinking about tonight's lesson since the last one had ended Thursday. And vowing not to give in to temptation, no matter how hard it was to ignore. Teaching Jess to defend herself was more important than his libido. She needed every tool he could give her just in case, by some slim chance, Brit was able to get to her in an unguarded moment.

Which sounded all noble and shit. Too bad his cock wasn't listening.

Jess's eyes were round saucers as she stared at him kneeling on the mats. "What?"

He waved a hand at the cool blue surface beneath his knees. "Down. Come on, Jess."

She licked her lips. Even having to hold back a groan, he appreciated the fact that Jess didn't live behind pretenses. All that she was, all that she felt was right out there for anyone to see—and what he could see was that she wanted to be beneath him as much as he wanted her to. If that made it even harder to keep himself professional, well, there were worse things to have to deal with.

But under the heat in her eyes—oh yeah, she knew where this was going too—he could see the beginnings of fear. His heart clenched. He held out his hand, coaxing her like the doe she'd once reminded him of. "It'll be all right, I promise."

Jess took his hand, easing down to sit in front of him, then lay carefully on her back. Her thick hair spread over the mat like it would a pillow. Her curves were emphasized by the slim fit of her workout clothes, the perfect mounds of her breasts a mouthwatering temptation he tried hard to ignore. He clenched his teeth, focused his gaze on her face instead of her body, and scooted closer to set his palms on her knees. "Open."

Slowly Jess slid her feet out, allowing him access to the narrow V between her legs. It shouldn't have been erotic—it never had been before. But he was learning fast that Jess wasn't any other woman, and everything with her made him think of sex. Covering her as he was about to do would cause a major glitch in his ability to compartmentalize his libido from his teaching.

Leaning over, he settled his heavy weight above her, keeping to his knees and elbows. Every fantasy he'd had that included getting Jess into this position, every minute he'd spent jacking off imagining this, scrolled like a porn film through his mind, and his shaft jerked against his lower belly.

He ignored it.

Grabbing her hands, he trapped them securely above

her head. The move stretched him out along her body, brought her breasts higher until the tops brushed his chest. Damn it, her nipples were hard. Jess stared up at him, trust and a hint of hunger in her eyes. He had to earn one or the other, but he couldn't earn both. *Get to work.*

"The hardest time not to panic is when you're trapped," he said, his voice sounding like he'd swallowed gravel. "Just remember, if you still have your clothes on and his hands are holding yours down, he can't rape you, can't hit you. He has to move *something* in order to further his goal, and it's when he moves that he's vulnerable." He demonstrated by adjusting his grip, transferring both her hands to one of his before shifting so he could lift his free hand toward her breast. That close, he had to swallow hard before he could get more words out. "See how my body tips to the side? Shifting my weight puts me off balance. Now's the time to make your move."

"What move is that?" Her voice sounded breathy, aroused but trying to hide it. Sweat gathered on his upper lip.

"It's called bridging. I want you to form the shape of a bridge with your body. Lift your hips as far off the floor as you can, creating an arch from your shoulders to your feet, knees in the air."

"Like the backbends we used to do as teenagers?"

"That's it."

The moment she started to lift her hips off the floor, he knew he was on thin ice.

"Umph. Like this?"

"Yeah, that's it." A near-silent groan welled in his throat as her pelvis brushed his erection.

A blush crept across her cheeks. "Sorry."

He cleared his throat. *Ignore it.* "Try to lift your weight up and tip me to one side, giving you room to maneuver—that's the objective when you're standing up, and it's the objective when you're on the ground. Make room, strike out if you can, get away. Same objective; same targets too."

"Same objective; same targets." Jess caught her lower lip between white teeth, her concentration palpable as she seemed to consider that. "Okay."

She lifted, tipped. Conlan gave way, allowing her to push him off. A moment's reprieve, not much. Not enough to catch his breath before he moved back over her. Jess opened her legs to him willingly. The feel of her soft thighs against his hips was way too good. What he planned to do next, though, threatened to destroy him.

"Now the real thing." Settling his hands on either side of her shoulders, he laid his entire weight down on her. *Holy fucking hell.* She was soft beneath him, so sweet, from the cradle of her hips to those full lips mere inches from his. She wasn't breathing either. As he watched, her pupils dilated, almost as if she needed to take in as much of him as possible. His cock thumped hard against his jockstrap, pressing into her lower stomach.

Nowhere to run, nowhere to hide.

His gaze locked with hers. Jess sucked in a breath, pushing her breasts harder against the solid wall of his chest. The breath choked off midstream.

If it weren't for the flush of hunger riding her cheeks, the need reflected in her eyes, he would be worrying about a sexual-harassment suit right now. The clues were there, though, even if he hadn't known from her invitation Tuesday night: she wanted him, maybe as much as he wanted her. And damned if that nagging voice that was supposed to be reminding him what a bad idea this was, replaying images of Lee to warn him, hadn't gone silent beneath a swell of the most painful need he'd ever experienced in his life.

"Ready?" Jess asked.

"Huh? Oh, yeah. I'm ready."

There, that hadn't sounded too horny—

She shoved up abruptly, surprising him—man, she learned fast—and brought her elbow around toward his temple in the same moment. As he tried to counterbalance her move and keep himself atop her, a solid strike landed on the side of his head. He jerked back instinctively, his weight working against him, pulling him even farther off balance, and at the same time, Jess curled a foot up to her middle and struck out, landing a concrete kick to his chest. Laughing, rolling away, Con put his hands up defensively.

"I give! I give!" he said, but she was having none of it. Jess scrambled on top of him, reversing their positions as she straddled his hips, her hands pinning his beside his head. A smug smile lit her face.

"Gotcha!"

"Oh, now you're asking for it," he growled. Twisting his hands, he circled out of her grip, forcing her to scramble for position as he bridged and rolled. She shrieked as her back hit the mat but managed to get one knee tucked up to her chest. Con landed with his elbow near her head, his weight already tipped. Jess, seeing her chance, pushed, the press of her knee sending him back over onto the mat. With a firm grip on her shoulders, he took Jess with him.

She hovered above him, her hair hanging in a curtain around her face, shielding them in their own private space. Laughing. The light in her eyes pulled him in. Without thought he speared his fingers through the thick brown strands of her hair, needing to feel them, to feel her—to hold some small part of her to him. Only when she moaned did he realize what he'd done.

"Jess, I—"

She blinked down at him, once, twice, then leaned in, and her lips settled deliberately against his.

9

W armth and salt and man. He tasted so good she knew she'd never regret taking advantage. And his lips were a perfect fit. He didn't jockey for position; he used his grip in her hair to adjust her, control her, put her exactly where he wanted her. Oddly enough, the thought didn't generate panic. She knew he wouldn't hurt her.

A trickle of sweat seeped down the crevice between her breasts, but it had nothing to do with exertion and everything to do with the hunger burning inside her.

Conlan's tangled fingers drew her away. She held her breath, afraid of what he'd see, afraid he'd call a halt. The opposing fears warred inside her head as she waited. When he didn't move, she tried to, needing him, wanting him, but he tightened his hand in her hair, holding her still. She fought the moan that struggled to escape.

Conlan heard it anyway. Enjoyed it. "That's right," he crooned, his warm breath highlighting the wetness of her lips. "Tell me all about it, baby."

"Con, please..." *Don't stop. Don't turn me away. Don't say no.*

He didn't; instead he brought her down to him, nose to nose, eyes locked. He slid the tip of his tongue along the open crease of her mouth. This time, wanting to please him, she let her moan whisper out into the tiny space that separated them.

He rewarded her with the delicate rub of his lips across hers. With short, rough nips that made her head spin. The soft touches tenderized her heart; the hard ones revved her higher. Only his grip kept her anchored in the moment—his grip and her need for more. She couldn't help pushing forward, pressing, needing his tongue in her mouth, begging for attention until at last his firm lips settled atop hers with a hard, hungry pressure that caused a loud whimper to escape.

God, he could give her lessons anytime if they all ended like this. The man was an expert, and not just in self-defense. He made her hunger in a way she'd never experienced before, to the point where the past, the fear, the uncertainty fell away and all that was left was him. So good, and yet still not enough.

And, maybe, not enough for him too. He tilted his head, his mouth slanting solidly over hers, his tongue taking advantage of her parted lips and delving inside, heavy and searing hot. He explored her, rasped across her teeth, smoothed the inside of her lower lip, traced the ridges along the roof of her mouth. His hands gripped tight at her hips, his hold unbreakable, conquering her even as she surrendered. Giving him words was impossible, but she gave him sounds, little tiny mews that couldn't have been clearer if she'd tried—except she could, when his mouth gentled and his power mixed with tenderness. She speared her fingers through his short hair, mimicking his hold, and said the only word her brain could come up with. "Yes."

That seemed to be all the direction he needed. He released her hair, freeing his fingers to trace the heated skin of her neck, her shoulders, her back. Her T-shirt was so thin she might as well have been naked. All the better to feel his touch—if she'd been truly bare, her heart might give out. His hands on her body, the heat of his firm belly between her spread legs. The craving to be closer to him, to feel his skin, his muscles, his rigid length against all of her built and built and built—and still she arched over him, unable to tip herself over the edge of restraint. When Conlan's hand smoothed down to rest on the sensitive small of her back, circling, demanding, urging her to lie flat against him, she whined her frustration into his mouth.

Conlan separated them, his breath a harsh rasp in the silent room. Jess let her head hang from his grip, down between her shaking arms, and tried hard to breathe with him.

"Damn, woman."

A ragged laugh escaped. And then a gasp as, with heart-stopping ease, Conlan clasped her rigid forearms and pushed her up. Her elbows bent, folding in as if obeying his unspoken command, and then he had her against him, laid out along his torso. Beneath her, he opened his mouth to take hers, controlling her even flat on his back, his kiss hard and rough and possessive. It was all Jess could think about until his hands gripped her hips and pushed, centering her over the rigid shaft along his lower belly.

A strangled sound burst from Conlan's throat, half laugh, half groan. It sent pleasure shooting through her, mixing with the eye-rolling feel of his sex against hers. Rough hands grasped the waist of her yoga pants and pushed, forcing the fabric down to rest below her butt cheeks. Embarrassment choked her until his palms, burning hot, cupped her there, covering her, kneading her. Holding her still as he ground his erection between the spread lips of her core.

Frantic, desperate, their searching mouths and hands and hips came together in ferocious need. Jess was lost in Conlan's dark taste, the scent of him filling her lungs, the rhythm of his hips taking her over into mindless want. Nothing else mattered. Nothing else existed.

A primal moan rumbled deep in his chest. Her nipples tightened in response, and she wished so many layers didn't separate them. She wanted to feel his skin under her hands, against her naked breasts. Just the thought of his mouth on her sensitive nipples, drawing, sucking, tightened something deep in her belly, as if a cord attached her clit and her womb and the tension was twisting so tight she wouldn't last until the breaking point.

Conlan tore his mouth away from hers. "Jess—"

Tap tap tap.

Conlan's hips lifted off the mat, driving harder against her.

Tap tap tap. "Con, are you still here?"

Jess jerked at the sweet voice breaking through the fog inside her head. Breath sharp, fast, she tried to make sense of the sound until her world tilted. Conlan sat up, not even bothering to lift her off him. His arms were solid around her, keeping her safe, holding her to him, but nothing could erase the swift heat of humiliation when she realized what that voice meant. Lori had come into the room, was probably looking straight at her.

Or at her bare butt.

A hasty grab for her pants found them already pulled

ELLA SHERIDAN

back up to her waist. She dared a glance at Conlan, but he was staring toward the door. If it weren't for the red flush across his cheekbones, she would think he'd been totally unaffected by what just happened. Of course, with their bodies so close together, another part of his anatomy also served as evidence that she hadn't just imagined the hunger between them.

Thank God.

"Lori?"

An embarrassing pause stretched out. Finally, a hint of laughter in her voice, Lori called, "I'm sorry. I thought you'd be..."

Teaching? Jess turned her head, catching a glimpse of Lori lingering by the doorway. The receptionist was trying hard not to smile—unsuccessfully.

A suspicious hitch interrupted Conlan's breath. "Did you need something, or are you just here to cramp my style?"

"I needed your signature. Cramping your style is a bonus," Lori said.

Oh God. First Conlan turning her down, and now this. She just couldn't catch a break, could she?

Another hitch from Conlan spilled into laughter. He still held her against him, so she didn't have much maneuvering room, but she managed to squeeze in a punch to the meaty part of his biceps.

"Ow!" he wheezed. And laughed harder. A feminine chuckle near the door had Jess hiding her face. Where was her freaking protector now? Oh, right. Laughing at her. Or with her. Or at the situation... Whatever. All she could do was wait it out and pray that, just this once, the floor really would open up and swallow her whole.

Easing back into a lazy chuckle, Conlan stroked a hand

72

along her spine and called out to Lori, "Just put the papers on my desk. I'll take care of it first thing in the morning."

"You got it, Boss. I'm headin' out." The sound of footsteps, then, "Night, Jess."

Jess waved behind her without raising her head. Not until the *snick* of the door confirmed its closing did she dare to look up at Conlan again.

"Well, that works almost as well as cold water."

Jess raised both eyebrows. "Really? And you would know this because...?"

"Because I've experienced it often this week," he said, the words light despite the weight of their meaning. Without elaborating, he shifted her on his lap, and Jess's grip on him tightened as his hard shaft slid along her sensitized clit. A strangled sound escaped without her permission.

Conlan tugged her chin up to give her a quick, hard kiss that said he felt the same. He leaned forward, and their foreheads met. Jess closed her eyes. He couldn't keep this up, hungry one moment, tender the next. Her heart couldn't take it. If she was going to do this—and her presence on his lap, against his erection, said she was—she had to keep her heart free. The world had taught her long ago not to hope for miracles; she wouldn't believe Conlan could be the first.

Still, the touch of his skin and the feel of his breath calmed her, eased the cold sting of embarrassment.

He held her for long minutes, and when he finally pulled away, he took the earlier warmth and freedom with him. Her skin constricted, threatening to choke her. Obviously the mood was dead, but she wished it wasn't. *Back to square one.*

Forcing her feet to move, she managed to stiffen her muscles enough to stand. Conlan followed, and a glance up confirmed that the laughter was gone, replaced by a pensive look that didn't bode well for the rest of tonight. Not knowing what to say, she opened her mouth anyway, but Conlan got to it first.

"We need to talk."

———

AFTER CHANGING out of their workout clothes, he led her across the fourth floor to the opposite side of reception, down another hallway, and into what she presumed was his office. His, Jack's—she didn't care if it was a supply closet at this point; she was too busy trying to figure out what the hell he wanted to talk about. What had she done wrong? Had he not liked something?

Maybe he hadn't wanted his employee to know he was having sex with a client. The thought that he might be ashamed of being with her made her cringe.

And then she took a good look at him as he turned to lean his hips against a big-ass desk taking up way too much space, and realized...she didn't care. If he had a problem, it was his problem, not hers. She wasn't accepting blame for another man's emotions or thoughts—she'd done that once, and she wouldn't do it again. She was responsible for her, no one else.

"Come here," he said gruffly, holding out his hand.

She moved to him. Conlan took both her hands in his, the way young girls did, almost as if he would start swinging them. The refrain from "London Bridge" whispered through her head, and Jess had to fight a nervous desire to laugh.

"I told you I was unavailable."

And yet I threw myself at you. That she had to take

responsibility for. She hadn't taken his no for no. She flinched. "I'm sorry."

"Don't. This is not your fault." A sigh escaped, loud in the quiet between them. He raised his head and stared hard into her eyes. "I've been giving you some pretty mixed signals."

A frown pinched the skin between her eyes. He had, kind of. So... "Why?"

"Because I want you. Because the heat between us burns me alive."

"So it is mutual." At least her instincts hadn't got that wrong.

Conlan lifted a sleek brow. "There is absolutely no doubt about that, sweetheart. When I've got you against me, my cock could pound nails. I want you until the burn wipes out any good judgment I might have. It would take hours, days of you beneath me before I could get this god-awful need out of my veins."

Her belly clenched. No one had ever needed her, wanted her like that. She was wallflower Jess, invisible to everyone but, apparently, Conlan. The idea that this big, beautiful man saw her... God. What could she say to that?

Before she came up with an answer, Conlan went on.

"But I don't want you to expect something I can't give."

"And that is?"

"Commitment."

She swallowed. Silence.

Her nerves stretched and stretched and stretched, so far she thought they'd snap. "So, let me make sure I understand this. You say you're unavailable, but what you really mean is you're available for a fun time in bed but not, what, a relationship?"

"Exactly."

It was her second-best option, so why wasn't she happy? "Why?"

He left the desk, left her to walk toward the wall of windows lining one side of the office. Con lifted a muscled arm to rest his forearm above his head on the glass. "Do you know what JCL stands for?"

"No." *Does it matter?*

"It stands for Jack, Conlan, and Lee."

"Who's Lee?"

"He is...was...best friends with Jack and me growing up. He died." A heartbeat. Two. "We were on tour in Afghanistan. I was wounded in a convoy attack. Lee was killed trying to save me."

Her chest ached just picturing it. To watch a friend die right in front of you... But— "What does this have to do with us?" She wasn't heartless to his pain, but she *was* confused.

"He did it on purpose. His girlfriend dumped him a couple of weeks before. Told him he wasn't worth waiting for. Truth was, she'd found someone else as soon as he was out of sight."

"So she was a bitch."

He choked out a brittle laugh. "She was." He dug a rough hand through his hair again, as if he could pull his tension out along with a few strands. "She was, and she wasn't the only one."

It was Jess's turn to be silent.

"The three of us, we met in middle school." Conlan turned to rest against the window, those thick arms crossed over his chest. "Lee's mom was already out of the picture; we never did figure out where she ran off to. Jack's mother died the year before"—a brush of his hand said that was a story for another time—"and my mother, Delia, died in a car accident that year."

"I'm sorry."

"Don't be. Delia was almost as much of a bitch as Sarah. Not at first; at first she was everything she thought my dad wanted. Until she realized she had to share him with me. Then she got very unhappy very fast." He shook his head. "The only good thing about my childhood was that my dad saw it happening and did his best to protect me from it."

Something in his tone shook her, and that word, *protect*. Had Delia been more than just a bitch? Thinking about the little boy he must've been, how vulnerable his body and spirit would've been, made her heart ache.

"So..."

"So." He raised his head to meet her eyes. Steel glinted in his darkened pupils. "My dad managed to get free—and me with him. Lee wasn't so lucky. Even knowing Sarah had cheated on him, was planning to marry someone else, for fuck's sake, he loved her anyway. He loved her enough that he couldn't bear living without her. He didn't kill himself, but the bullet he didn't bother to dodge did the job just as well."

And that was why Conlan didn't want a commitment: he'd watched his father be hurt by his mother, watched his friend die, all for love. And he didn't want to follow in their footsteps.

She could've told him love wasn't always like that; on some level he probably knew it too. She might not have experienced it for herself, but she'd seen it clearly with Cris and Steven. Heck, she and Conlan weren't even talking about love between them—they'd only known each other a week. So why spell out his past for her? She had no doubt he'd hopped into any number of beds between Lee's death and now. Why not jump into hers and get it over with, then walk away?

Because he was afraid he wouldn't be able to. And so was she. Only she was brave enough to take the chance. Conlan was determined to walk away afterward no matter what he felt.

"You know, I didn't take you for a coward."

Conlan jerked away from the window, his body going rigid. She might've laughed at the surprise on his face if her heart wasn't threatening to beat out of her chest.

"What—"

"If you're that worried about it, walk away, Conlan. Really. The only reason you wouldn't walk away is because you can't, because this thing between us scares the shit out of you. Well, guess what?" She paced closer. "It scares me too. I sure as hell don't want to fall for a guy who just wants a week fucking me."

His eyebrows rose at the word. Jess's did too. She'd never actually said that aloud, but it felt good. Inhibitions were for somebody who had much less to lose than she did.

"I can walk out that door right now, schedule my lessons with someone else, and make sure I never see you again. If that's what you want, let me know. Otherwise, man up. Life's too short to spend it worrying about this stuff."

As they came out of her mouth, she realized those last words were for her too. She didn't know how much time she had left; no one did. She'd almost died once. She sure as hell didn't want to waste any more time if she could help it. That was the best *fuck you* she could give Brit, and the best gift she could give herself.

Conlan leaned back against the window once more. A grin pulled at one side of his full lips. "So, is that a yes?"

Crossing her arms over her chest, she tried to actually think out her answer this time. She raised her eyes to the view of faint stars above Conlan's head. "That really depends on you." When she dropped her gaze, it was to meet his. "I can't be someone I'm not. I don't know if I have casual in me; that's just the way it is. I can only promise I won't lay claim to anything you don't want to give me." Even if it killed her. "How you react to that, and what you choose to give, is on you, not me."

Conlan straightened, squaring his shoulders. He stalked toward her, and Jess fought the urge to back up. Fought the need to speak. It was past time for words.

Conlan thought so too. He didn't open his mouth until it met hers, and then it was only for the roughest groan to escape. He took her, with his tongue, his breath, his hands holding her still. Hunger flared fast and bright, sweeping through her like a lit match striking lighter fluid.

Their tongues tangled. Hands groped. Jess whimpered —too many clothes, too much space between them, too big a chance that he'd stop before the hunger inside her was sated. When his head lifted, she clutched hard at his shirt, trying to bring him back.

Conlan smiled. "All right."

She might've laughed at his acquiescence if it weren't for the tremble in his voice, his hands. "All right," she said back.

One more hard kiss and Conlan took her hand. "Good." He tugged her toward the door, digging in his jeans pocket to pull out his keys. "I hope you don't have anywhere you need to be, because if I don't get you naked right now, I'm gonna die."

10

————

Conlan helped her off the motorcycle before dismounting himself. She was in his arms a moment later for a long, dizzying kiss before he linked their fingers together and tugged her forward. "Ready?" he asked.

She tried to decide as they walked toward his apartment. *Yes? No? How in the hell would I know?* She already knew she wouldn't be able to do this and walk away with her heart intact, but even heartbroken, it would be worth it. She wasn't going to deny herself whatever small part of him that Conlan was willing to share.

She smiled back without speaking.

Conlan unlocked the door and led her through before locking it behind them and tossing his keys on a nearby table. Half a second later, he had her backed against the door.

His kiss—aggressive, commanding, hungry—seared her lips. He delved deep, his tongue hard against hers, tempting her to suck on it. When she followed the instinct, the light pull drew a harsh growl from his throat. Shivers exploded down her spine.

Tilting her head, she opened more, forgetting to breathe, forgetting everything but the need to surrender to him. When he pulled away, it was her turn to growl.

Watching Conlan grip the hem of his T-shirt and strip it off was worth his absence. His broad, muscular chest was revealed—smooth, beautiful skin stretched across powerful ridges of muscle; pecs topped with a smattering of dark hair and dark brown nipples. Saliva rushed to her mouth at the sight.

He flicked open the button of his jeans and slid down the zipper, but his workout shorts worked as well as boxers at blocking her view of more. Still, he was right in front of her, right where she could reach him, touch him. She swore her knees wobbled. All that warm muscle, just waiting for her. He didn't give her time, though. His arms encircled her, hauling her tight against his chest, and her knees did give way. Nothing had ever felt as good as this. Nothing ever would. She knew, at that very moment, that Conlan was setting a standard she would judge every man in her life by. And none of them would ever meet it.

His lips came back to hers. Parted. His kiss wiped away thoughts of the future as the slick slide of his lips and the demanding thrust of his tongue became her world. All she could do was move in time to the rhythm he set, savoring his presence in her mouth, feeling the need in his touch. Hard hands clamped on to her rear and lifted, and she instinctively wrapped her legs around his hips. There was no fear of falling, of being too heavy and having him drop her. Conlan gave her that confidence, and she trusted him. When her back met the wall, she arched against it, forcing her pelvis harder into his.

He broke the kiss. "God, Jess." One hand reached between them and undid the button of her jeans. "Now."

"Now." Absolutely.

He unzipped her pants, then reached around to secure her to him once more. Pulling away from the wall, he moved unerringly across the dimness of a living room, hallway, bedroom. She didn't pay attention to details; she was too busy burying her nose in the curve between his shoulder and neck. The scent of sweat and man and musk filled her lungs. His skin was tough, salty. When she instinctively bit down on his pulse point and sucked, Conlan stumbled to a stop, his grip on her hips digging deep. A harsh sound rumbled through his chest, morphing into rough words.

"Yes yes yes."

It took a few moments to get them moving again, moments in which Jess did her best to torture her would-be lover. The hard throb of his erection against her belly and the agonized pace of his breathing were her reward.

And then they were walking into what must be a bathroom from the glimpse of tile she got. Conlan let go with one hand to touch a light switch, and dim fluorescents came to life. As he walked her toward a wide granite counter, Jess glanced around. The room was easily the size of her kitchen, with a garden tub that could fit four and a large glass-enclosed shower. She had a feeling she was going to see the inside of that shower—and Conlan covered in nothing but clear water droplets and soap suds. A hungry shiver ran along her spine.

"Conlan?" Heat rushed to her already warm cheeks.

The counter was hard beneath her, much harder than Conlan's grip had been. He didn't waste time with words now that his hands were free. He simply reached out, lifted her shirt over her head before she could utter a protest, then went for her bra. The lacy fabric surrendered to his demands and found itself on the floor next to her T-shirt. Jess found herself bare, exposed to a man for the very first time in her life.

Instinct demanded she cover herself, but as her hands lifted, Conlan growled, stopping her short. *He wants to look at me.* Her breath hitched at the realization. Carefully, holding that black, hungry gaze, she leaned back until her spine hit the cold mirror. Arching her back lifted her breasts for his touch and left her feeling like a naked feast on display. The way Conlan eyed her breasts, she had a feeling that's what he saw too.

He leaned in, gaze wicked, breath hot. It hit her nipple, and the bud crinkled up tight. The instinct to push closer to his lips was uncontrollable. He wrapped them around the tip of her breast, the touch of his tongue scorching her naked skin. Jess jerked, a high whine of surprise and pleasure escaping. Holding her nipple in the light clasp of his teeth, Conlan sucked.

"God, Conlan!"

His hands went to her hips; hers went to his shoulders. Both strong grips anchored her in the moment. The hard pull at her breast was like nothing she'd ever experienced before. He almost seemed to draw her very essence from her body.

Just when she began to wonder if orgasm was possible from nothing more than his mouth on her breast—and her body screamed that it was—Conlan backed away. Jess clenched her hands into fists, needing him back at her breast, needing him to give her the satisfaction that seemed to wait mere seconds away. But Conlan resisted. His breath was so ragged he couldn't speak.

"What is it?" she asked, almost as breathless as he was.

Conlan chuckled. "I'm— I need to breathe."

She glanced down. There, peeking from the top of his shorts, she could see the barest tip of his penis, wet, almost purple with need. Maybe she hadn't been the only one close, and from so little. She couldn't help a tiny grin at the realization.

Ignoring his body's demands, he grasped the waist of her open jeans. "Lift." Gulping, Jess complied. Her pants and underwear joined her other clothes on the floor, along with her shoes. His big hands gripped the inside of her thighs. Jess's muscles went rigid.

Conlan met her eyes, a hard glint of need clear as he stared at her. "Trust me," he said, the two words low and heavy and rough as gravel. He licked his lips, his tongue leaving a wet trail behind that shone in the dimness like a spotlight. "You'll love this."

He bent toward her, his aim much lower than her lips or nipples, and Jess's mouth went dry. She should tell him she'd never done this before, but then, did it really matter? Did anything matter but giving him what he wanted and being pleasured in return? Decision made, she forced her muscles to relax, her legs to open, and watched in awe as Conlan buried his nose against the top of her mound and breathed deep.

Firm, calloused hands pushed her legs farther apart, opening the center of her body to him. Giving him access. A smile of deep satisfaction on his face, Conlan tipped his chin up to meet her eyes, staring with searing intensity as he slid his hands up, up, up, until sure fingers settled on her outer labia and eased them apart. Cool air collided with the heat of her most private skin.

It was too much, too intimate. The connection to him was like a rush of fire through her veins, overwhelming, devastating. She closed her eyes and rolled her head against the mirror as her breath locked in her lungs.

At first the gentle prodding against her clit didn't register, just tiny tingles of sensation that grew harder and more insistent. When firm lips clamped down and suction pulled her clit from underneath its hood, she wailed at the sharp spike of pleasure. The climb toward ecstasy that had begun with her breasts resurged, centered at the apex of her thighs, behind her eyelids, on and on and on, until finally, oh God, finally she exploded in his arms.

By the time awareness returned, Conlan was naked, and a pleased grin lit his face. He lifted her until her feet touched the floor, made sure she was steady, and drew her to the shower, where the water was already running. Her eyelids heavy, she watched as he stepped through the open door and under the spray, giving her the first good look at his nude body. It was like watching a Celtic god basking in the sun. She'd already seen the muscle that roped his arms and chest, but seeing it roll under his skin as he ran his fingers through his hair to wet it? Wow. The sprinkling of dark hair arrowing down his six-pack drew her eyes to a sexy-as-hell belly button she wanted desperately to nibble. The treasure trail didn't end there, though; it swept down to a tangle of dark curls that encompassed his sex.

His very aroused sex.

His cock, thick and long, stood straight against his lower belly, playing tag with his navel. A thrill of feminine anxiety hit her. There was no way she could take him. He was too much—not just there, but everywhere. He overpowered her senses until she couldn't breathe with wanting him, until taking that final step into the shower seemed like jumping off a cliff.

"Come here," he said, and she realized he'd been

watching her examine him. A flush swept up her neck to blaze in her cheeks. "Come to me, Jess."

Embarrassed or not, she obeyed. Her bare skin met his, and it was... *Oh yes.* The feel of all that rough, masculine skin had her rubbing against him like a kitten. She was pretty sure she even purred—she couldn't help herself.

Conlan pushed closer, his erection digging into the softness below her belly button. His hands coasted up her arms, trailing water, to grip her shoulders. His mouth met hers, open and hungry. She groaned against his tongue.

It was all too much, more than she'd ever expected. He was hers—right here, right now, Conlan was hers.

She'd climaxed mere minutes before, but already her body screamed for more. Spreading her fingers to take in as much warm, wet flesh as possible, she dared to stroke down the crevice of his spine to the firm globes of his butt and palmed him. Conlan threw his head back, his pleasured growl aimed at the ceiling.

A tiny male nipple pebbled right in front of her. She leaned in and sucked.

"Jess!"

"Conlan." The word was more moan than language. This was going so fast, flying by, and she wanted to slow down and savor him but she couldn't. She needed him now.

Conlan understood. He stepped forward, pushing her before him until her back met the steam-warmed wall. Taking her mouth with a desperate kiss, he brought her hand to his rock-hard shaft.

"Touch me," he demanded against her mouth.

The feel of him was at once shocking and, somehow, familiar. Desperate to please him, she copied the way he'd touched her, kneading and molding, moving up the length of his erection to explore the tip with the pads of her fingers.

His hips shifted forward, pushing him harder against her hand. His breath blew hot between her lips, but it was the intensity of his eyes as he stared into hers that spoke his pleasure the loudest. That look filled her heart to over-flowing.

She slid her fingers down, tracing the vein that ran along the underside of his shaft. Cupping his sensitive sac, she rolled it in her palm. His head dropped to the side until it met her shoulder, and she could hear him gritting his teeth.

"Yes," he bit out.

Oh, she liked this. She liked holding him, having all that power and masculine drive in the palm of her hand. She continued to rub, to entice, barely noticing when his teeth lightly gripped her neck and he sucked. One hand gripped her thigh. He lifted her leg to prop her foot on a nearby shelf, knocking off a bottle of shampoo, but neither of them paid attention. What she did notice was the feel of his fingers as he sifted through the curls covering her mound.

This was it. Conlan was going to take her. She tried to relax, to focus on the feel of him, hard and dominant, in her hand rather than the nerves tightening her muscles. She didn't need tighter; his heavy length was intimidating enough as it was.

A whisper of cooler air washed across her heated core as Conlan separated her tender folds. She didn't know if she'd ever get used to that feeling, or the next one: a single finger rolling up and around her throbbing clit. Jess's grip tightened, and she couldn't control the need to beg. "Con— please. Please, I need you."

He circled, teasing her flesh, setting a rhythm she met with small pulses of her pelvis. She could feel her body weeping, cream dripping down her thigh, and knew she was as ready as she'd ever get. When he pushed back to rim her sensitive opening, she met him with a hard thrust, on the verge of exploding.

"So good, Jess. You feel so good," he said against her breast. He slid across her opening, just barely, just enough for her to feel his fingers.

She needed more. Pushing against him, she tried to impale herself, but Conlan drew back. Forward, retreat. Again and again until she thought she'd scream.

"Now, damn it!" She was frantic, needing it, needing him inside her. She didn't care if it hurt. She had to have him.

And then she felt it. His fingers advancing into her— one, then two—until he hit the barrier that she'd give anything for him to breach.

He stopped.

"Jess?"

11

Her name escaped, resonating on a pitch of confusion. Unable to believe what he knew was absolutely true, he slid the tips of his fingers against the thin veil of flesh inside Jess's body. She flinched, but his palm grazing her clit had her eyelids sliding gracefully closed. She was so fucking beautiful in her need. And so very new to it. Her hymen screamed that news in his head, the news that, when he took her, Jess would be his alone. Deep down, where all those feelings men denied actually existed, a primitive roar echoed through his soul, a masculine triumph so fierce it shook the foundation of the man he'd thought he was. The violent need to take the gift she offered—and do it as fast as possible—surged inside him.

And turned his hunger to ash. Because taking her now wouldn't be a one- or even two-night stand. No, taking her now would mean forever.

When he didn't move again, Jess dragged her eyes open, the effort it required obvious in her scrunched brow. "Conlan?"

"You're a virgin." The words barely escaped over his tangled tongue.

His fingers twitched inside her, and Jess nudged her hips forward, pressing down on his palm. "Yes..."

Conlan didn't think, didn't stop to consider. He had pulled his hand back and was across the length of the shower before he'd blinked again. Water splashed into his eyes as he retreated from the one thing he knew he couldn't overlook.

Jess didn't follow him. She moaned, curving down around the hand pressing hard against her lower belly. She stayed like that for long minutes as Conlan battled for control—of his body, his emotions, the driving instinct to protect and comfort the woman huddled against his shower wall. Any idea he'd had about that disappeared when Jess straightened, her blazing eyes meeting his like a lightning flash.

"What. The hell. Is wrong now?"

If it wasn't for the sick churning in the pit of his stomach, he might've laughed. She was all hellcat now, spitting fire, venom dripping from every syllable. The sight hardened his cock despite his command to fucking *stand down*.

Jess ran a hand over her wet hair. The move lifted her breast too, aiming a taut pink nipple in his direction. His brief curse made her flinch.

"Conlan—"

"You're a virgin. Why didn't you tell me you were a virgin?"

"Because I didn't think it mattered." Her tone tacked a *dumbass* on to the end of that sentence.

"You didn't think it mattered? I told you I don't want a commitment. Virgins are all about flowers and hearts and white-picket fences and *commitment*."

"I told you I wouldn't ask for a commitment."

"That's not what your body's saying."

She shook her head, the anger in her eyes settling to a mild boil. "My body doesn't speak for me. Con..."

She took a step away from the cool tiles, toward the warm water and his too-warm libido. His hand jerked up on instinct, warding her off. Jess stopped like she'd hit a brick wall, and her eyes, those beautiful doe eyes that had captivated him from the start, went blank. She squared her shoulders despite the shiver that racked her body.

His hard-on died a rapid death. "I thought—"

"Thought what?"

He swiped at the water running down his face. "I just assumed you had been with Brit or someone at some point, before... Most relationships involve sex, Jess. Hell, most women lose their virginity way before graduating college." Lord knew he had. "I thought you'd been with at least him, even if..."

"Even if what? If he was a bastard now? I mean, I got off so easily for you, surely I could've done it with him, right? For how long, Conlan? I was with Brit for a year. Part of that I spent mourning my parents, oblivious to pretty much everything around me and just obeying commands, going through the motions. It would've been the perfect time to give it up. Even if he treated me like shit. Even if I hadn't necessarily enjoyed it, at least it would've been out of your way. Is that what you thought?"

He dropped his gaze to the water pooling at their feet, unable to bear her scrutiny.

"You'd rather I had a bad sexual experience than no experience at all? Guess what? You almost got your wish." Her breath hiccupped over the last words. "If he hadn't been so busy grooming me to be his little doormat, he might've pushed harder, might not have waited till he had me good and secure under his thumb. Except then he got tired of waiting. I came way too close to being raped—by the bastard you were hoping I'd had sex with."

He jerked his head up. Jess wasn't looking at him; she was staring at the tile in front of her as if it held the memories that had to be swirling in her head.

"He brought me home from a charity dinner I hadn't wanted to go to in the first place. He was drunk and wanted to have sex. I told him no." She shrugged, the move anything but casual. "He said he deserved it. Saying yes would've been a lot more convenient now—and a lot less painful then."

The dead tone to her voice was worse than having her scream at him. Worse than her punching him. In fact, he wished she would; maybe, in the short-term, that physical pain would dull the agony already in his chest. He closed his eyes, but his brain supplied the pictures anyway: Jess so small and defenseless; that big blond bastard hurting her. "Jess, I—"

"Don't say you're sorry."

He'd told her that before, hadn't he? She hadn't had reason to be sorry; he sure as hell did.

"It's the truth. But Jess"—he gestured between them, amazed his hand was actually steady—"you shouldn't do this. You shouldn't give up your virginity for a one-night stand. On a whim. You certainly shouldn't give it to someone who..."

"Someone who doesn't want it?"

Her brittle tone flayed him like shards of glass, but the cuts could never go deep enough to dig out what he'd done. What he'd said. "I just—"

"Forget it." Jess turned away. With a push, the shower

door opened. She pulled a towel off the rack as she stepped through, and wrapped it around herself, tucking the end in tight, hiding her body from his gaze.

He shut off the water, stepping to the shower door mere seconds behind her. "Jess—"

But she was already walking out of the bathroom, scooping her clothes off the floor as she went. She didn't look back. "Save it."

He paused, one hand on the shower door, and watched her exit the room. *Fuck.*

He'd handled that like the biggest shit ever.

He needed to follow her, needed to go in there and fix the problem, only...there was no fixing it, was there? As much as he wanted to heal her hurt, he couldn't go back on his decision. Just the thought had the noose around his neck tightening.

What a fucking mess.

Giving her time to get dressed, he dried himself and walked into the closet to slide on a fresh pair of jeans. He snatched up a T-shirt and tugged it on roughly as he crossed to the bedroom door.

Jess was sitting on the chest at the end of his bed, lacing her shoes. His heart clenched as he watched her struggle to tie them with shaking fingers.

"Jess."

She didn't look up. "I want to go home, please."

Please. The tiny little word came out in a whisper. He closed his eyes against it, feeling like the complete dick he knew he was. That didn't stop him from opening his eyes and crossing the room toward her. "Jess, we need to talk. I need to explain... Damn it, look at me."

She squared her shoulders and met his gaze head-on as

he came to a stop just beyond her knees. "It's fine. Just take me home."

"After we talk." For some reason he didn't understand, he needed her to get it, to see that he was right, that this would only end up hurting her, hurting both of them in the long run.

"And what if I don't want to talk about it? God." She pushed to her feet, going toe-to-toe with him. "I'm not a child. I don't want to talk. Take. Me. Home."

"Not until you listen to me. I know I handled this wrong. I know I was an ass—"

Her entire face went blank in mock innocence. "Ya think?"

He reached for her, needing to hold on, to control the crazy spiraling this situation had fallen into. It was only Jess stumbling backward, panic on her face as she avoided his grip, that brought him to his senses. He snatched his hands back.

Just stop. Just...

He closed his eyes. Fisted his hands. Counted long breaths in the faint hope he could regain control.

Another breath. And another.

The calm he'd lost somewhere back in the shower didn't return, but he manufactured a weak facsimile of it before he spoke.

"I'm sorry, Jess."

She seemed to get that he wasn't just apologizing for scaring her. "Me too."

"Look at me please." He kept himself quiet, still. Arms crossed protectively over her chest, she raised her eyes to his. "Baby, you are very desirable; you have to know that by now. So damn desirable, but—"

A snort made her derision clear, but the glistening of

tears in her eyes told the true story. "Yeah, I got that from the way you couldn't back up fast enough." Apparently done with the whole thing, she started across the bedroom. "I'll call a cab."

"No! No, I'll take you. Give me just a minute."

The longest seconds of his life passed like cold molasses; then Jess blinked, and the sweep of her lashes erased all trace of tears from her eyes. "Fine."

He kept his gaze on her as he backed toward the bathroom. It stayed on her until he had no choice but to turn. Even then, her image lay, superimposed, over everything his sight took in. The scent of warm woman and water lingered as he grabbed socks, shoes, wallet. It was the only time he'd smell her here, he knew. Not just because she was a virgin, but because she brought out something in him he couldn't control—and control was everything. Telling himself to keep his emotional distance didn't work with Jess; it never would. He knew that now.

He grabbed his keys on the way out. Jess stood stiffly by the front door, waiting. Conlan didn't touch her when he escorted her to his car or as he drove her back to her place. They sat in silence, a sense of finality filling the seconds as they stretched into minutes. When he pulled up to her apartment building, Jess didn't look back.

"Goodbye, Conlan."

And that was it. He didn't know what he'd expected her to say, but those two words didn't even come close. Watching her walk through the glass door, he knew this might very well be the last time he saw Jess. It was a bit ironic that she was the one walking away.

12

She pushed through the door of her apartment, spinning around to close it quickly, but not quick enough. Brit was in before she could protest.

"Brit, I'm tired." *And you're drunk, she wanted to say but didn't. Her heart was already pounding. That sense of walking on tiptoes, at first so subtle, was now an ever-present reality she couldn't escape. She needed to soothe him, not because she loved him, but because she was afraid of what he would do.*

She was afraid. And there was no one here to help her.

Brit turned those cool blue eyes her way, and her blood froze in her veins. It was that look, the one that preceded snide comments on something she'd done wrong, someplace she wasn't good enough, some expectation she hadn't fulfilled to his exacting degree. If she was lucky. If she wasn't...

The ice crept through her muscles, holding her as tight as any shackles ever could.

"You're always tired," *Brit said with a twist of his lips.* "Maybe I'm tired." *He stepped into her space, his lean body belying the power she knew it held.* "Maybe I want you to make me feel better."

"Not tonight." Not ever if she could help it, if she could get herself out of the trap she'd let herself fall into. She'd always wondered how women could stay in an abusive relationship, could let a man treat them that way. She didn't wonder anymore; she knew. The subtlety, the creeping tentacles of control that wrapped so tight around your throat you couldn't even scream. Oh yes, she knew. She looked into Brit's eyes and saw power and knew herself to be powerless. But there was one thing she wouldn't hand over.

Her body.

"Not tonight," Brit mocked. "Yes, tonight. I want some relief, and you're going to give it. No more dicking around."

His voice rose with every word he spoke, warning her that the alcohol was stealing his patience more by the minute. Before she could dodge, he had her arm, fingers hard, hurting. Brit spun her around.

"Brit, no."

"Yes." The alcohol-scented word hit her ear as his body met her back. The hard jut of his erection had her swallowing hard.

"I mean it," she told him, forcing the words not to wobble. "You need to go home and sleep it off."

"I don't think so." His fingers bit into her arms, refusing to allow her to move. She could feel the echo of her racing heartbeat in the throbbing pain in her biceps. "How many months have we been together? How many months? I've waited. I've been patient. More patient than anyone else would have been. Maybe more patient than I should have been." His fingers dropped to circle her wrists. A small shove into her back propelled her across the room toward the dim hallway. "Maybe I'm tired of being patient, Jess. Maybe the time for patience is over."

Panic blossomed in earnest. She lunged, hoping to escape, to reach her room and lock him out, only to be yanked back by the sudden digging of his fingers into her hips.

Stay calm, *she told herself.* If you stay calm, he'll let go.

A tugging at her side registered, then cool air on her skin as her skirt dropped to the floor.

Fuck calm.

"What the hell are you doing?" Jess scrambled for her skirt. A heavy jerk at her back busted the buttons down the front of her shirt.

"I'm doing what I should have done a long time ago. Taking what's mine."

The sound of her sharp scream startled her awake. She shot up, clutching her shirt, gasping a stream of panicked cries that reminded her far too clearly of what Brit had done. It didn't matter that he hadn't succeeded, that her screams had convinced the neighbors to call the police, that the sirens had scared Brit away before they could find him there. It didn't matter, because when she went to sleep at night, she relived it over and over again. Every word, every touch, every violation. She might've escaped him once, but each nightmare assured her he still controlled her in every way that mattered.

"No! No, he doesn't." She forced herself to swallow through a tight, dry throat, to breathe when her lungs refused to fill. "Just shut it down. It's okay; you're awake now."

A rough, desperate scrub of her hand wiped the lingering sleep from her eyes and the feel of Brit's breath from her neck. The dream faded slowly, leaving Jess chilled and clammy in the cool air-conditioning of the apartment. It took long moments before she could finally force her shivering limbs to carry her to the bathroom and the splash of tepid water on her face, her wrists. When her heart no longer felt like it would tumble out of her throat, she braced her hands on either side of the sink and met her reflection's eyes in the mirror.

"You're okay. It's gonna be okay."

She had to believe that. She wasn't Brit's mouse any longer; she wasn't anyone's mouse. Even big strong Conlan had taken the easy way out, but she wouldn't. She planned to live, even if it hurt.

Rough terry cloth absorbed the water on her skin and woke her up just a little bit more. She tossed the towel aside and headed down the hall toward the kitchen and coffee and breakfast. She would eat, relax, maybe call Cris... The thought of the interrogation she would get nixed that idea. Maybe later. For now she just wanted peace and quiet.

Jess carried her food down the hall to her office and settled in at her desk. She sipped the warm, vanilla-flavored coffee and nibbled bites of her breakfast as the computer booted. When the blue welcome screen popped up, she clicked on the e-mail icon and ate while her mail loaded.

Spam. Sales alerts. She finished off her coffee, her gaze on the screen. Nothing important. She scanned and deleted and shuffled things to particular folders for later, until she reached the bottom of the screen and the latest e-mail in the list.

You are mine.

The subject line seemed to flash a warning in neon lights. "Jesus, no." It couldn't be. But the echo of those words in Brit's cultured, commanding voice told her otherwise.

Half of the message was visible in the preview pane. No, not a message, a picture. It looked like the roof of a building, the vaguest hint of light shining off it.

Moonlight. An apartment building. Conlan's.

Her mind screamed at her to ignore the e-mail, not to click on it, that she didn't want to know what it contained.

Her finger ignored her mind; it clicked automatically. The picture loaded on her screen, an image of Conlan and Jess arriving on his motorcycle at his apartment building last night. Conlan had one foot on the pavement, his fingers at the strap to his helmet. Jess gripped his hips.

A single line of text beneath the photo took over her entire field of vision, her every thought, even her breath.

You are mine.

The coffee that had calmed her earlier rolled in her stomach now.

The e-mail program beeped. Another message, no subject. Same e-mail address. Jess clicked. The screen filled with a picture.

Same night, same parking lot. An embracing couple. Her gut went cold, the ice spreading out to freeze her legs and arms and fingers and lips just like it had in her dream. Even her scalp squeezed tight. It was her, this time wrapped in Conlan's arms, his mouth on hers, his fingers palming her rear to drag her close. The remembered feel of his heat ghosted over her, the pulsing rhythm of his hips against hers, his tongue stroking into her mouth. And then he'd taken her inside—and dumped her because she was a virgin.

One man hadn't wanted her, and this one...this one refused to leave her alone.

A message waited at the bottom of this e-mail too: *No one touches what's mine.*

The pulse in her temples was loud, a clanging drum in the absolute stillness of the room.

Ding.

A third message.

This time the picture showed Conlan leading her toward

the door of his apartment. Their fingers were twined together. Intent obvious.

Get rid of him or else.

She shuddered, bile rising.

The angle of the picture was down, as if it had been taken from a tree...or a balcony, but it was close, too close. He would have to be standing directly above them. Surely she wouldn't have missed...

No, had to be a telephoto lens. Please, God, let it be a telephoto lens.

The e-mail address on the message originated from an online hosting service—no tracking the information, if it was even true, which she knew it wasn't. No way to retaliate against Brit—and no way to stop him from doing it again.

Her hand was on her phone before she even realized what she was doing. Shakily she dialed Detective King. It was a Sunday morning; he wouldn't be there, but she could leave a message. While she waited for his voice mail to pick up, the computer beeped one more time. Another message. It contained only two words, written over and over and over again: *You're mine.*

Wouldn't Brit be pleased if he knew she still hadn't given any man what he'd wanted so desperately? The irony made her giggle. Then laugh. A totally inappropriate response, she knew, but after last night and the nightmare and now this, she couldn't help it. The sound got louder, more hysterical, but cut off abruptly when the voice-mail prompt sounded in her ear.

At least she had some small bit of control left.

Her voice was steady as she left the message for Detective King insisting on a meeting Monday morning. She even managed to tell him why. She stayed detached. Firm. After hanging up, that same detachment had her watching as her finger automatically tapped out Conlan's number. He needed to know; he could tell her what to do. She needed his support.

Except he wasn't offering support, was he? After last night he wasn't even offering to teach her self-defense anymore. He was shunting her off to someone else so he could go on his merry little way and not have to worry about getting too attached. Maybe if she could scrape together enough money to officially hire JCL for security, he would find someone to babysit her, but not him. Not anymore.

She managed to hit End Call before it started to ring.

She couldn't call Cris; her friend had other things to worry about. She tapped in Saul's number, her fingers starting to shake, only to be sent directly to voice mail. The tinny sound of her godfather's voice in her ear slid over her like ice.

She punched Off.

Staring at the phone, she saw instead Detective King and his smug superiority, the way he'd brushed off her fears and her injuries and swallowed Brit's alibi like the good dog he was. She'd been lying in bed with bandages covering the gouges in her neck where Brit had choked her with her own necklace. A brace had supported her broken and bruised ribs, and her hair had been put up to cover the patch they'd had to shave for the twenty-four stitches necessary to close her split scalp—but King had stood there and told her she must be mistaken about her attacker's identity.

She saw Conlan's face when he'd told her he was unavailable, the panic as he backed away from her in the shower after touching her so intimately. She felt the chill of the water on her naked skin as her heart shattered into pieces.

She looked close, and saw her own eyes staring back at

her, reflected in the now blank screen. Eyes she'd gazed into this morning and vowed to keep going, no matter what. To be strong. That vow hadn't been predicated on having someone beside her or even having someone believe her. It just was. No matter what.

So fuck them.

The phone hit the opposite wall of her office before she even realized she'd thrown it. She listened to it clatter onto the floor while she reached for the keyboard to pull it closer. The mouse came next, and she clicked the Reply button for the last e-mail. Brit might not receive it, might not even be using this address anymore. She didn't care. She was giving him a little piece of what he'd given her.

He thought she was his? She'd see about that.

The new message screen opened, and Jess typed the words she wanted to say, the words that bubbled up from deep within her soul. What she hadn't been able to say when she'd been Brit's cowering, scared little mouse. Once she was finished, she looked the words over, and a smile that felt as icy as her heart touched her lips.

Go back to hell, you son of a bitch.

She clicked Send. The program's progress bar tracked the journey of her retaliation back to its rightful owner. She was done belonging to anybody. Her life was her own, and she would damn well live it, with or without support.

On her way out of the room, Jess's foot scraped across a sharp edge. She looked down to see her phone lying amid the broken pieces of its case. Studying the jagged shards, too many to put back together, she caught herself blinking back a flush of tears. Was she like that, too broken to heal?

She didn't know. She looked at the shattered pieces of plastic and knew, no matter the glue, no matter the repairs, the cracks would always be there. Hers probably would too.

But one thing she did know for certain: If she didn't stop Brit, there wouldn't be enough pieces of her left to find, much less put back together. This had to stop. Had to.

Careless of the broken edges, she took a step and kicked the pieces hard, scattering them across the room.

———

"So Lori said your lesson went better than expected last night."

Jack's tone held a snigger. The man was far too smug for their usual Sunday evening beer ritual. Con eyed him as the waitress set two brown bottles on the battered table between them.

"Thanks, darlin'." Jack winked, causing the cute brunette to blush as she turned away. The man didn't even notice, just kept right on grinning at Con from across the table. He'd watched perfectly intelligent, mature women swoon at that grin. They fell to worship at Jack's feet when he flashed it. Con just wanted to punch Jack's teeth out, but he picked up his beer and took a long, icy swallow instead. Jack was part bloodhound, and any other reaction would lead him down a path Con really didn't want to take, not tonight.

Jack ignored Con's sour disposition. "Come on, man. You can't tell me you don't want to spill the details."

"Didn't Lori already give you those?"

It wasn't that they hadn't swapped stories before; they had, both of them, on other occasions—rarely, but it happened. Men didn't talk feelings; they talked lays. This thing with Jess shouldn't be all that different, except it was, and he didn't want to talk about it.

"I mean, hell, you did her on company property; techni- cally I'm entitled to know what went on in my—our business," he clarified at Con's snarl, though his grin never wavered. "Unless... You didn't clear the security tapes, did you? I could just wa—"

"I didn't do her."

Fucking understatement of the year, his cock reminded him.

Jack paused, beer raised halfway to his open mouth. "No way. Lori said you were halfway there right on the mats. You've got to be lying." He shook his head. "You know I'll find it, right? All it'll take is a few minutes' search to—"

"Jack."

"What?"

"Not. Another. Word."

"Oh, come on! I just wanna know if she—"

"No."

"But—"

Con surged up out of his seat.

"All right, all right." Jack laughed against the mouth of his bottle. "Sit your ass down. I get it—no touchy." At Con's continued glare, he held up both hands, one clutching his beer. "Not even virtually, I promise." He paused. "Maybe."

Con shot him the bird.

Jack smirked. "Besides," he said, "Lori already cleared the tapes."

Con grunted his approval.

"Cock blocker."

Just couldn't resist that final dig, could he? The truth stung, even if Jack didn't mean it. Even if it wasn't how Jack thought it. The memory of Jess walking away from him last night flashed in his mind. The regret that sliced through him wasn't a surprise anymore.

Something on Con's face must've registered, because

Jack's beer went back to the table before it could touch his lips again. "You didn't."

"Didn't what?" As if he didn't know.

"Jesus, you didn't."

Con let a twist of his mouth answer for him.

"Son of a bitch." Jack shook his head, but it was the concern lurking in his eyes that really pissed Con off.

"You'd actually prefer it if I had fucked our client?"

"Maybe, yeah!"

Conlan ignored that in favor of finishing his beer in one big swallow. Their blushing waitress had come and gone again, leaving behind two fresh bottles, before either of them broke the silence.

"Jesus, Con."

"Just shut the hell up."

"No." The word was sharp, hitting harder than Jack's fist on the table, which hit pretty damn hard if the shaking that ensued meant anything. The sudden switch from humor to violence shocked Con speechless. Jack was deadly when he wanted to be, when the situation warranted, and his temper wasn't anything to turn your back on, but not with friends, and never with Con.

"Why would you do that—to yourself or Jess? It's not like it hasn't been building from the first moment you laid eyes on her."

And that was the problem. Jess had been different from the very start. And Jack damn well knew it. "You know why."

"I know why, and I think it's stupid. She's sweet and nice and hot, for fuck's sake. And so what if she might want a little something more than a roll in the hay—she just might be the best damn thing that ever walked across your path, and you're throwing it away? Over the vague possibility that she might eventually want an actual relationship?"

"Yes! Yes, that's why I can't—" Chest tight, breath like a freight train, Con struggled to control the anger threatening to take the top of his head off. "I can't let myself have her, because...she might...she deserves..." *So much more.* He couldn't say the words, but they were there all the same, deflating his anger as quickly as it had come.

Jack hung his head, shaking it and giving a weary sigh. "You know, sometimes I wish Lee was here so I could kill him myself."

Con reared back. "What the fuck?"

Jack leaned across the table, his entire body pushing his point. "Come on, Con. When are you gonna face the fact that Lee and Sarah never had a real, healthy relationship, that what happened to him—what he allowed to happen— had nothing to do with reality and everything to do with some sick obsession neither of them wanted to let go of?"

The beer in Con's stomach threatened a return appearance. "No. It wasn't like that. She dumped him after jerking him around for years of his life."

"And he let her!"

No, it wasn't true. What had happened to Lee was Sarah's fault. She might as well have aimed the gun at him herself.

Jack wouldn't stop. "Lee should've bowed down and thanked that woman for finally hooking her claws in someone else. She gave him a gift when she walked away, but he was too obsessed to see it. Hell, she probably got off on knowing he was dying inside—then she had two men to dangle on her puppet strings. What the two of them had wasn't love; it was a sick two-way street neither of them really wanted off. I loved Lee like a brother, you know that, but I wasn't blind to his faults." Jack picked up his fresh bottle and drained it in two big gulps. "I sure as hell refuse to let Lee's dumbass choices rule my life," he said, voice gruff from the alcohol, gaze making it clear one of them was doing just that.

Con opened his mouth—to deny that Jess meant anything beyond a dumped one-night stand, to argue Jack's claim, to defend Lee somewhere beyond his own mind...he wasn't totally sure which—when his cell jangled along the table. He glanced down on instinct to catch the first line of a text message that flashed across the screen.

The first word was all he needed: *Jess.*

Still pissed and grateful for the reprieve, he tapped the screen.

Jess is mine.

He squinted, the message not truly registering for a moment. A second buzz sounded.

Disappear or she will.

A curse broke from his lips.

"Con?"

The number wasn't one he recognized, but then, when you were one of the biggest security companies in Atlanta, you got weird contacts all the time. When you specialized in defending abused women, threats weren't uncommon either. Jess's name was—he only knew one, and only one reason to threaten her.

"Something interesting?" Jack asked.

"Yeah. Take a look at this." Turning his phone toward Jack, Conlan ran the message back through his brain.

Jack's gaze locked with his over the phone. "Who is this?"

"If I had to guess, I'd say it's the guy Jess needs protection from."

Jack dropped immediately into work mode. "Name."

"Brit Holbrooke."

Jack's eyebrows hit his hairline. "You know who that is, right?" Jack waved the waitress, who'd stopped to pick up their empties, away. "The Atlanta Holbrookes? They run their own tech company?"

"No. I must've missed that with all the other touchy-feely shit going on around here." But it explained why Holbrooke had seemed familiar. It also explained a bit about the man's arrogance, and how he'd found Con. Having his phone number wasn't that unusual—it was listed on the company website—but tracking him down, just from seeing him? That was a whole other level of skill, a level that made him decidedly uneasy.

Jack ignored the dig and rubbed his chin, thinking. "They're Atlanta elite, keyed in to every major family and office in the city, including the mayor."

"Might be why Jess said the cops came up empty," Con told him, air quotes giving the final word an opposite meaning.

"Not surprising." Jack tapped his phone, sitting on the table near his beer just like Con's, and typed in a note. "I'll do some digging and find out who handled the case. What'd she say about it?"

Con told him what little he knew from Jess, as well as what Lori had shared from her paperwork. His encounter with Holbrooke at the coffee shop. The longer he talked, the tighter his muscles got, just thinking about that asshole anywhere near Jess. His heart sped up, the metallic taste of fear lacing his tongue. He reached for his beer, needing to drown out the taste, and came up empty.

"Sounds like someone doesn't want to relinquish owner-ship," Jack observed, nodding down at Con's phone.

"Would you?" Con asked, not really considering how much the question acknowledged until the words left his lips. Jack lifted a brow at him but didn't plow into the hole he'd just left wide open.

"How bad was last night?" he asked instead. "Any chance she'll continue her lessons? Because I gotta tell ya, Con, this whole situation sets off every alarm I've got, but that"—he pointed a finger at the now blank screen—"blows them all to hell. You knew from the get-go that he was stalking her, but it's not just her anymore. He's taken the time to find out who you are, how involved you are, which means he's following her close."

"Close enough to track me. Threaten me. He knows who I am, but he's not afraid." It wasn't ego to say most men were afraid of him. He'd taken the time to make sure of it over the years.

"My guess? If he's following that close, he saw you last night, saw something that pushed him too close to the edge. Any closer and he'll take the first opportunity he can to get physical again."

Con swallowed against the sharp tang of fear on the back of his tongue—not for him, but for Jess.

"She needs help," Jack said. "If she won't accept you to do it, we'll sub someone else."

"Not someone else. You." He wouldn't—no, couldn't—trust Jess's safety to anyone else. And he wouldn't leave her unprotected, no matter how much the thought of even his best friend that close to her rubbed him raw. Christ, he wasn't much better than Holbrooke in some ways, was he? "When she's not at work or at JCL, I'll keep watch." She might not know he was there, but it was all he could give her. That and, if he was lucky, Brit's head—preferably disconnected from his body.

"I'll have Lori contact her. Con—"

He met Jack's eyes, read the conflict there, and knew

what his friend wanted to say. "I can't, Jack. I just...can't."
Even now.

"You can; you're just too much of a coward to do it."

A laugh, more broken than he'd like, escaped. "That's what she said."

"Smart girl." Jack rapped the table with his knuckles. "But I'll do it. We'll need to be careful. This guy's obviously got more resources than your average abuser."

"And more balls," Con said, the words bitter. He glanced back down at his phone. *Disappear or she will.* Heat washed over him. It wasn't a question anymore: Brit intended to hurt Jess. Con intended to stop him. The fucker was going down; Con would make sure of it.

13

She was almost home Monday night when her cell phone rang in the seat next to her. "Hello?"

"Jess."

Conlan.

She didn't know what to say, so she didn't say anything. She let the silence stretch as she pulled into her parking lot and angled the car into a space.

She couldn't tell if Conlan felt...well, anything. This was the first time they'd spoken since he'd rejected her, but his voice was blank as he asked, "You called to cancel your lesson?"

"I did." Lori had asked why, but Jess hadn't been up to explaining. If the sweet Southern receptionist hadn't figured it out from her unexpected interruption Saturday night, her boss could tell her.

"I don't think that's a good idea."

Her laugh came out a bit more on the hysterical side than she'd like. "Really? You still want to teach me?"

A heavy sigh sounded in her ear. "Jack will likely take over. It's for the best—"

"For whom?"

The silence crackled with awkward tension. Jess shook her head as she gathered her things, fishing for her key card and wishing she could just hang up the phone before she embarrassed herself more. Was she standing up for herself, for what they both knew they felt, or just being a bitch? She couldn't tell anymore, and honestly, considering the way her life was going and the ulcer her stomach was probably working on after the last few days, she didn't think she cared. She just knew she was at the breaking point and even the detective assigned to her case didn't have time for her. If she couldn't be honest with the man who'd seen her naked, who'd had his fingers inside her, for goodness' sake, who could she be honest with?

The sound of her car door slamming shut was loud in the gathering twilight. "Look, Conlan, I need to go."

"I got a text yesterday."

"I'm sure you get them every day. Why is that important?"

"Because this one was from Holbrooke."

The e-mails she'd received—and her response—flashed before her eyes. She ignored her sudden shaking and swiped her card in the door. "Wh-what did it say?"

"It said, 'Jess is mine. Disappear or she will.'"

She stumbled across the threshold before managing to right herself. "I—" God. She headed toward the elevator, searching desperately for a response, but there was just... nothing. *Disappear or she will.* Brit had actually declared, to someone besides her, that he wanted to kill her. So another man wouldn't have her.

That pesky hymen problem rearing its ugly head again. Maybe she just needed to hire someone and get rid of it once and for all; it seemed to be the only option, considering she couldn't get the man she wanted to take it willingly.

"It's okay, Jess. Nothing I can't handle."

You, maybe. What about me? "It's not okay. It's— Grrr!" She ground the heel of her palm against her eyes, her purse smacking her chin in the process. "Why is he doing this? Why?"

But she knew why.

Conlan was talking in her ear, something about tracking and police reports and Jack, but she wasn't listening. She was tumbling out of the elevator as fast as her legs would carry her, digging in her pocket for her keys. A few feet from her door, she dropped her files, fumbling with the phone to keep it in her hand as she scrambled to hold on to everything. Finally she just dropped it all, all except the phone and her keys, and walked the few steps to her door.

It was open.

"Conlan."

Something in her tone registered with him; she knew because he went silent. Then, low and deadly, "What?"

She was already backing down the hall. One foot landed on her purse, and she tripped, almost going down.

"Jess? Talk to me."

"I—" The elevator appeared on her right. Eyes focused on the door to her apartment—the open door—she fumbled for the Down button. "I—"

"Jess?" The word was breathless, as if he was running. A slamming door. An engine rumbling. "What's going on?"

The elevator dinged its arrival. "My apartment—I think it's been broken into."

The squeal of tires came across the line. "Get out! Get out now, Jess. I'm on my way."

"Okay."

The elevator doors narrowed, focusing the image of those few inches between her door and the jamb it should've been locked into, down, down, down until it disappeared from sight. Then she was dropping, her stomach sinking like she was on a roller coaster.

Conlan's voice throbbed with adrenaline. "I want you to hang up. Call 911. I'm on my way." When she didn't respond, he practically yelled, "Jess! Do it now!"

"Okay."

The word was sickly. She fumbled for the Off button as she lurched down the first-floor hall toward the back door. Only the sight of the black night waiting on the other side of the glass forced her to a stop. No way in hell was she going out there alone. Which was how she found herself huddled in the corner off to one side of the door, waiting on the arrival of the police. The fact that she was on the line with the dispatcher, giving him information, describing what she'd seen, receiving assurances that a unit was on its way, registered somewhere between the heart in her throat and her unseeing eyes, but not fully. What she really wanted was Conlan's arms around her, his heat warming the ice taking over her body. That wasn't going to happen, though, was it? Because she was a virgin and he didn't do virgins. If the reason hadn't seemed stupid before, it did now.

Hilarious.

The need crawled under her skin anyway, doubling, tripling, until she thought if she had to sit here one more second, alone, waiting for something to happen without the buffer of Conlan's reassurance, his touch, she would absolutely friggin' screa—

A sharp series of raps ricocheted like gunfire in the tiny entry. Jess jerked, pushing herself as far into the corner as she could. Even as she slapped a hand over her mouth to stop it, she sucked in air for the first swelling shriek.

The rapping came again, loud and startling, then a faint, "Jess! It's Con. Open the door!"

The starch went out of her so fast she almost slumped to the floor. She forced herself to walk the two paces to the door instead.

Conlan stood on the other side of the glass, only this wasn't her Conlan. No, the grim-faced man looking back at her was hard, dangerous. Different. Definitely not the same man who'd touched her with such tenderness in the shower.

She had the door open in a heartbeat.

Her Conlan or not, the hardened warrior who came through the door reached for her without hesitation. "Come here," he said roughly, and the next thing she knew, his heavy arm gathered her close to his side, and he refused to let go. His heat sank into her bones, slowing the shakes that had taken hold of her, softening her muscles until she couldn't resist anymore and melted against him. But even his touch couldn't erase the sense of looming disaster that filled her, especially when she caught sight of his opposite hand hovering over the gun strapped to his hip.

A sudden squawking sound came from her hand, and Jess looked down at it, finally registering the dispatcher's demanding voice. Con took the phone before she could send the signal to her muscles to raise it to her ear.

"Hello, Conlan James speaking, JCL Security. Your name, please?"

The ease with which he took over left her flattened. He couldn't be bothered to sleep with her, but he could ride to the rescue like a freaking white knight. She opened her mouth to protest, but Conlan stared her down, that same mean stare as before, daring her to reach for the phone, daring anything and anyone to interfere with what he wanted, and eyeing his muscles, she knew resisting would do no good. The impotence of it all built, and by the time he tapped her phone off, Jess felt like a pressure cooker ready to explode. "What the hell do you mean—"

A surprised look came over Con's face, but it passed quickly as he glanced out the door. "The cops are here."

"Con—"

"Jess—" Tough. Low. Implacable.

A rap on the glass. The moment was lost as Conlan pushed the door open, admitting two uniformed policemen.

The next couple of hours passed in a blur as Jess recounted her story more than once, answered questions about her apartment, and watched what seemed like half the Atlanta PD traipse in and out of the home they wouldn't allow her into. By the time they did, she wished she could've waited a bit longer.

She didn't care if he wanted her to or not; she gripped Conlan's hand like the lifeline she knew it to be.

"There are just a few things to remember first, ma'am," the officer said as they stood outside her apartment.

Jess nodded woodenly.

"Be certain not to touch anything. We are still in the process of taking pictures, so we don't want anything moved or changed. We will fingerprint you at the station later to eliminate your prints. And you, Mr. James."

"They're on file for business purposes," Conlan said, warrior face still firmly on display.

The cop nodded. "Make note of anything you think might be missing," he told Jess, then hesitated, a look of sympathy softening the harsh, proper lines of his young face. Not enough experience to be hardened to a victim's suffering, she thought, thankful he and his partner had been the ones to respond to the 911 call. "You should be prepared. There are…"

"There are what?"

Con grunted, jump-starting the cop where Jess's words hadn't.

"Uh, messages…on the walls."

Shock tingled up her spine. "Messages?"

"Yes, ma'am." He went on without addressing the issue further. "Thankfully your building has tight security and several cameras in this area, so we might've got the perp on film, but just in case, we need to know if anything sounds or looks familiar. Any clues you can give us would help, okay?"

Clues? They wanted clues? She'd already told them who'd done this, not that it would do any good. She knew that and wanted not to, wanted to believe the sincerity in this cop's concerned eyes. But even if he was sincere, it wouldn't matter. Whatever Brit had done inside her apartment, it wouldn't be laid at his feet.

She kept her pessimism to herself and stepped through the door behind the officer. She tried to brace herself, knowing Brit wanted to hurt her, pretty sure this was retaliation for her *fuck off* message yesterday, but nothing could prepare her for what waited on the other side of the door.

"Oh God." *Breathe.* A weak giggle escaped when Conlan whispered the same word in her ear. She swallowed it back. And stared.

Total devastation glared back at her from every corner of her home. Shards of glass from the mirror over the mantel created a minefield across the carpet, mixing with stuffing from the furniture and pages— Damn, not her books. Tears welled as she scanned the bare shelves of her bookcase. Her precious books, the source of so much of her comfort, her passion, lay scattered in pieces across the living room. Not one that she could see had survived intact. Neither had her curtains. Lamps. The blanket that used to rest on the back of her couch.

The presence of a crime-scene tech taking pictures barely registered, the bright white of the camera flash turning the frightening images of destruction into a surreal flash frame of deepening horror, pain, and anger.

Shredded bits of leather over exposed springs.

Flash.

Paper confetti, the printed words torn to small bits of gibberish.

Flash.

Cris's smiling face, slashed to pieces in a twisted picture frame.

Flash.

Strangers' eyes staring everywhere she turned.

Flash.

Even worse—if it could get worse—were the brutal words painted across her now bare walls. The artwork she'd saved for months to buy, the awards from school and work, all had been torn down, creating bright white canvases for slashes of vibrant red paint. The words sank into her soul and, oddly enough, sparked a strange sort of relief. This was familiar, at least.

Whore.

Slut.

Cunt.

Every derogatory epithet she could think of glared from the walls that had once kept her safe, screaming into her mind. She felt dirty in a way she didn't think a thousand showers could ever remove, a way that was as familiar as the words she read. The warm slide of Conlan's arm around her shoulders registered briefly before he tugged her toward him. She fisted his T-shirt at the base of his spine, needing a handhold, something solid, grounding.

"Come on, Jess," he said softly, reaching with a tissue he got from God knew where to wipe her face. "They need to know if anything's missing."

Her laugh was incredulous, the rising hysteria obvious even to her ears. How the hell could she tell? But she pushed forward without asking that. People talked around her, asked questions, snapped pictures, bagged evidence, but none of it truly registered anymore.

The kitchen... Well, walking farther than the doorway was impossible. Even the fridge stood open, food spilled inside and out, adding insult to injury.

The hallway light drew her attention to great slashes of crimson almost as tall as Jess. The edge of what she could handle approached fast, but she couldn't stop herself from reading the message left for her:

I warned you.

Yes, you did, she thought, the pictures she'd received flashing in her mind. She'd chosen to fight rather than ignore them. Apparently Brit got her message.

Her stomach churned.

She moved forward.

Her bedroom door. *No more waiting.*

Inside, red paint showered the ripped mattress and torn bedding; the scattered, slashed clothing; her shattered laptop, looking as if a ball-peen hammer had taken it apart piece by piece. But it was the final message, dripping garishly above her headboard, that truly chilled her blood.

Mine. My fucking mouse.

Jess gagged.

"What is it, baby?"

Conlan's voice was a mere whisper in her ear. Without

thought, her hand rose to stroke the barely visible scars across her throat, a throat closed tight with fear as memories rushed her.

Mine. My fucking mouse.

Yeah, he'd got her message. And sent one back. She understood it loud and clear.

"Anything you can tell us, Ms. Kingston?" the young cop asked. "Any of this familiar?"

She kept her eyes on the message until Conlan spoke. "Jess, tell them."

She turned to stare into his stormy gray eyes. "Doesn't matter. They won't believe me now any more than they did before."

In fact, she very much feared they wouldn't believe her until she was dead. If then.

14

"Ms. Kingston."

Detective Gaines zeroed in like a hawk spotting a rodent in a field. On the outside he looked like an accountant—a well-built accountant, but still, an accountant. His hair wasn't buzz cut like a normal policeman; instead, the soft blond waves tickled his ears, hiding the earpieces from his wire-rimmed glasses. His suit was dark, his hands masculine but manicured, and his formal politeness made her feel like she was anticipating trouble from the IRS. An audit would have been a cakewalk compared to the look he gave her now, however.

The detective leaned forward on the gray metal table separating them, his clasped hands a paperweight holding down the scattered notes and files he'd been perusing. That eagle-eyed gaze never let up. "All right, let's talk about tonight."

She was sure the words were meant to be reassuring—okay, maybe not—but somehow she couldn't get past the sense that she'd done something wrong. Gaines's light eyes asked her to explain, and she couldn't. How could you explain a psychopath?

Where the hell was Conlan? He'd taken a detour between fingerprinting and here, promising he'd be back shortly. That was twenty minutes ago. Since the moment they'd walked into her apartment, he'd been close, a rock, as if their argument never happened. She knew she should take care of this on her own, stand on her own two feet...but after the day she'd had, that was impossible. She didn't want to think about the future; all she wanted was for him to get his ass back in here.

Gaines flipped through notes from the scene. "You said you know who broke into your apartment."

"Yes." She tried to put every ounce of conviction she had into the word, which of course made it sound the opposite. "My ex-boyfriend, Brit Holbrooke."

"Holbrooke? Any relation to Holbrooke Technologies?"

The suspicion in his tone drew steel into her spine. Brit had the backing of a powerful name and a powerful family, and she didn't. That fact had been borne home to her after her attack, but it didn't make him any less guilty.

"Yes, it's the family company. Brit is the technology director there, his father's vice president."

"Ah." An attempt to frown barely pulled at the edge of his lips, they were so tight. "And how do you know he is responsible?"

She raised an eyebrow, then glanced down at the notes in front of him. The manila file at the bottom of the stack was clearly visible. She was tired and off-kilter, but not stupid. "I think you already know that."

Gaines shuffled the notes aside and flipped the case file open. There, pinned along the inner edges, flashed full-color photos of Jess—not just the cream of her skin or the brown of her hair, but black and blue and red. Close-ups of her body, her injuries, the agony clear even with her eyes closed. Jess couldn't help the catch in her breath, the way her eyes flinched away.

And Gaines was watching it all.

"I've skimmed the reports, but Holbrooke had an iron-clad alibi."

She'd had this argument with Detective King too often to hold out any hope that Gaines would believe her, but she couldn't help a bitter, "And he probably will tonight too. Money talks—or makes sure you don't."

"So, despite no evidence that your ex was involved in your attack, you claim tonight is an extension of that incident."

The cop tone and lingo were grating on her already frazzled nerves. She closed her eyes and breathed in, trying to control her irritation—and her fear; it was unavoidable when the memories had to be faced. When her skin stopped feeling like she was about to burst out of it, she looked at the detective again. "Brit returned to town last week," she told him, working to keep her tone even. "Or at least that's the first I saw him. He's been stalking me ever since." She explained what had happened, searching her mind for details, all the while trying to squelch any hope that tried to rise.

When she finished, Gaines's gaze bored into her. "And tonight?"

"I know it was him."

"I can't build a case on knowing, Ms. Kingston. We might get some forensics"—his tone said he doubted it—"some video, but barring that or a witness..." He shrugged.

The smack of Jess's hand hitting the table startled them both. "I know it was him! No one else cares enough to follow me around town, follow me home. No one cares who I see or warns me to stay away from men. No one ever called me 'mouse' but Brit, and no one would know about it because he only did it in private. What is it going to take for you to believe me—a body? Because he isn't going to stop."

By the last word, she was breathless, voice shaking and eyes watering from the force of the anger inside her. Gaines stared, searching for she knew not what—and didn't really care. Finally, the lines between his eyebrows deepening, he asked, "Why did he call you 'mouse'?"

Yeah, just what I wanted to share. She looked down at the table, focusing on her fingertip tracing the scratches and dents in the surface. "Because he said I was too quiet, always hanging around in the corner like a mouse. He wanted me to be more assertive, more outgoing..." *More willing to have sex.* "*You even squeak when I touch you, you damn mouse.*" She laughed, the sound bitter even in its softness. "Of course, when I came out of my corner fighting, he liked that even less."

A rattle of the doorknob preceded Conlan stepping into the room, Jack following close behind. She didn't stand. Gaines did, extending his hand for a brief, firm shake for each man before resuming his seat.

Conlan took the seat next to her, pulling the chair close enough that his shoulder nudged hers. He reached over, grabbed the hand currently tapping out a fast tattoo on her pants leg, and settled it with his own on the thigh closest to her. Jess felt the denim of his jeans, the solid heat of muscle beneath the cloth, and let Conlan's closeness shore up her shaky defenses.

"Jack. Good to see you. And Con." Gaines's gaze turned from Jack to Conlan and dropped to the hand held so carefully in his lap. "What brings you two into this fine mess?"

"That's pretty obvious, Patrick," Jack said quietly. "Let's not play games."

Gaines held his hands up and chuckled, becoming the unassuming accountant once more. "No games, Jack. Just asking."

Jack took the last battered metal chair around the table. Once settled, his dark brown eyes centered on her. Jess didn't have a smile left in her, but she managed a nod toward Conlan's friend. "Jack."

"Rough night, darlin'?"

"Rough night," she confirmed.

Jack turned narrowed eyes back to Gaines. "What have you got so far?"

"Now, Jack, you know I can't share that with you, even if I had it—which I don't. It's too soon for anything to be in." He glanced down at his notes, pulling everyone's attention to the obscene display of photos still laid out. Jess felt Conlan stiffen before Gaines flipped the file closed. "Con, I understand you were on scene when the unit arrived. Were you with Ms. Kingston when she discovered the open door?"

Jess bristled, reading Gaines's implication clearly, but Conlan shrugged the question off. "I was on the phone with her when she discovered the break-in. She needed me. I came."

I wish.

"Because you're dating?"

Conlan did squirm at that.

Figures.

"We met last week. Brit had her cornered between two cars in a parking lot."

She'd already told Gaines all this, but he made no mention of that fact.

"So Ms. Kingston told you what she saw, then called 911, but you arrived before APD. Must've been close."

"I was." Conlan's fingers tightened on hers briefly. "I was following her home, but had to make a quick stop. That's why I called. I wanted to have at least some contact if I had to be out of sight for a few minutes."

The shock of his words took a moment to register. Why? Why refuse to see her again but still follow her? Oddly enough, she didn't jump straight to *I have another stalker*. No, if Conlan was following her, there had to be a reason.

Gaines obviously thought so too. "Because...?"

Shifting to one side, Conlan fished his cell phone out of his back jeans pocket. "Because I got a text message from the bastard yesterday, and I wanted to be close in case he showed his face again."

Gaines turned to Jess. "How about you?"

"I...I did. Not a text. An e-mail. Or, e-mails."

"What did they say?" Gaines demanded. Jess explained what Brit had sent her. Jack and Conlan cursed in unison.

Gaines rubbed his chin thoughtfully. "And you?" he asked Conlan.

He tapped on his phone, then passed it to Gaines. Whatever it said made Gaines's eyebrows meet halfway up his forehead. He passed the phone back. "You ran the number?"

Jack was the one who answered. "Of course we didn't. A friend did." Jess didn't believe him and she didn't think Gaines did either, but the detective didn't press. "Throwaway cell."

"Figures. How long were you on Ms. Kingston's six?"

Conlan related the details of his day, even down to giving Gaines Lori's contact information to confirm. While Gaines wrote the information down, Conlan asked, "Any witnesses? What about cameras?"

"Canvas found no witnesses yet. We'll run the security tapes tomorrow, see if any clues are there."

"Start with the camera over apartment thirty-one. It's pointed directly at her door. No way could it have missed a direct shot of anyone going in," Conlan said.

Gaines frowned. After consulting his notes again, he said, "The office records don't say anything about a camera in the hallway. At either end, yes, but not over one of the apartments."

"I saw it while we waited for y'all to do your thing." He named the brand, and Jack whistled.

"Popular with high-end security teams and high-end thieves."

Jess was starting to get an even worse feeling than she'd had for about four hours. "Are you saying he's not just following me, he's videotaping me?" She'd known about the pictures, but video? *Inside* her apartment building?

So he'd followed her, taken pictures of her at intimate moments, tracked down her e-mail address, her new apartment... "I think I might be sick."

One side of Gaines's mouth quirked down in something vaguely resembling a grimace. "We don't know that for certain," he said, overriding Conlan, who'd opened his mouth to answer. "And even if we did know someone had a camera placed in that location, we haven't tied it to Holbrooke."

A long look passed between Jack and Conlan, one that Gaines intercepted.

"This is an official APD investigation. I'm assuming I'll have your full cooperation, gentlemen?"

"Are you asking us not to butt our noses in?" Jack asked.
"Yes."

Jack shrugged. "Sure."

They all knew he was lying, but Gaines didn't pursue it. After making a final note, he began gathering the papers. When all was neat and tidy, he leaned forward, resting his clasped hands against the table.

"I can tell you that I will investigate, Ms. Kingston— without prejudice. What we'll find, I don't know." The predator was back in his eyes, and Jess braced herself for his next words. "Holbrooke's position in this city is not a factor for me, but neither will he be my only focus. When the evidence comes in and we have more to go on, we will definitely be in contact with you. Officer Davies is supervising the scene until the crime techs are done, and he will allow you to pick up some personal items. We'll need to know how to contact you."

"How to...? God, I didn't even think..." She couldn't go home, not for more than to pick up a few things, if she could even find a few things intact.

Conlan squeezed her fingers again. "She'll be with me. You have my information."

Jess's breath stuttered. "What?"

She wasn't the only one surprised. Jack jerked his head around, staring at Conlan for a few moments before a small, satisfied smile touched his lips. Jess couldn't begin to guess what that was about; she was too busy reeling from Conlan's declaration.

"I-I can call Cris. I should—"

"Holbrooke knows you, Jess. If you aren't at home, where's the first place he'll look?"

He was right; he'd go straight to her best friend. "Still, I—"

"With me, baby, and that's final. You need around-the-clock protection until this is over."

Baby. How she loved hearing him say that, enough so

that his last words almost slipped by her. "I can't afford around-the-clock protection."

Jack chuckled. "I don't think he's planning on charging you."

Jess shot him a glare before turning back to Conlan. "Wouldn't your address be easily available? I mean, he saw us together. He knows your name, your phone number."

"Trust me; I'm not worried about him. I protect people for a living, remember? For tonight at the very least, you're stuck with me."

"I don't th—"

"Don't think, not right now."

Which was how she found herself sitting in Conlan's car a few minutes later, headed toward her apartment. At almost midnight, traffic was sparse, but even so, she couldn't help wondering at the normalcy of people going about their lives, hanging with friends, doing whatever. She was headed to her trashed apartment to see if she had any clothes left, then going home with the man who'd refused to sleep with her but now wanted her living in his pocket. Her world was so far from normal it wasn't even funny.

A flashback of her apartment blazed through her mind. Definitely not funny.

They didn't speak until Conlan steered the car into the parking area near her apartment building, now devoid of flashing lights and police cruisers. The white tech van taking up the two spaces nearest the door was all that remained. Conlan shifted into park and turned off the engine, then reached for her hand. "Look, Jess, I know we're not exactly on solid footing right now, but it's the middle of the night. Let's get some rest, get our heads on straight, and then..."

He seemed at a loss for what came after *then*. She didn't help him out.

Finally he sighed. "Just let me take care of...things for tonight."

"Why?"

She didn't miss the hesitation. It hurt, but hell, she needed whatever he was willing to give.

"Because I'm a friend."

"A friend?"

"Yeah." The smile he gave her was a tired facsimile of the wicked grin that made her melt.

The ring of her cell phone blared through the moment.

Without thinking, Jess tugged the slim cell out of her pocket, her eyes still on the man beside her. "Hello."

"Jess. How was your evening?"

The breath froze in her lungs at the sound of Brit's voice in her ear.

"What's the matter, mouse? Cat got your tongue?" His chuckle sent a shiver of fear down her spine.

"What is it?" Conlan asked.

"Is he still with you?" Brit kept talking in her ear, but her gaze stayed glued to Conlan, to the concern on his face, the rising anger. "Maybe my message wasn't quite clear enough."

"Who is it, Jess?"

"Why are you calling me? Why are you doing this?" Jess asked Brit.

"Because I can, little mouse. You belong to me."

"No!" Jess twisted toward the door, one hand rising to ward off Conlan's efforts to take the phone. "I don't belong to you; I don't belong to anyone. You stay away from me!"

Conlan's white face got right in hers. "Give me that damn phone now."

Brit's voice hissed in her ear. "Oh, Jess, you're mine. You always will be. You might've escaped for a little while, but it was only a matter of time before I reeled you back in. It's time you came home."

The phone cut off just as Conlan ripped the handset from her. Punching his finger at the screen in desperation, he growled when nothing came up. It was as if she'd never even received a call. *Maybe I imagined it,* she thought a bit hysterically.

Jess barely blinked before Conlan was out of the car and around to her side, pulling her out, but it was just long enough. Bile rose, sending her sprinting for the bushes nearby. Racking sobs mixed with the spasms fisting her belly as she emptied her stomach, continuing to heave clear fluid even then.

Minutes, maybe hours, later, gentle hands pulled the hair away from her face and stroked her back, easing her tears enough that she could lean against the brick building at her side, waiting for the trembling to still. A white tissue, stark in the darkness, appeared under her face, and Jess realized she was still doubled over facing the ground. She took the square and cleaned herself, using a second ghostly offering to clear her mouth before standing upright. Conlan's angry face swam in front of her.

"Okay?"

She nodded.

"Good. Upstairs," he said.

15

"Jess!"

Conlan's hoarse cry cut through the dark, dragging her submerged consciousness out of another nightmare and into reality. After forcing her eyes open, she met his concerned gaze as he hovered over her.

That look confused her until she realized she was fighting for breath. The more air she pulled, the emptier her lungs felt, until panic surged with her racing heartbeat. She gripped the firm biceps caging her and focused on Conlan's face, his lips. They were tight, angry. What had she done?

"I'm sorry." The words were squeezed through her closed airway, low and raspy. Had she been screaming? Maybe that's why he was angry—she'd woken him up. She looked for a window, a clock, anything that could tell her if it was the middle of the night. Oh God, she hadn't meant to wake him up.

"Jess, stop." Firm hands framed her face, stilling her search. "Shh, look at me. It's all right. Just breathe." The anxious tone of his voice was cutting through the panic in her mind. "It's all right. I'm here."

As if her brain had finally clicked online, Jess realized where she was, where they were. In Conlan's apartment. In his bed. Vague memories of arriving, Conlan helping her undress, and the cool crispness of fresh sheets against her skin flitted through her mind. She shifted, feeling the soft covers and her mostly bare body.

Bare.

Conlan was leaning over her, securing her to the mattress. His elbows were braced just outside her shoulders, keeping most of his weight off her and his chest hovering above. The muscled expanse rose and fell, drawing her eyes, her hands like a lodestone.

His skin warmed her palms. Filling her lungs in rhythm with his became her center, her only focus for long moments in time. *Breathe. Just breathe.*

A flinch went through her when Conlan moved, easing away.

"Awake now?"

That's right, not supposed to be touching anymore. She took another lungful of air, responding on the exhale. "Yeah."

"Good," he said. His eyes glimmered in the moonlight streaming through the curtains. "You scared the shit out of me."

"I'm sor—"

Conlan cut her off with a shake of his head. "Don't," he said. "Don't apologize to me. It's no wonder you're having nightmares with the shitty experience you had tonight. Last night." He shook his head again. "Whenever it is."

Jess closed her eyes, trying to block out the distance between them, but flashes from her dream brought them back open. Brit, a hand around her neck, screaming, pain. A whimper choked off in her throat.

"Shh." Conlan lay down, his strong arms turning her

toward him, gathering her close. Her silk-clad breasts hit his bare chest, her pelvis fitting right against his, and suddenly nightmares were the last thing on her mind. No, now she couldn't breathe for a whole different reason.

"Con?" She glanced up, meeting his shadowed gaze, and time went as still as her breath. Something hovered between them, something she couldn't name, but it sizzled and snapped along her senses until remaining still was impossible. On reflex, her tongue sneaked out, wetting her suddenly dry lips. Conlan cursed.

She went to speak, and Conlan's mouth dropped to meet hers. She opened to him instead. Her hands, her skin, every molecule soaked up the heat of him, the intensity, the hunger. It quivered through him and into her. The nightmare couldn't have her back. She was Conlan's; she lived for his kiss, his taste, his touch. A hiccupy sigh escaped between kisses as the present overtook the past.

Conlan shifted restlessly, pulling her closer, then closer still. His knee nudged between hers, then up toward the apex of her thighs. The hard, muscled length of his leg wedged itself against her mound, and she actually smiled. So much better than the past.

He settled back into stillness. Jess stirred, restless, and Con's limbs clamped down on hers to keep her still. Was that it? Surely he wouldn't just leave things there—they were in bed, skin to skin, for goodness' sake.

Snuggling in, she breathed softly against his chest. Even in the dim room she could see his nipple tighten. "Conlan?"

"Ssh. Just go back to sleep."

———

CONLAN FORCED his breathing to calm, even if he couldn't force his erection to do the same. It was screaming its need, throbbing like a son of a bitch, but he wouldn't give in. *Go to sleep.*

The quiet lasted about two seconds more before Jess moved. She arched into him, her pebbled nipples clearly felt, brushing across his chest—once, twice, again. He leaned back, certain she wasn't aware enough to understand what she was doing, although the bulge between his thighs, so tightly tangled with hers, had to be a big clue.

Jess whimpered, her fingernails digging into the muscles of his arms, urging him closer.

"Jess."

She tilted her head away from his chest and glanced up from under her lashes. Residual fear and rising desire warred in the depths of her soft brown eyes.

"What is it, baby?"

Jess answered him without words, arching again, the movement dragging her pelvis along his rock-hard shaft. Low groans escaped both of them.

He wanted to give in. He wanted to close his eyes and forget day would ever come and just lose himself in the pleasure she could give him. But that was impossible, because day would come and, with it, reality. So he forced the pleasure away.

Jess wasn't quite so willing.

Stretching up, she brought her mouth to the sensitive notch of his neck and shoulder and bit down, holding him close as her pelvis rolled into his again. The sound that escaped her turned into a whine of pure sexual need, jacking him even higher. He squeezed his eyes shut. No, he couldn't do this. They had to stop.

His body wasn't listening. Lightning quick, he had her

rolled beneath him and his mouth on hers, taking her breath and giving her his in a hot tango of lips, tongues, and teeth. Jess gave as good as she got, devouring him immediately and completely. Lust shot an electrical charge up his spine, urging him on, tempting him to let go and take what she was offering all the way to its natural conclusion. That decision was made for him when she reached around to unhook her bra.

The feel of her full, round breasts pressed directly against his skin fed the red haze taking over his mind. He transferred his hand to the curve of her butt cheek, digging his fingers deep, bringing his other palm up to cup her nape. Her moan tasted of surrender.

One strong, slender leg dragged restlessly up his hip. The minute the warm wetness soaking her panties registered along the back of his cock, he felt the tightening in his balls that signaled climax and jerked himself out of her arms. Next thing he knew, he stood across the room with his back to Jess, breath loud, ragged in the sudden silence.

The slide of cotton sheets dragged his gaze back to the bed. Jess fumbled with her bra, straightening the straps before sliding them up her arms. Her hands shook; he could see that, even in the dark. Something deep in his chest squeezed tight.

"Jess..."

Scooting to the edge, she went to get up, then sank slowly back down amid the tangled covers. A lost look filled her eyes. "I just realized—I can't leave. I don't have anywhere to go."

"God, Jess, I just—"

She held up a pale hand. "I don't want to hear it. *Again*. It seems like every time we start to get close—" The rest of the sentence dropped with her hand. She grabbed a blanket from the end of the bed. "I'll sleep on the couch."

"No." He stepped in front of her as she rounded the bed. Reaching out to clasp her arms, he tried to explain. "Tonight, the apartment—I just don't want you to make a decision you'll regret in the morning."

Yanking herself away, Jess glared up at him, her anger sudden and hot and palpable between them. "And *I'm* tired of everyone trying to make those decisions for me. Jesus! If I want to make a mistake, then by God, I'll be the one to make it. I know what I want, damn it!" She began to pace, steps sharp, angry. "It's the shower all over again. What, are you only good at teasing a girl, is that it? Because really, I'm beginning to feel like reverse cock blocking is all you're good for."

"What? No!" He took a single step toward her but stopped when she shied away. Rough breaths escaped her heaving chest. When a tear fell from the corner of her eye, he knew he had to explain or die trying. "Look, I— Saturday, I...I panicked."

She shot him an incredulous look. "Right. The whole picket-fence-and-love thing. Well here's a clue, Con: I'm not thinking about a picket fence. Or commitment. I'm thinking I just want to forget for a little while, feel good, share...*something* with someone that is my choice. I don't think it's all that scary, especially for a big tough guy like you."

Well when she put it like that... He dropped his head. In the silence he watched his hands fist and relax, fist and relax, again and again until the rhythm calmed his panic and settled his breathing. And as he breathed, he realized she was right. It wasn't so scary—unless it was between him and Jess, and then it terrified the shit out of him because she wasn't just any woman. She was the one who could change everything. He hadn't believed he wanted that, hadn't let himself acknowledge exactly what he was feeling for her—but pushing her away was killing him. He wouldn't do it anymore. She deserved better. And Jack was right; it was time to stop living in the past.

Jess had chosen to move forward instead of always looking back. Maybe he needed to take lessons from her instead of the other way around.

He glanced up. Jess had crossed her arms, one hip cocked out, her plump breasts raised as if in offering to him. The sight brought a hot flush to his cheeks.

"You're right. This is your decision, not mine." A sigh escaped. "And I...I want you, more than I've ever wanted anyone in my life. So, if you're sure this is what you want, that it isn't just today or the past or anything but pure need, then"—he held his arms out to his sides—"you win." He took a step toward her.

"God, really?" she scoffed. "Don't do me any favors."

He could read the hurt in her eyes, but the heavy ache between his legs added irritation to his concern. He indicated his erection, still proudly displayed behind his white boxer briefs. "Does it look like I'm not ready and willing? 'Cause I assure you, baby, I'm both—and more."

Jess's gaze zeroed in on his rock-hard, painful shaft. She licked her lips, and just like that, the anger in the room fell away. All that remained was the hunger running through them both. Damn if the woman didn't have a shitload of power over him—now, tomorrow, hell, maybe forever.

He needed to get a little of that power back. "Strip, baby."

At the command, she jerked, muscles quivering, fingers tightening into fists.

"Jess, it's your choice. Either give me the control, or take over. Either way, I'm yours." *And you are mine.* He didn't use those words, the same ones Holbrooke had used. He didn't mean them the same way her ex had, but he wouldn't add to the volatile mix of emotions in the room by saying the wrong thing. Again.

She didn't need the words—what he'd said was enough. The heat that flashed in her eyes told him so. God, it felt like she was burning him alive. Finger by finger, her hands relaxed until they lay completely open, and then, so slowly, Jess slipped the strap of her bra off one softly rounded shoulder, tugging it down until the pink-tipped globe popped out.

He swallowed hard. "Good girl," he said in a hoarse voice. When she did the same on the opposite side, he shifted restlessly. Without conscious thought, one hand came up to grip the base of his cock and squeeze down hard. *Just a little longer.*

Jess ducked her head, but not before he glimpsed a small smile tilting her lips. *That's right, baby. Make me lose control.*

The bra hit the floor with a soft *thud*, and Jess turned her attention to the silky white panties covering the place he most wanted to see. She shimmied them down, swaying her hips far more than necessary, he was sure. The expression on her face when she raised her head said she knew what she was doing to him and she was enjoying it.

So was he.

"Now me," he commanded.

She lifted an eyebrow in challenge, and Conlan gave her a firm look. She must have read the determination in his eyes, because she stepped forward and hooked her thumbs in the top of his boxer briefs before lowering them carefully, down, down, down, until they dropped to the floor at his feet. His erection tilted out, weeping already in anticipation of her touch. Silence hung heavy in the room as she looked her fill, her breasts swaying softly with every deep breath she took.

"On the bed," he told her. The sight of her rounded ass as she turned to obey had him squeezing his sex again. Damn, forget foreplay. At this point he didn't need it, and if the cream shining on the insides of her thighs was any indication, neither did she. When she turned to lie on her back, watching him, he stalked forward, letting her see his intent —to take her hard and fast, to force her beyond any inhibitions and concerns and problems and emotions that filled her mind and into the oblivion that could only be found after explosive passion. She needed it—they both did, so damn bad—and he was just the man to give it to her.

After a quick detour to the dresser for a condom he went ahead and slid on, he climbed onto the bed, his gaze riveted to her silken body. God, she was beautiful. All womanly curves and moist, hidden places. Just looking at her, he knew he wouldn't last too much longer before he shot his load on the sheets. "Cup your breasts, Jess. Offer them to me."

Her eyes went wide, but the sensual grimace that crossed her face as she arched her back told him the words turned her on. When she lifted her breasts, the nipples jutting proudly upward, the best kind of present, his mouth watered and he leaned forward to reward her with a nip to one sensitive tip.

"Oh!"

He latched on, pinning her rigid nipple to the roof of his mouth as he drew on her hungrily. She tasted good—sweet, hard as a berry, and so sensitive her entire body strained upward to give him more. Sobs fell from her mouth as he devoured her, kneading the firm flesh of her breast in his hand, unable to hold back or soften the power of his sucking. He could stay at her breasts forever and never get enough.

She writhed beneath him, lifting her pelvis to rock against his swollen shaft. "Conlan, please! I need you."

He raised heavy eyes to stare down into her face. "Do you ache, baby?"

Sweat glistened along the creamy skin of her chest, and her eyes were frantic. "God, yes."

"Good." Just where she needed to be. He focused his attention on the opposite breast and lowered one hand to the juncture of her thighs.

Pushing his fingers between her legs, he urged them apart, making room for himself and settling there. He rolled his palm against her mound, beginning a deep massage that matched the rhythm of his suckling, intensifying the desire that trembled through her body.

She was wet—damn, so wet that she dripped onto his fingers, the scent of sex and anticipation spicing the air. Her nipples jutted up in sharp points as he switched between them. Watching her face, her breathing, he traced her slit from front to back with two long fingers, opening the plump lips, delving inside to run his fingertips around her clitoris. She pushed her knees out even more, opening herself, allowing him access as she thrust against his hand. Her steady cries rent the air.

His body shook with the overwhelming need to finish. The strain pounded in his cock, but only when her hands came up to grip his head, fingers digging deep into his hair to clutch handfuls in ragged desperation, did he dare to dip a single finger into her opening. That first touch seemed to set her on fire.

"Conlan," she shrieked, pushing down, forcing his finger deeper. She moaned, the sound dark chocolate and drugged with passion. "So good."

He couldn't wait much longer. Based on the slick feel of her, Jess couldn't either. Praying for control, he impaled her fully on a single digit, circling, thrusting, opening her to him. She was tight. He withdrew his finger and returned with two, stretching her, scissoring, preparing her. Her moans drove him wild, breathy, sucking gulps of air that made him wonder what she would sound like with his cock inside, stretching her taut. The thought brought a pulse of precum to spill from his tip.

Jess seemed lost in the moment, her eyes closed, her body undulating as she pushed against his fingers. So beautiful in her hunger. A tingling warning shot down his spine just watching her.

Time to go.

"Open for me, Jess." Conlan thrust his fingers in hard.

Jess accepted every inch, her thighs stretching wide, no hesitation as she gave him his first full, unhindered view of her body. She was dark pink, glistening, her pretty opening clenching around his fingers, the tiny pearl at the top peeking out from its hood and hard in her arousal. He looked up, wanting to praise her, to thank her for her trust, and was just in time to see her fingers grasp a swollen nipple and pinch hard. The sight was all he could take. He replaced his fingers with his throbbing cock, moving up over her body, breathing her name as he took her mouth in a raw, starving kiss.

He struck quickly, surging forward into her glove-tight passage, praying to God he could hold it together a few minutes more. He felt what was left of her hymen give as he moved, felt her jerk, heard her harsh cry echo between them before he was seated to the hilt. He couldn't have stopped the second thrust if his life depended on it, but he was able to moderate it, a short, hard dig before he held himself ruthlessly still and allowed his climax to wash over him. Heart near to exploding, he took a moment to breathe, to relish every spasm of pleasure shooting through him as her walls clamped down on him like a vise. His body screamed at him to move, to claim her in the most primitive way possible, with thrust after hard, desperate thrust, anything to extend the goddamn ecstasy rushing through his veins, but he fought the instinct and won. Instead he soothed his mouth over the tears on Jess's cheeks and waited for her to open her eyes.

———

THE SHARP, tearing pain obliterated all else for long seconds. Through the haze, she felt Conlan's second short thrust, spasming her muscles as they protested the foreign presence in her body. Even as a strange warmth bathed her electrified core, shock traveled from her body to her brain, freezing her in place.

The pain faded as moments passed, but the need for climax, so strong before his penetration, went with it. She held deathly still, afraid even to breathe in case the hurt returned. Not until a wet drop slid into her ear did she realize tears trailed along her face.

It was done. Finally, after so much frustration and waiting, she was no longer a virgin. She tried to inspect that thought, to decide if it was relief she felt, but the pressure of Conlan inside her cast everything else aside. She hadn't expected to feel like this, the sheer overwhelming invasion of not just her body but her heart. She was taken over, possessed, enslaved by the man whose body still filled hers.

"Jess." Wet warmth traced the lines her tears had left across her cheeks. Hot breath dried the moisture. Conlan's gentle lips touched hers. His weight settled onto her, and he rocked back and forth, soothing her and, strangely enough, pleasuring her. There was no more pain, no more than a dull ache. Jess sighed in relief, shifting her legs instinctively to let him closer.

"Easy, baby," he whispered against her mouth. "Just give it a minute."

So she did. The soft rocking continued, the gentle rasp of his chest against her nipples, his pubic hair against her clit. It didn't take long before the sensations lit a tiny spark of hunger within her once more.

Opening her eyes, Jess focused on the dark shadow hiding Conlan's expression. He went still, tilting her chin up with a determined finger. "You okay?"

She swallowed hard. "It hurt."

"I know. I'm sorry." Before she could register that Conlan was apologizing, he dipped his head to whisper in her ear. "The pain's over now, though." Slowly, carefully, he eased his hips back, sliding out of her body, then eased in again. No pain, just... *God.* She couldn't hold back a moan.

"That's it. That's my Jess." His mouth met hers, his tongue delving deep in a slick imitation of what he was doing between her legs. Her insides clenched around him, and this time he moaned. "Holy sh—" Conlan bit down on his lip as he stared into her eyes. "You feel so damn good, baby. So good I came. Two strokes. That was it; that was all I could take." He chuckled. "Nothing has ever felt as good as you taking me in. I've never come that fast. Never."

A small, silly burst of pride flashed through her. Without

thought her pelvis titled up to his, the rigid length of his cock scraping her clit. Jess's breath caught in her throat.

"That's right. Now it's your turn, baby." He thrust again, then again, sending a thrill of heat rushing through her. Her body melted into the mattress in an unconscious signal even she could read.

When she tried to speak, her voice was a mere whisper in the dark. "Can you... I mean, are you—"

The grin that spread across his face sent another thrill of pleasure through her. "Does this feel like I'm done?" With a flex of his hips, he glided back fully, then thrust forward with a hard push. His pelvis ground against her clit. A high squeak was all the answer she could provide.

Conlan lifted a breast to his lips, his thumb circling her softened nipple until it lengthened once more, begging shamelessly for his attention. She clutched at him, raising her legs to ride his hips, needing more than the lazy rhythm he set. "Please. Con, please."

His teeth nipped the taut tip in response, causing her to jump, before he sucked her in hard. His cheeks hollowed as he drew on her. A path of sexual need burned from the end of her breast to her clit, pounding out the rhythm of his sucks, shoving her closer and closer to orgasm. He picked up the pace, sliding easily in and out, filling every available breath of space until he nudged the opening to her womb. So full, so good.

"Con. Oh God. It feels..."

"That's right, baby. Right there." He punctuated the words with a sharp thrust. She strained toward him, wanting more, wanting to give him everything.

"Please." She needed, that was all she knew. She needed, and with every push into her body, he met that need, until she was at the top of the cliff again, wanting nothing more than to dive off and take him with her. He had to go too.

"Con, plea—" She squeezed around him, tightening, feeling him swell against her walls as he thrust faster. They strove together, pushing, straining, fighting for their pleasure.

"Jess. Jess, now!" Con shouted, his cock jerking, filling her with that heavenly warmth a second time, and she convulsed again, allowing the pleasure to take her, remake her, as she lay safe in his arms.

16

Muted light filtered through the blinds as Jess stirred the next morning, the scent of coffee teasing her into wakefulness. Stretching automatically, she winced, then smiled, feeling the tug of muscles she had never been aware of before. It was oh so worth it. She couldn't have asked for a better first time—a better any time—than Conlan. The man's moves were magic.

Seeing her duffel bag on the floor near the door, she gathered clothes and hurried into the bathroom, anxious to join Con. She'd like nothing better than to spend the day together, no commitments, nowhere to go, just the two of them and an empty house, empty bed. Instead there were issues to deal with, plans to make. A girl could dream, though.

She groaned into the water as it filtered down from the top of her head to her aching thighs, letting the heat ease her muscles even as anticipation tightened them. She didn't care how sore she was or how much she had waiting for her to do—she wouldn't miss a single opportunity to be with him, to feel him, to love him.

God, she loved him.

Her heart had the damnedest timing, didn't it? Even if they'd known each other longer than a week and a half, it would be too soon, not to mention how fucked up her life was. Flashes of her apartment came back to haunt her, making her shiver despite the heated droplets raining down on her. So much was going wrong right now—except Conlan. He was everything that was right. It hadn't even been the sex that had done it. It was standing in that room last night and yelling at him that it was her decision, and having him offer what she'd so desperately needed. It had been the generosity of his lovemaking and the power of the emotions arcing between them.

And now she was getting ready to face him once more. What if he regretted their time together? What if he didn't?

She'd deal with it when it came. Future or not, relationship, commitment, whatever, this was her first—and maybe only, based on her not so stellar track record—chance to have a lover, and she wouldn't waste a minute of it. The future would just have to take care of itself. For however long she had Conlan, in whatever form, she would enjoy him.

She dressed quickly in a pair of khakis and a nice, if not totally work appropriate, T-shirt. How even a few clothes had managed to survive the destruction, she didn't know, but their familiar presence soothed her nerves as she hurried to brush her hair back from her face and then picked up her phone. She left a quick message for Saul saying she would be delayed getting in to work but would stop by a little later to explain. She didn't want to deal with the details right now—not before her first cup of coffee, and not before seeing the man she'd given her heart to.

Conlan was leaning against the counter in front of the coffee maker, a full cup in his hands, when she walked into the kitchen. He was dressed in a pair of worn khakis and a button-down left open to reveal the muscles of his chest. The perfect view for breakfast.

"Cream and three sugars, right?" he asked, turning to grab an empty cup waiting on the counter.

"Yes, please." Taking a chance, she snuggled close, enjoying his firm butt nestled into her belly. His warmth heated the part of her deep inside that even the shower hadn't been able to touch.

Con stepped out of her hold and headed for the fridge. *Or maybe not.*

She watched silently as he fixed her coffee before passing it to her, handle out, careful not to touch. Determined to ignore the obvious attitude, she focused on the rich aroma filling her nose. A quick sip of the steaming brew brought a moan of pleasure. "Perfection."

She took another taste of her coffee, seeking courage in the caffeine, followed by a deep breath. "So...I do have to go in to work for a little while, at least. I'm sure there are things I need to follow up with Gaines too. What's on your agenda for today?"

Conlan stared into his cup, frowning. He cleared his throat. "I think we need to talk before we decide that."

Dread filtered slowly through her veins, tightening muscles, clenching her teeth. *Breathe. You've survived worse. You can survive this too, remember.*

Yeah, but that didn't mean it wouldn't hurt like a son of a bitch.

"I think I've heard those words before." She turned her

back and headed for a barstool. When she was seated, her cup warming her icy hands, she looked over at his dead-serious face. "Spill it."

"Jess, last night was..."

She let her eyelids slip closed at the standard speech. Had he rehearsed it, or did he already know it by heart?

"It was amazing, Jess. Thank you."

Her eyes popped back open, round with surprise. Not what she'd expected to hear, but she was afraid to hope. His expression didn't shout happiness—it shouted, *Get me out of here!*

"Are you okay?" he asked.

Well, my nipples feel bruised and my pelvis aches and all I really want is for us to go at it again and forget the concept of talking ever existed.

Yeah, she didn't think she'd answer that. At least not honestly, not when they were right in the middle of the I-don't-think-we-should-see-each-other-anymore speech. "I'm fine."

He cleared his throat. "Good." Another sip, another throat clearing. "We... The condom we used...last night. It... it broke."

Her lungs collapsed under a shitload of *crap!* She set her cup down with extreme care on the cool, smooth countertop.

Conlan was still talking. "I take full responsibility. I should have been paying attention. I should've noticed. Changed condoms. I was supposed to before the second time anyway. I just...didn't. Notice, I mean. Or remember. I — It was too—"

"Amazing."

The coffee swirling in his cup seemed to fascinate him. "Yes."

Jess's gaze was stuck on Conlan. She'd thought she would hear *It was great, but...* not *You might be a mommy.* Shouldn't she have noticed? She remembered the warmth deep inside when Conlan climaxed, but she'd been too inexperienced to think about the fact that the sensation wouldn't be normal with a condom. At least, she assumed it wasn't normal, now, after...

Jesus.

The silence was loud between them, so loud Jess prayed it covered the pounding of her heart. It wasn't fear. The thought of carrying Conlan's child, now, before she was ready, before he had the chance to change his whole anti-picket-fence stance, didn't scare her nearly as bad as she thought it should. What scared her was his reaction—or lack thereof. She searched his face, coming up empty.

Okay, well... She cleared her throat.

"God, I feel like a nineteen-year-old caught with his pants down."

The image was so unimaginable Jess couldn't hold back a laugh. Conlan glanced up from under his lashes, watching her hold her belly and laugh hysterically, and a sheepish smile touched his lips before he set his coffee cup down and came around the end of the bar. His arms settled around her the way she'd wanted them to when she'd walked into the room, and then he was replacing her giggles with his tongue. Jess swallowed the taste of coffee and amusement and Conlan.

When he finally stopped kissing her, Jess gulped in a breath. Conlan nuzzled her nose with his. "Good to know I can make you laugh."

"It's either laugh or cry," she said, smiling up at him.

His gaze went serious. "I'm sorry. Shit, when I realized..."

He shook his head. "And you've got enough on you right now without this."

Staring up at him, she considered the options. Considered her mental state. The thought of getting rid of a possible baby, *Conlan's* baby... No, she couldn't think about that. "To be honest, I don't feel like this is something I can make a choice about right now. I'd be more worried if it was last week, but as it is..." She shrugged. "My period is due any day."

"So..." His warm hand rubbed up and down her back. "Okay."

"What...what about you? What are you thinking?"

"I think I'll stand by your decision no matter what. And"—he hugged her tight to him, tucking her head against his chest—"I won't be so careless with you again."

Her throat tightened.

Conlan held her a moment longer before clearing his throat. "Okay." He tilted down, his mouth settling on hers, and time slipped away as she lost herself in his kiss.

The ringing of her cell phone back in the bedroom finally brought them up for air. "That's Saul," she said as she ran her hands down the firm muscles of Conlan's chest, her fingertips catching on his pointed nipples. "It is safe for me to go, right? It's broad daylight."

His breath hitched as she played with the firm nubs. Conlan seemed to struggle to gather words together. "I'll take you." He cleared his throat with a growl. "I can't concentrate when you do that." His hands gripped hers, drawing them to his mouth for a kiss, then away from his body. She didn't protest—too much.

"I have to hit the office for a couple of meetings I can't miss, but even during the day, I'm not taking chances. How long will you be?"

She thought about what she needed to take care of. "A couple of hours, maybe."

"Okay. I want you at JCL when you're done. I'll send someone for you."

"Conlan—"

"Uh-uh," he warned before she could get any further. "It's an escort or nothing, baby. Even if I wasn't sleeping with you, I'd be making sure you were safe. But I am sleeping with you—and hope to do it again very soon—so you might as well get used to this. I'm not taking chances until we know this bastard is gone."

She stared into his eyes, and the certainty she saw there, the firm emphasis he put on *very soon*, made the decision for her. It was still difficult to believe that this beautiful man cared about her, wanted her, that he didn't see her as just a client or an inconvenience. She needed to work on that, the part of her that didn't believe she was worthy, of him or anyone else. In the meantime she rewarded him with another long kiss. "Okay."

"Good." This time Conlan kissed her. His lips were hungry, hard. One rough hand slid under the edge of her T-shirt, calluses scraping along her skin until it reached the silk of her bra, and Jess forgot she needed to go anywhere except back to bed.

It was another hour before they made it out the door.

His "you stay safe" rang in her ears—along with a few other things, like "broken condom"—as she went through the motions at work, settling things, gathering materials, explaining to Saul what her psycho ex-boyfriend had done this time. His sickened expression and the desperation with which he hugged her was a balm to her somewhat tattered psyche. She hugged him back, and when he insisted she return to working from home, she didn't argue. She had too many good things in her life to risk Brit's craziness, against her or them; the idea that he might come to her work and manage to make it inside, just like he had at her apartment, scared the crap out of her.

Freedom was overrated when it put the people you loved in danger, and Brit was a danger to them all. She no longer had any doubt about that.

Nicolas, Conlan's employee, was a brawny man with coffee-colored skin and eyes to match. Those eyes reassured her; they never stopped moving, watching, searching. Even Saul came under intense scrutiny when he stopped by her office to say goodbye. Jess gave her godfather another long, careful hug, and allowed Nicolas to escort her out. The intense Georgia sun blinded her as they made their way to the company Jeep Nicolas had driven over, but his solid hand guided her as they crossed the few feet of hot asphalt to the waiting vehicle. A smile pulled at her lips as she stepped up onto the running board of the Jeep and into the dark interior, not quite able to get past the feeling that she was a valuable package being delivered to an exacting owner. Nicolas might not use kid gloves, but he was very careful. The man obviously understood the threat they were facing—and the boss demanding her safety.

The cool dimness was a welcome relief as they slid into the confines of the parking garage at JCL. Nicolas didn't bother pulling into a space; he parked in the aisle, a few feet from the elevator. "Wait for me," he warned as he opened his door, but Jess already had her fingers on the handle, instinctively tightening. He exited the driver's side as her door popped open. With a grimace Jess waited for him to round the vehicle, feeling a bit ridiculous to have him escort her but unwilling to defy the man whose job it was to keep her safe.

Through the gap between the door and Jeep, she heard a distinct *crack*, the sound echoing against the concrete walls of the garage. Instinctively Jess stuck her head out—and watched Nicolas hit the pavement, one side of his head busted open and bloody. The red liquid spread across his buzz-cut hair and down over his closed eyes as Jess sat, frozen, half in and half out of the Jeep.

She didn't see Brit coming until it was too late. A bestial growl warned her mere seconds before the door was yanked out of her hand, a hard grip jerking her from the seat. She stumbled, numb, her gaze glued to Nicolas. Only when a wrench of her arm pulled her off balance, her feet unable to keep up as her body flew forward, did she turn her head and meet the hate-filled eyes of her ex-boyfriend.

Jess screamed.

Her knees hit the pavement, the impact shooting agony through the bones and muscles. She crumpled, needing to curl into a ball, to grab her pain-filled legs and ease the throbbing hurt steeling her breath, but Brit refused to let go. He dragged her forward, the movement increasing the torment racking her body, his sharp "Shut the hell up, bitch!" ringing in her ears.

No way in hell.

She screamed again, and despite the protests of every body part, curled herself around and lashed out at Brit's legs. She missed the first one, sailed right past, and scored a glancing blow to his standing leg. It buckled, but Brit managed to catch himself. He turned, his fist bouncing off her skull. Stars filled her vision. The shock of pain, of Brit's attack tried to pull her into protective blackness, but she fought it as hard as she fought him. Kicking, flailing, rolling. She didn't care if he dislocated her shoulder, gave her a concussion—whatever it took, she wasn't letting this man have her without the biggest fight of her life.

"Jess!"

The voice rang out over the sounds of her battle with Brit, but whomever it was, Brit heard it, and the distraction was just enough for her to wrench her hand free of his grip. She fell with no warning, hitting the ground so hard her teeth clacked together, catching her tongue between them. The pain was enough to keep her on the ground, but it was the sudden burst of shattering impact against her head that forced her beyond caring and into blessed unconsciousness.

17

The buzz of fluorescent lights scraped Con's already raw nerves like sandpaper, and the scathing looks he was getting from Cris, so different from her friendly glances at the coffee shop, compounded his irritation until he wanted to rage at everyone in the room except Jess. Jess, who lay unconscious in a stark white hospital bed because Con hadn't gotten to her quick enough.

The truth was, Cris couldn't condemn him any more than he condemned himself.

He hid it like the good soldier he was. No emotion, no looking back, just keep moving forward until the enemy is obliterated, no matter the odds. But when those odds lay pale and battered under the harsh light overhead, he couldn't stop the truth from burning in his chest, where no one could see. He hadn't protected this woman, and she had come very close to dying because of it. A millimeter off and Holbrooke's heavy boot could've caught her temple, her eye, could've stamped out the sweet light and heat that was Jess, mere hours after he'd allowed himself to admit that he could have her, could maybe even keep her if he didn't fuck up the future with his overblown fears. Turns out it wasn't his fears that had fucked things up; it was his complacence.

Jack's grip settled heavily on his shoulder, squeezing down, dragging him out of the cycle of self-pity circling his personal mental drain. Jack could read what Con didn't want to reveal, damn it. And even though his first instinct was to shrug out of his friend's grip, he didn't. It wouldn't do any good, and honestly, without Jack standing at his back, he just might hit his knees if Jess didn't wake soon.

"Why the hell weren't you there to meet her?"

He met Cris's gaze across the hospital bed but didn't answer. Didn't argue the obvious. None of it mattered anyway. Jess was unconscious, and Holbrooke had escaped. Those were the only two relevant facts at the moment.

Jack wasn't so easygoing. "If he hadn't been on his way to meet her, she'd be gone. Or dead."

The brutal truth hit Cris like a blow. Con, knowing her condition from talks with Jess, raised his hand to Jack. "It doesn't matter. All that matters is that Jess and Nicolas are all right."

Steven, Cris's much less volatile husband, Con had learned, rubbed a hand along her back. "How is your man?" he asked.

Jack shrugged, his tension still communicating itself through his grip on Con but not evident in his voice. "They're still evaluating. Holbrooke left a tire iron at the scene. Nic took a direct strike to the back of the head. We're just thankful right now that his neck wasn't broken."

Jack let go of Con, stepping over to the window. His stare might seem blind to the others, but Con knew differently. He was assessing possibilities, considering scenarios, and hopefully coming up with answers Con just couldn't find at the moment. All he knew was the fragile coolness of Jess's hand in his and the unending agony of not knowing whether she'd wake. The doctor had assured him she would, but he wouldn't allow himself to believe it until he saw it.

Cris wasn't deterred by the change in topic, nor by Jack's attempt to draw her attention away from Con. "He was waiting for her, right there in the garage," she said, her voice wavering. Con let her pain pierce his armor, knife him in the heart. He deserved it. "Didn't you expect him? Didn't you think the sick son of a bitch would come after her?"

"Cris, hon, stop." Steven rubbed a hand soothingly over her trembling shoulder. "None of us expected him to be this brazen. He covered his tracks well enough to not be convicted of beating her half to death; he's careful. Who thought he'd be crazy enough to attack in the middle of the day, in a public place?"

"We should have," Con admitted.

"He's escalating," Jack said.

Cris began to cry once more, her sobs wrenching something deep in Con's gut. "Should you be here?" he asked Steven, now hovering protectively over his weeping wife. He'd called knowing they wouldn't want to be kept in the dark—at least, not any further than they'd already been—but Jess had shared her concerns about Cris's pregnancy. He didn't know if emotional upset could put her at higher risk of miscarriage, but he didn't want to be responsible if it could.

Cris raised those angry eyes to his again. "Yes, I should be here," she hissed. "I should have been there last night. *You* should have called to tell us what was happening with *my* best friend."

"Hon—"

The tiniest whimper sounded from the bed between

them. Like heat-seeking missiles, four pairs of eyes all zeroed in.

"Jess?" Leaning down, Con reached for her, hesitated, then allowed himself to carefully cup her sheet-white cheek. "Jess, baby, can you hear me?"

Eyelashes fluttering, Jess moaned again. It took several heart-stopping minutes before those beautiful doe eyes opened fully. Jess squinted up into the glare of the overhead lights. She frowned, jerked her head to the side. A startled cry escaped.

"Shh." Con stroked her cheek gently. "Easy. No head banging for you yet."

Jess slitted her eyes and met his. Con didn't think anything could be sweeter than seeing the comprehension filling her soft gaze. Damn it, he was getting sappy.

Cris had stood when Jess opened her eyes, and now she grabbed Jess's other hand. Jess turned toward her friend, grimacing with the movement.

"You need to sit," she told Cris.

A single tear drizzled down Cris's flushed cheek. "Don't you be telling me what to do. I'm mad at you. God, Jess..."

"Shh. 'S all right." She pulled on the hand Conlan held, trying to reach for her friend.

Con tugged her hand back down. "Don't be moving. You've got an IV."

Steven stepped in, easing Cris back into her chair and using a tissue to mop up his wife's face. Jess stared down at her hand, encased in Con's. He knew she must be sore, her wrist slightly swollen from Holbrooke's grip, mottled bruises already rising to the surface around her wrist and elbow. He watched her take in the sight, watched panic rise in her gaze and squeeze his heart with the knowledge that he hadn't protected her, hadn't kept the bogeyman away like he was supposed to. That one look condemned him, though Jess didn't know it, didn't even intend it. But Con knew it, and the black marks on his soul would be there forever.

"Where is he?" Jess asked.

Another mark seared him. "He got away." Con had been more concerned with her crumpled body than Holbrooke's escape. Jack had searched but found nothing but the discarded weapon lying next to Nic's unconscious form.

Jess gasped, struggling to sit up despite her weakness. "You get her out of here, you hear me? Get her out!"

Cris reached for Jess. "Calm down. It's okay."

"It's not!" Jess wavered, sinking back onto her pillow, but her frantic need to protect Cris blazed from her eyes. "You have to go. Steven, take her somewhere safe."

"Not until I know you're okay." Cris stood again, her tone firm. "We're fine here for now."

"No—"

"Jess. Jess!" Con reached for the bed controls to lift her head, bring her closer to him. "It's all right. We have a guard outside the door. I wouldn't let Cris come if I didn't know it was safe."

Cris opened her mouth as if to argue. Con slashed a warning look her way.

"Just relax, baby. It's okay. Just relax."

Silent tears trickled down Jess's cheeks. He could almost see the pain that must be pounding in her head. Wiping the wetness from her skin wasn't enough; seeing that she was awake and aware and not a vegetable didn't help. He needed to feel, with more than just his hands, that she was okay. Ignoring everyone else, he rounded the bed, lifted Jess as carefully as he could, and slid beneath her, settling her on his lap. With a near-silent sigh, she laid her head in the hollow of his shoulder, and her body lost some of its rigid tension under his hands.

As she quieted, he murmured in her ear, told her again how safe they were, that she and Cris were protected, that Gaines would be here soon as well. Jack stood before the door, thick arms crossed as if he dared anyone to come in. Jess relaxed bit by bit until their bodies melded fully together. Feeling her breathe allowed him to take small, rusty breaths of his own.

God, he was so in over his head, but he couldn't let her go.

The door opened, hitting Jack in the back. He refused to budge until he verified the identity of the visitor, Jess's doctor. The tall, slender man sported faded green scrubs and a worn expression, one Con sometimes spied in his own mirror. The ER saw domestic violence cases almost as often as he and Jack did.

"I see you're awake, Ms. Kingston. I'm Dr. Bryant. How are you?"

"My head feels like someone's using it for a chopping block," Jess mumbled.

Dr. Bryant chuckled, switching his attention to Con. "Would you mind—"

"Yes, I would." He'd just gotten Jess in his arms. He wasn't giving her up now unless it was absolutely necessary. It wasn't.

"I see." The doctor shrugged philosophically. "Well, let's see what we've got going here." He flipped a penlight out of his pocket and began his exam. Jess moaned at the light, her pain clenching Con's gut, but endured stoically, even when Dr. Bryant fingered the massive knot on the back of her head. Con didn't tell her they'd had to shave a small patch of hair to get to the wound. She could worry about it once she was back home safe with him.

Assuming she felt safe. And that she'd stay with him. But he'd worry about that later too.

She might have doubts, especially after this, but even the nagging voice he'd used to keep himself out of harm's way the past few years couldn't change his mind. The more he examined his fears, the more he found he just didn't give a fuck anymore. Jess was his, and she belonged with him—in his lap, in his bed, in his home, and most definitely in his life.

"Well, you are certainly lucky," the doctor finally said. Cris's snort of disagreement was plain to the whole room. The doctor's lips lifted in a small smile. "Actually it's true. The force of that kick alone could've killed you. As it is, you've got a concussion that will give you fits for the next few days." He pulled a pad from his pocket and began writing a prescription. "Take these for pain." He ripped the small blue sheet off and handed it to Conlan. "Take her home and put her to bed"—Jess snorted at that one—"but wake her every couple of hours for the first twelve just to be sure. If there are no changes, follow up with your regular physician."

The doctor began removing her IV. Jess watched him but didn't comment. Only when he placed gauze over the entry point did she stiffen. "Con," she said, voice strained, "did you tell them..."

He looked at her, at the IV, and a lightbulb went on. "It's okay; I warned the nurse."

"Of course he did." Cris's tone was more frigid than the air spewing from the vent overhead. "And don't be thinking we won't talk about that later, young lady. I don't know what you were thinking."

"It's not like we planned on it," Con said.

"She'd just had her home vandalized. What were you thinking?" Cris asked.

Jess tilted her head up to meet his eyes. A slow but definite grin appeared on her lips.

Cris saw it and sputtered, "Okay, I do know what you were thinking, but still..."

Conlan laughed, quiet but as definite as Jess's grin had been. When Jess joined him, the sound reverberating against his chest, he knew he didn't care what anyone else thought. Jess knew the truth, and she could laugh despite the hell she'd been through. She was a miracle; she really was.

After seeing to a couple more minor details, Dr. Bryant released Jess to go home. As he opened the door to leave, Gaines stepped inside.

"Ms. Kingston."

"Why do people keep calling me that?" Jess muttered into Con's chest. "If they hadn't pumped me full of feel-good stuff so my head didn't explode, I'd probably get violent."

Gaines chuckled. Jack's eyes rounded, and Con realized his friend was staring at Jess. The look she was giving the detective must be a doozy.

Con couldn't help the itch that had him surrounding Jess, trying to cushion her from blows he knew were coming and he couldn't do anything to stop. Jess's fingers curled around his wrist.

"Whatcha got?" Jack asked.

"Not Holbrooke," Gaines said. "He seems to have disappeared."

"And..."

Gaines perked up. "Preliminary evidence is in from the apartment. That should help us get a warrant."

"You should be able to get a warrant from the fact that you had an eyewitness to him beating her," Con growled.

"What did you find?" Jack asked, cutting off any further words from Con.

"You were right." Gaines threw Con a wary look. "There were remote cameras positioned on her floor of the building and throughout the apartment, mostly in light fixtures. None were currently sending, so tracing the signal is out. We also found bugs in the—"

"We don't need to know where," Con warned him. A shiver shook Jess hard, and her nails bit into his skin. Gaines glanced at her, sympathy in his eyes.

"Is there any chance he...that he was in the apartment? While I was there?"

"We just don't know," Gaines admitted, his tone a degree softer than before. "The cameras don't record; they send a signal to an outside server, which might or might not record the feed, but unless we have the server, the point is moot."

"This guy's too smart to record himself," Jack muttered.

"Or too arrogant to not record it," Con countered.

Jack nodded. "True."

Jess shifted, whimpered. That tiny sound, so small, so quiet, shot through Con like lightning. Rage boiled up—at Holbrooke for doing this to her, and at himself for being so damn impotent to do anything about it. He'd spent his life training for the moment when he'd need to protect those around him. To watch Jess, so fragile, being torn to bits by this bastard who believed he could dictate her life was like watching the Titanic sink without a life raft to help—the situation was disintegrating by the second, and there was nothing he could do. Except maybe get his hands around the fucker's scrawny neck—

He glanced down at Jess, saw tears on her wet lashes,

and knew that, given the opportunity, he would kill Holbrooke. He would guard Jess with his body for now, but in the end, that bastard was going to disappear. Permanently.

Gaines was still talking. "The warrant will take time. We're hindered by the fact that both Holbrooke's office and residence are technically owned by his father. We're currently trying to find a judge that's not a family friend. We'll get it, though; don't you worry. As you said, we have an eyewitness." Gaines rubbed long fingers across the lines in his forehead.

"No traces from the cameras, though," Jack observed.

"No fingerprints or anything of that nature, though we're working on tracking down where they were bought. I don't think we'll find anything going that route, but we'll do it anyway. Like the phone calls and texts, there's just no way to trace the feed. Too much throwaway tech these days."

"What phone calls and texts?" Cris asked.

Gaines explained, his voice grim. "Unfortunately it's fairly easy to stalk these days without getting caught."

"He didn't just stalk," Cris said. "He beat her. Not once but now twice. It seems fairly easy for this dick to get away with anything, not just stalking."

Gaines shifted uneasily. Con's gaze met Jack's, and he could see the lightbulb go off behind his friend's eyes just like it had Con's. Gaines was right; it was easy to get away with some things. But Holbrooke wasn't getting away with something easy. The technology he had access to helped, but this man knew what he was doing. He had to have done this before.

"Any clues or contacts in his past that might help?" Con asked, forcing his voice to stay casual.

"Nothing."

Jack's brow scrunched up. "He's awfully good at covering his tracks for someone who is so obviously on the edge of crazyville."

"You'd think," Gaines agreed, "but I haven't found anything."

Jack met Con's gaze once more, the light in them assuring Con he would find what Gaines couldn't. He could do it too. Knowing Jack's infamous hacker skills were in charge of the search, that he could go where Gaines feared —or wasn't allowed—to tread, eased the boiling emotions swirling in Con's chest.

"So basically we know nothing and have no real options unless we can get a warrant." Jess's voice was heavy with resignation. She'd been down this road before.

Gaines didn't deny it. "Which is why we need to get you someplace safe. We need to buy a little time."

"She can come home with us," Cris said firmly.

"No." Jess and Conlan both spoke at the same time. Ignoring Con, Jess pushed up from his chest to tell her best friend, "I will not bring this mess into your home right now."

Cris opened her mouth to argue, but Jess got there first. "No. Absolutely not. I love you—and you too, Steven—and I appreciate you wanting to help me, but that baby comes first. Besides, you can't go home."

Steven's face was filled with understanding. And worry. Cris frowned.

Jess's voice gentled. "That's why I didn't call, and why I'm not going anywhere near your home. That's the first place he will look. You are going to your mother's house and going straight back to bed like your doctor told you to. No arguments. You have to keep yourself safe right now."

"But—"

"She's right, hon," Steven insisted, concern throbbing in his voice. "You're not abandoning her. Conlan will take good care of her for us."

"Like he did before?"

Jess shook her head. "Con isn't to blame for today; neither is Nicolas or me. Brit is the one to blame."

Con didn't believe that, but he let the point go. "I will keep her safe," he said instead. When Jess shot him a look of thanks, he leaned over and lightly brushed his lips across hers. "I'll keep you safe," he whispered against her mouth. Those four words were a vow he would keep this time, even if it meant his life.

Gaines broke into the moment. "What did you have in mind?"

"I have a place up by Lake Lanier that's completely private, off the books. The cabin's in my grandmother's maiden name, so there's no real connection unless someone wants to do a helluva lot of digging."

"Other than a safe house, that's probably the best we can do. We just need a couple of days to find him; then you should be in the clear," Gaines said.

Con knew it likely wouldn't be that fast, but frankly, he didn't care. This was the right choice; his instincts were screaming it.

Jess tugged at him. When he glanced down, worry stared back at him. "I thought..." She dropped her voice so only he could hear it. "I thought you said no commi—"

He brought a finger up to her mouth, cutting off that now hated word. "I know what I said." Leaning down until they were nose to nose, he held her imploring brown gaze with his. "I..."

He knew what he wanted to say, what Jess wanted him to say if the look in her eyes was any indication, but the words wouldn't come. Instead he tipped her chin up, took her lips, and told her how he felt in the only way he could.

Long moments later, Jess pulled back. She sucked in a deep breath, letting it out in a soft puff before saying, "I guess the lake it is."

18

It was early evening before they arrived at the lake house. They'd grabbed fast food on the way and Jess had taken more pain medication, so she was visibly drooping as they pulled into the attached garage. Con turned the key to Off, listening to the hot engine tick in the silence for a moment before he turned to Jess.

"Let's get you settled."

She gave him a wan smile. "Sounds good."

He ushered her in, taking note of her reactions as she wandered through the light, sunny yellow kitchen and into the open living room. He'd raised the ceilings throughout when he remodeled the original family home, adding warm natural tones to mimic the wooden deck and forest waiting outside the full wall of windows along the back of the house. The glittering waters of Lake Lanier were just visible between the green leaves and rough trunks of the trees. Knowing the glass was bulletproof would take away the beauty for Jess, but for Con, it settled something inside him that needed desperately to know she was safe. There was no better sanctuary than this cabin; he'd made sure of it, first for himself, and now for Jess.

He let her look while he unloaded the bag Jess had brought to his place and a few groceries Jack had gotten before they left. Jess transferred her attention from the outdoors to him as he put the food away.

"Nice," she said, a hint of amusement in her dark eyes.

"What?"

"A domesticated man."

He laughed as he stowed soup in the cabinet. "I can open a can, at least. And make coffee."

"That's the most important thing."

"Not *the* most important."

Her eyes went wide as she caught his meaning, and then she smirked. "So that's two things you do well."

He waggled his eyebrows and reached for her luggage. "Come on. I'll show you the bedroom."

"I'll bet you will," she murmured as she followed him down the hall. The heat in her words started his heart beating a bit faster. A stern reprimand didn't seem to slow it back down.

He had Jess lie on the bed while he emptied a couple of drawers and put her clothes in his dresser and closet. Her eyes remained half-open, though, watching him instead of dozing off. Was she afraid to sleep after all that had happened today, or was her body refusing to rest after being unconscious for so long?

Not sure which it was but determined that she relax enough to fall asleep, he went into the master bathroom, turning the lights on low with the dimmer switch near the sink, and crossed to start the water in the whirlpool tub he and his dad had installed last year. The dark, earthy tiles and dim light made for a warm, intimate feel in a space that was the size of a small bedroom. What could he say—he was a big guy, and he liked a big bathroom. The tub itself could fit him and two other people, not that he'd ever tried it. The possibility of trying it with Jess had his erection throbbing behind his zipper.

Just don't think about it, dickhead, and maybe it'll go away.

Not likely.

Leaving the water to run, he went back into the bedroom to find Jess stretched out, dark circles under her closed eyes, attesting to the strain of the past few days. She stirred as he stepped up to the bed. "How about a bath?"

Jess stretched, the sound she made like a feminine purr as muscles elongated and tension was forced out. "Sounds wonderful." She sat up and turned toward the edge of the bed, scooting until her lower legs dangled. Con stepped in, making a place for himself between her knees, and grasped the hem of her shirt. With a gentle pull, he revealed her smooth skin and mounded breasts—framed in a mouthwatering display by a lace bra—before easing the material over her head. As it cleared her face, her eyes met his.

When he didn't speak, Jess did. "What is it, Conlan?"

"You're beautiful."

For one breathless moment they stared at each other. Jess recovered first, leaning in until her soft lips brushed his T-shirt directly over the trail of hair that traveled from his navel to his crotch. His dick thumped against his zipper at the touch. "So are you," she whispered into his skin.

Shuddering, forcing himself under control, he reached behind her back and opened the catch of her bra. Jess arched, giving him space to maneuver. He slid the material away. The move put the naked, rosy tips of her breasts within inches of his mouth, and he couldn't resist a light nip. She jerked, and her nipples budded hard beneath his gaze.

Ignoring the hot surge of lust in his blood, he laid her back on the bed, reached down, and eased her pants and panties—lace to match the bra—off, along with her socks and shoes. "Come on. The hot water's waiting."

Jess hesitated beside the tub, her look of delight warming him in a way he didn't want to examine. The heady smell of vanilla filled the room, coming from the bath oil he'd mixed in the water. Vanilla was her scent, reminding him of the sweetness of her body, the taste of her skin, the creamy desire that coated her center. He hadn't been able to resist the bottle on an endcap at the drugstore when he'd stopped to fill her prescription, visions of steaming water and naked skin filling his head. Jess's closed eyes and deep breathing said she seemed to like the added touch as much as he did.

Jess turned, her eyes warm with approval. Those eyes drifted over him, all the way down to the hard bulge at his crotch. He mentally shrugged. Hiding this level of arousal was impossible; he wasn't going to apologize for what seeing her naked did to him.

She didn't look like she wanted an apology, though. More like a taste.

"Join me?" she asked.

His heart skipped a beat.

All thoughts of leaving her to relax sank like a rock with those two little words, shaky and almost uncertain. She needed; he supplied. It was a biological imperative he was starting to become intimately familiar with.

With a sharp nod, he began to strip, watching carefully as she lowered herself into the water. Her breasts bobbed on the surface, and he jerked the zipper of his jeans a bit harder than intended, drawing a hiss as the metal nipped the tip of his cotton-covered cock. He ignored the pain adding to his already aching body and finished getting naked in record time. Then he was easing himself down behind Jess, her silken body cradled between his thighs, his erection hot and shamelessly hard against the small of her back. He circled his arms around to rest tightly just below her breasts; she sighed and relaxed back into him.

When the water was up to her shoulders, he reached out with a foot and turned the faucet off. Jess giggled.

"What?" he teased, nuzzling the top of her head. "Didn't you know I'm talented from head to toes?"

"I think I did know that, yes."

They lay in silence for a long while, soaking in the quiet. Jess trailed her fingers through the hair covering his legs, the soft touches mesmerizing, relaxing. Con forced himself to let the outside world, the events he couldn't change, the worry and concern and anger and fear—*and lust, don't forget lust*—fall away until all he knew was this moment, the feel of this woman in his arms, the faint sound of her breath and the smooth caress of her skin against his.

When she arched her back to rub lightly against his semihard erection, he groaned. "Baby," he whispered in her ear, "you better stop that. You need to rest."

"What if I don't want to rest?" Jess slid against him again, harder this time. The ridge of her tailbone ground into the base of his cock, making him groan.

"You have a concussion. Sex isn't in the cards tonight."

Jess grasped his hands where they lay on her stomach, and pushed them up until they cupped her spiked nipples. He couldn't keep from rolling the silky mounds of her breasts in his palms.

"I think it can be," she whispered between hitches in her breath. "It's been too long already since I felt you taking up every empty inch of space in my body. And after today..."

She pressed his hands harder against her and groaned. "I need you. I…"

"You've been through too much already."

She had. She'd been through a battle he hadn't been able to fight for her. Con thought back to the times he'd seen action, the times his body had heated with so much need and adrenaline that finding the nearest willing body had become his number one priority. He didn't think Jess was choosing him because he was available, but her body and her heart trusted him to take care of her.

It was a normal reaction to combat, but he couldn't give in. Not with a concussion.

"We just have to be careful," she assured him with another suggestive roll of her hips.

"Jess…baby." They shouldn't do this. He wanted to, but they shouldn't.

Her taut nipples beckoned, and he grasped them, ever so lightly pulsing their hard lengths between his thumbs and fingers. The hot, explicit word that left Jess's lips shot his arousal up a hundred notches.

"You can do careful, can't you?" she asked. Her fingers drifted to the undersides of his thighs, tracing closer and closer to forbidden territory. "You can be slow. And careful. And—"

He nipped her ear, cutting off the seductive spell of her words. But he knew and she knew that he would give in. As he considered the safest way to please her, he circled her nipples with rough fingers, around and around until she moaned her pleasure into the steamy air. "No penetration," he whispered against her hair. "Very slow and very careful. I mean it, Jess."

"Yes." Jess nodded cautiously, then seemed to abandon words for throaty mews and gasps, rocking her hips ever so slightly against his cock in a compulsive rhythm that matched his movements at her breasts.

Con stopped the motion of his hands. If they were going to do this, he'd do it right. No risk to her. "Be still."

Jess froze.

"Absolutely still, Jess. Do you understand?"

"Yes." She drew the word out on a long, low breath.

Con reached down and gripped her inner thighs, pulling her legs up slowly to drape over his knees. His view over her shoulder showed her delicate slit, soft curls drifting with the movement of the water. His mouth went dry at the sight— what he wouldn't give to taste her. Instead he tightened one arm around her rib cage, forcing her to stillness, and used the other to tug her feminine lips open even farther until her gasp and shiver told him she was wide open to the water's hot caress. Allowing the heat to do its work, he once more caught her stiff peaks, and this time he rolled them between his fingers, gradually hardening his grip, squeezing her nipples with just the right force to make her sing for him.

"Conlan!"

"Shh, it's all right, baby. Let it build."

As desire rose, Jess began to writhe, too inexperienced to control the need to chase his touch. Con shifted, allowing the back of her skull to settle naturally in the hollow between his shoulder and neck, and leaned his chin against her, holding her head immobile as he resumed his torture at her breasts.

Panting and the gentle rippling of the water filled the silence for long moments. When Jess's panting became moans, she arched, her ass alternately cushioning and squeezing his aching sac. "Conlan, please," she whimpered.

Those two simple words, spoken with such desperate

need, spiked his hunger with a suddenness that left him gasping for air. His balls drew up tight, hugging the base of his hard shaft, ready to spill at any moment. Determined she would go with him, he trailed his hand down to cup her intimately.

Jess whimpered his name again, laying her hand over his, her pelvis tilting to urge him on.

Keeping her head as still as possible, he plucked at her clit, teasing the hood down and up, savoring the burn in his sex as he waited for her. Water sloshed up the sides of the tub, but he couldn't care less. As her cries became deeper, more needy, her muscles tightening against him, he moved lower, spearing two fingers into her tiny opening. His palm rasped her hardened nub with every thrust inside. One stroke, two, three and she was spasming around his fingers, crying out his name, her short, frantic movements grinding into his cock until he shot his seed along the delicate furrow of her spine.

In the aftermath, holding Jess, lax and warm, against him, he let his lips fall once more to her temple and whispered her name. His Jess. She'd changed his life and his heart forever. He might be the one with all the experience, but she was the one who knew how to love, how to risk it all for what she wanted. The pounding of his heartbeat was in his ears, in his throat, choking off his breath, a rhythmic claim of *mine, mine, all mine.*

He couldn't lose her. God help him, but he couldn't.

19

The *snap* of a twig nearby had Con bringing up his gun, sighting, slipping his finger down next to the trigger, all in one smooth motion that stilled as a timid doe entered his gun's sights. He hunched down in the predawn light, cursing the edgy feeling that had him up and roaming the woods around the lake instead of curling around Jess's warm body in the middle of the big bed they'd shared for the last two nights. The doe swung her head in his direction, belatedly sensing danger, and with a running leap, escaped over the ridgeline to safety.

Con stayed down, still, waiting for the woods to quiet. The geese at the water's edge, used to the antics of the deer, barely paused in their morning baths. They dunked and fluttered, telling Con no unusual human presence was nearby. The animals here knew him, were used to his scent all over these woods; hell, he'd played here years ago as a boy, he and Jack and Lee, learning to hunt and fight and become one with nature. As long as he was quiet, careful, they'd ignore him in favor of the water.

Continuing his slow, low trip around the cove, he couldn't shake the itch along the back of his neck, no matter what the natural alarm system of the wild told him. All was quiet, normal, but something wasn't right. He knew it, felt it. He just couldn't find it.

Or maybe there's nothing to find.

Maybe.

Maybe what he was sensing wasn't coming from outside.

A thick stand of trees waited ahead. Con slid into them, maneuvering through dense brambles and underbrush and heavy, intertwining branches until he came to the area where the hill began its second rise toward the ridgeline. Buried beneath a mound of fallen leaves, Con found the latch for the hidden door and tugged it. The lock held. No one was getting into the house through the tunnel. Many of the safety features in the house, like the glass, had been part of the construction when he'd renovated, but he and Jack and his dad, Ben, had built the underground passage themselves, over several years, ensuring no blueprints or specs were filed in an office or government building somewhere, waiting to come back and bite him in the butt. Even if someone did realize the tunnel existed, its sophisticated locking mechanism could only be bypassed with his or Jack's thumbprint. Otherwise, from the inside or the outside, no one was getting through this opening.

The knowledge eased some of his anxiety as he recovered the door and his tracks, making his way around the far end of the inlet and around to the north side of the woods near the house, keeping his eyes peeled for anything that might spell trouble on its way. There was nothing. Everything was quiet. Untouched.

No, the problem wasn't out here. It was inside his head.

He'd never been paranoid, but now, with Jess in his home, in his bed, he was jumping at his own shadow. Hunkering down between two boulders, he let the soft lap of the water against the sandy shoreline calm the faster beat of his heart, the frantic pulse of *not safe, not safe, not safe*. It wasn't working. The words grew stronger with every breath he took, never letting up, over and over and over until he wouldn't hear a bull charging him, much less a stalker in stealth mode. The pounding thoughts had nothing to do with an external threat and everything to do with his own fear.

He looked down at his hands. The faintest tremble shot through them.

"Jesus."

He'd never had this much at stake, never had so much to lose, and it made him afraid. If he lost Jess, he'd lose himself. They'd known each other a mere handful of days, and yet they were so tightly intertwined that he knew he couldn't lose her. He had to protect her, much, much better than he had before.

Like a hundred-pound weight, the image of Jess on the ground, Holbrooke's boot making contact, hit him in the chest. It hurt so bad he couldn't breathe, could only wheeze with the need to stop it from happening. But there was no stopping it; it had already happened, and he hadn't been there in time to prevent it.

Get. It. Together.

Breathe.

He barked the command in his head, the sound so much like his first—and most hated—drill sergeant that he had no choice but to comply. Swallowing the bitter taste at the back of his throat, he stared down the shoreline toward the house, still and dark, and just breathed. In and out. Again and again, using the sound of the water hitting the shoreline as a guide. Deliberately he thought of Jess as he'd left her, continuing to sleep in that big bed in his solid, safe house shadowed by the surrounding woods. The would-be tints of dawn struggled to lighten the sky, and Jess still slept, he hoped for a while longer. She needed the rest, the time to heal, the escape from this hellish limbo. And he needed the time to get a good goddamn grip on himself.

He couldn't hold back a heavy sigh as he continued along a parallel path to the bank, searching the likely hiding places, keeping an eye out for scuff marks on the rocks, tracks and broken plants in the underbrush, anything that might indicate a visitor other than the normal wildlife. Nothing was disturbed. They were safe, at least for now.

He was a hundred yards from the house when his cell phone vibrated, the quick one-two-three buzz that indicated Jack was calling. Settling with his back against a thick maple tree, Con dug the phone out of its holster on his belt. "Yeah."

"Don't you sound chipper this morning."

Con couldn't hold back a snort. "What's up?"

"A lot."

His entire body tensed. "Well don't hold back on my account."

"I won't," Jack said. His words were flat, ugly. "I really want to kill this bastard, Con."

"Don't we all?"

Jack grunted. A pause, some paper shuffling. "I managed to unlock Holbrooke's juvie record. History of stalking, including two restraining orders, escalating until his eighteenth birthday. No convictions."

"And no record of anything after that?" Con asked.

"Nothing. I did find mention of him connected to two investigations, one Jess's, the other a Rebecca Wellsley."

"Who is she?"

"Holbrooke's previous girlfriend. Appears he collects them like someone else would china. Same MO as Jess: father died just before they got together, no mom in the picture, became very isolated from her friends…"

"I'm seeing a pattern here." *And not getting a good feeling about it.*

Jack grunted. "No kidding. Holbrooke chooses his victims carefully. Actually made it to the fiancée stage with Wellsley."

Thinking of Jess tied that closely to Holbrooke tightened his gut. "Why is there a case file on Wellsley?"

"Because she disappeared a couple of years before Holbrooke met Jess."

"Shit." The word *disappeared* rang in his head like a gong. "Any connection between Holbrooke and the disappearance?"

"No more connection than there is between him and Jess's assault, which is to say there's lots of conjecture and no hard facts that aren't contradicted by his alibis. I checked through old newspaper articles, gossip-column stuff, and found a rumor that Wellsley had moved out to Arizona, but according to a police report filed in Tucson, she never claimed her apartment. The rental company reported her missing after several months went by. No movement on credit cards, bank accounts; no record of her name, driver's license, anything turning up in any reports anywhere in the US."

"Think she's in hiding?"

"No, I don't," he said, shades of the Grim Reaper clinging to the words. "The investigation was turned over to Atlanta

PD when it was determined no evidence existed that Wellsley had even entered Arizona. Once here, it was shuffled to some newbie detective who didn't really pursue it, said there were no leads, and the disappearance landed rather quickly in the cold-case files. Since there was no one looking for her here—Holbrooke included, apparently—no one noticed."

"Sounds like a cover-up," Con growled. Maybe it was the similarity to Jess's story, the knowledge that if no one had cared about Jess, if Cris and Saul and Steven hadn't existed, she might've vanished just like Wellsley, that made it feel fishy, but he didn't think so. He smelled dirty cops, dirty politics, and dirty money all over the case, and he and Jack had seen it often enough to trust that instinct. "So one or more of the local PD are on the payroll."

"More likely higher up. A grunt won't question his CO's command to look the other way and forget the whole thing. There's just no way to know for sure who the dirty hands belong to. What we do know is that Holbrooke's family has an assload of official and unofficial connections—and a fuck ton of money. Enough money to bury any involvement of their name deep. Deep enough I almost missed it."

"What about Gaines?"

"He brought the complete file on Jess's case to me. After I already knew it, of course, but he was up-front about it, and nothing was missing when he handed it over. I'm inclined to think it's not him. Not that I'd leave it to chance, which is why I picked through Patrick's personal history last night too. He's clean—and thorough, unlike the kid that handled Wellsley's case. Which reminds me..." Jack hesitated, then continued. "I did a search through the Georgia Missing Person's Database and came up with two possible matches, Jane Does that were never claimed. I have appointments this afternoon to meet with a couple of detectives farther south about them. I think it's a good possibility one might be her."

Con rubbed a rough hand down his face and back up, stopping to press against the pain throbbing between his eyes. "You think she's dead."

Jack's voice was quiet but certain. "Yes, I do. I just happened into some records from the Holbrooke family lawyers, Johnson, Grady, and Morrone."

Con grunted. "How?" Greedy lawyers had more protections on their files than the cops ever even thought about.

"Don't ask. Seems they've written more than one nondisclosure agreement over the last few years, all accompanied by large checks, all to young women in questionable entertainment-industry positions. Each woman had recent medical bills at the time of the agreements, one in particular with damage to her throat. Jess has scars on her throat, doesn't she?"

Con closed his eyes against the picture of the faint lines crisscrossing the delicate skin of Jess's neck. She'd never mentioned them, and he didn't ask. They looked as if something thin, a necklace maybe, had been used to choke her.

"Con?"

"Yeah." He cleared the tight pain from his throat, then said it again. "Yes, she does."

He could hear the jiggle of the phone as Jack nodded, but his friend didn't pursue the subject. "I'm sending a couple of people out to do interviews, see what we can find, but it's possible Brit got too rough with his 'play' and had to pay out hush money."

So he'd been practicing. Or possibly taking his aggression out on other women while he lured his more important victims, Rebecca Wellsley and Jess, in. With sick certainty Conlan realized it was probably her innocent reluctance that had attracted Holbrooke to Jess in the first place, and possibly to his fiancée as well. A willing partner would've been no fun for this man.

"Jack—"

"I know."

He did. They saw things like this quite a bit in their business, but it was different, so different when it involved someone you cared about. Someone you loved.

Jack cleared his throat. "One last thing. I managed to get access to one of the cameras in Jess's apartment. It remote links to an outside server to download footage and then erases its memory. I tagged it, and the server went live last night, just long enough to download the last of the footage and terminate the link. I was able to piggyback the download. Con, he was in her apartment."

"Of course he was. The bugs..."

"No, not just to place cameras. While she was there. Sleeping. Showering. There's also footage of him working on her computer, and I'd be willing to bet her cell phone is also implanted with a tracker."

The images Jack painted made Con feel sick. "The police have it. It's not here. None of her electronics are here."

Keep talking. Keep talking. If he didn't, he was likely to do something he'd regret later, like punch the helpless tree he leaned against. He didn't want Jess seeing him with bruised and bloodied hands.

"I figured." Jack sighed heavily. "This fucker's not playing around, Con. Most likely he's just biding his time. His resources are close to unlimited, his access to technology too, even on the run. Be careful."

"I will. We'll be fine here." They would; he'd made sure of it, no matter what the hair on the back of his neck said. "I'm keeping her under wraps until this thing is settled."

"And if it isn't?"

The words blazoned on Jess's bedroom wall floated through his mind. *My fucking mouse.* "It will be. He wants to finish this too much to disappear without her."

"That's what I'm afraid of," Jack admitted.

20

Jess stepped into the living room, gaze transfixed by the wall of glass that encompassed the entire back side of the open space. She hadn't left the bedroom yesterday; heck, Conlan had hardly let her leave the bed to use the bathroom, he'd been so worried over her injuries. Now she was finally getting her first glimpse of Conlan's house in full daylight, and it was amazing. Spacious. Beautiful. The cool greens and grays and browns of the living room made her feel like she was already standing outdoors. And the dappled shade of the deck made her itch to grab a book, to sit out in the cool dimness and lose herself in another world.

"Over here, Jess."

She turned toward the sun-filled kitchen, and there was Conlan, lean hips resting against a sleek granite countertop. The way his legs were crossed at the feet bunched the material of his jeans just right in the crotch. It took a moment to pull her gaze up from that bulge to notice the two coffee cups he held...and his smirk.

"I hope one of those is for me," she said as she walked over.

Con's smirk widened. "Of course."

When she would have taken one of the cups, he moved it just out of reach and leaned in, nuzzling her cheek before settling a quick coffee-flavored kiss on her lips. "Good morning."

Jess accepted her cup with a smile. "Good morning." The first sip scalded her tongue with rich sweetness. She savored it, closing her eyes in enjoyment before glancing around the kitchen. "Have you been up for a while? I don't remember you leaving the bed."

"That's because you were snoring."

Jess pulled back, doing her best two-cent impression of shock. "I do not snore."

"Yes, you do." Conlan bent down until his nose rubbed along the side of hers. "And even if you didn't, you'd never know."

She pinched his stomach lightly just for the twinkle in his eye. Conlan's laugh was as full and rich as the coffee he'd made, which she savored in slow sips while admiring the male beauty he so effortlessly displayed. God, no one should look that good in the morning.

He looks even better at night.

Yes, he did, no doubt about it. She hid her grin behind the rim of her coffee cup.

Con moved to the fridge and started taking out things for breakfast. "You like eggs?" he asked, head down near the shelves.

"Hmm?" She tried hard not to swallow her tongue at the view of his ass she was getting. "Sure."

Okay, so the word was slightly strangled. She could swear

she heard a muffled laugh from the vicinity of the fridge's open door, but she refused to acknowledge it. He had a big enough... ego...as it was without feeding it. "I thought you couldn't cook."

"Not couldn't," he threw over his shoulder, "just don't like to. But breakfast tastes better at home."

Jess smiled into her coffee. "So this house belonged to your grandmother?"

Conlan stood, arms stacked with way more food than it should take to feed the two of them, and kicked the refrigerator door closed. "Not in this incarnation, but the original cabin did. I rebuilt this place around the time my dad retired. We did the work together, and I brought in a team for the heavy stuff."

Jess trailed him across the kitchen to the stove. "Your dad's in construction?"

"From the time I was little, yes. I grew up around construction sites—slave labor, you know." He held up a package of bacon and a package of sausage. "Yes?"

"Uh, sure." Both? She shrugged and reached for the packages. "Let me help."

"Uh-uh-uh. You sit." He nodded toward the stools pulled up to a bar-like section of the counter. "Let me fix you some breakfast."

"You've been fixing too much the past couple of days," she protested, but she sat anyway, her hands soaking in the warmth from her coffee cup. Something about his protectiveness, the care he lavished on her, had gone farther toward making her feel better than any pain medication or time spent in bed. Not that time spent in bed was a bad thing unless you spent it there alone, which she had all day yesterday. Even pouting hadn't worked, but still some tiny part of her had melted at his adamant refusal to "hinder" her recovery, as he'd called it. If she had anything to say about it, her recovery would definitely be hindered today.

She divided her time between watching him fry bacon and scramble eggs and watching a couple of cardinals flitting between two feeders perched outside the window. The moment felt domestic, deceptively comfortable.

"How much do you know about Brit's background?"

The question jarred her out of domestic bliss. She shifted on her stool. "Not much. His folks have lived here forever. His father founded Holbrooke Technologies in the early eighties, and after college Brit came back and took the position he has now. He works a lot."

Silenced filled the next few minutes as Conlan dumped bread in the toaster and spooned fruit into a couple of small bowls. "Did he ever talk about past relationships with you?"

"Why does this feel like an interrogation?"

"Because it is?" Conlan stepped up to the bar, two plates in hand. "I need to know all I can about the enemy, Jess. Recon isn't possible; you're my best source of solid intel."

She struggled with that for a moment, with letting Brit into the space between them, but he was right and she couldn't ignore what was going on any more than she could ignore Conlan. Standing, she said, "He didn't really talk about other women." She rounded the bar to take the plates from him, then trailed him to the stove. As he dished up food, she continued. "I know he was engaged a couple of years ago, but they broke it off before the wedding. I was new at Ex Libris and not hanging out with my parents' crowd as much then, so I didn't know her, just rumors mostly."

They settled at a small table in the breakfast nook off the back of the kitchen. "So how did you meet?" Conlan asked, spearing a strawberry. His face didn't change, but his voice went tight.

He didn't like talking about this either. Somehow knowing that made it a little bit easier.

"My parents. They managed to rope me into attending an annual charity ball they helped organize every year, and my dad"—her voice teetered on cracking—"he introduced us. Said Brit had great potential." She managed a small laugh. "What he meant was Brit had money and was interested in his shy, awkward daughter."

She didn't glance up, didn't want to see pity in Con's eyes. Choking down a couple of bites of her breakfast gave her a minute to get herself back together.

"And then your parents were killed in a car accident."

She nodded. "We'd only been dating a few weeks, off and on." Mostly off. Even then something just hadn't clicked, but every time she saw her parents, they asked about "how things were progressing" with Brit. "I was pretty much a basket case after that, couldn't focus on anything. He just...stepped in. Took over. I didn't have to worry about anything, not at first." She pushed her half-eaten food away.

"Jess." Conlan hesitated, opened his mouth to speak, then hesitated again.

"What?"

"Did you know that Rebecca Wellsley, Brit's fiancée, lost her father right before they started dating?"

The scent of the food was making her sick. Blindly she stood, needing to get away, needing to get ahold of herself. She refused to throw up. She was stronger than that.

"No, I-I didn't know that. She...she had family somewhere, I think. She moved after they broke up. I remember my mother telling me about it when I first started dating him." She waved a vague hand. "I don't remember where. Maybe she can tell us something?"

When she reached the bar, she turned to face him. Conlan was already shaking his head. "I wish she could, Jess. But that's not an option."

"Why not?" She couldn't do more than whisper, couldn't get the question out past her strangled vocal cords.

"Because we can't find her. She's missing, and Jack believes...I believe...she might be dead."

Jess's knees buckled, forcing her to grab the edge of the bar. Con was across the room in an instant, his strong grip holding her steady, grounding her in a world she couldn't understand. "No, that can't be right. He couldn't have..."

"Did he ever mention her?" Con asked.

"No." Shaking her head made the spinning room speed up, but she couldn't stop, just kept shaking and shaking and shaking. "He...he never brought her up. He—" *It isn't true.* But it was. "You think he's done this before, that it...it didn't —" Staring into his eyes, she saw the truth blazing back at her. "Oh God, you think he might've killed my parents."

Conlan dragged her hard against him. His grip went tight, almost bruising, and it scared her even more, not because he hurt her, but because it told her without words that her guess was right on the money—and that it scared the shit out of Conlan too.

"No!" It was the cry of a mindless animal. Jess fought it, fought the pain and the terror and Conlan's grip, banging her fists against his solid chest and keening for release—from the idea that Brit had killed her parents or from Conlan, she didn't know. All she knew was the over-whelming wash of agony. It doubled her over, forced her forehead into his shoulder, her wide-open mouth against the caging muscles of his arm as she screamed and screamed and screamed. And still the mind-blanking terror remained.

How long she was lost in the dark, drowning in the turmoil, she didn't know. When she surfaced, every muscle shook, hurt, every breath scraped her lungs like shards of glass.

"It's not your fault, Jess. It's not."

A sharp hiccup. Her fist banged against Con's collarbone. "It is," she sobbed. "Don't tell me it's not!"

"I have to." Despite the blows, Conlan was right there with her, in the line of fire, absorbing her hits and her tears and her grief without thought to himself. His arms held her half-bent body against him. Through her crying, the ragged sound of his breathing, his voice was clear. "I have to tell the truth. This wasn't your fault."

"It was!" She twisted, but Con's grip might as well have been made of steel for all the give it had. "Three people are dead! Rebecca's father might be a fourth. Who knows how many more, huh? She—my parents—they're gone! Because I was too stupid to realize the man I was dating was an abuser and a murderer."

"We don't know that, baby," Con crooned. "We don't know. We're just speculating. We don't know."

"You do." She could hear it in his voice. Still, some part of her felt how badly he wanted to make this right, wanted to hide her away from the pain, not just with his hold or his body, but by saying whatever he had to, to get through to her.

Even so, she couldn't accept the lie. She wished she could, wished it so much she shook with it. Her fists wrapped in Conlan's shirt and shook him too. "I depended on him when my parents died, cried in front of him, kissed their dead cheeks—and he killed them. Because of me!"

"No, baby. Don't." Clasping her cheeks, he forced her to look into his sorrow-darkened eyes. "Please don't." He kissed her, soft and bittersweet. "You're killing me." He kissed her again, loved her with his words and his mouth and his touch until the tears died away, and even then he rocked her in the silence, the two of them slumped together, dazed in the aftermath like shipwreck survivors.

Long moments passed before he spoke again. "All victims blame themselves, Jess, but it's not your fault. It's that bastard's fault. He did this to you, to them, not you."

Turning her head against his shoulder, she met his eyes wearily. "And how many more people will he do it to? You? Jack? Steven and Cris and their unborn child? Who else has to pay for Brit to have me? Because if it's between me and them, I'll walk out that door right now and never look back. He won't hurt anybody else but me."

A snarl twisted Conlan's lips. "Never!" He shook her hard, one quick jerk. Her head flopped like a speared fish. "You aren't going anywhere that asshole can get his hands on you. He won't hurt anyone else—not you, not me, not Cris and her baby. No one!"

"You don't know that!"

"Yes, I do." He forced her close, every inch of her against every inch of him, his arms crushing her ribs until she thought they would shatter. "I do. I know. I'll keep you safe, baby, I promise, no matter what."

She didn't deny it, didn't want to. But they both knew that when this moment ended and they had to face the light of day, there were no guarantees. The future held nothing but uncertainties until Brit was gone.

21

"Where did you get a swimsuit?" Jess turned the top of the skimpy blue bikini inside out, searching for a tag. Her size too. She glanced up at Conlan, wary and faintly excited.

"Cris."

"No way!" Her friend wouldn't—she'd been mad at Conlan, not trying to feed their mutual attraction. Hadn't she? "When?"

"When she brought stuff to the hospital for you. I just kept it in my drawer for safekeeping."

"You mean you hid it so I wouldn't."

He shot her an unrepentant grin. "I think it's time we used it."

"We?" It was she who would be exposing herself.

He raised one wicked black brow. "We." He started stripping. "Let's go swimming."

She glanced a bit frantically around the room. "Where's your suit?"

"Don't need one. You don't either, but I figured you'd prefer something instead of nothing."

She gulped. Literally gulped. Skinny-dipping with Conlan. "I'll go change."

"Coward!" he called after her, his tone tinged with laughter.

"You bet," she shot back.

She didn't let her grin out until she made it behind the closed door of the bathroom. Just the fact that a grin was possible was such a relief she slumped against the door, the suit hugged to her belly. The past few days had been rough. Since what she thought of as the "kitchen incident," they'd cooked and cleaned together, worked side by side on their laptops, even played games and watched movies like they were a real couple actually living together, not just forced into proximity by a madman. Still, Jess had wandered through each day numb, just going through the motions. Feeling Conlan's concerned gaze on her and helpless to respond. Even his big body crowding her in the bed at night hadn't elicited a response. It was as if the overwhelming flood of emotion that day had wiped out her circuits and she couldn't find a way to reset them.

Eyeing the bikini, she wondered if maybe Conlan had.

After undressing, she struggled with the strings—strings!—but finally managed to get the tiny two-piece on. Did she need to shave? A quick glance in the mirror assured her she didn't. It also told her she might as well be naked, but since Conlan had seen it all, thoroughly, she sucked in her belly and walked out anyway. The sudden darkening of his gray eyes as they slid over her body was all the reward she needed. "Like?" she asked, holding her hands out and doing a little twirl.

"I'd have to be dead not to."

Judging by the stiffening of his penis, she didn't think he was dead. The sight added a definite bounce to her step as she preceded him out the door. Conlan groaned behind her.

The sun was hot on her shoulders as they left the tree line near the shore. She knew Conlan's home was located on a cove and that he owned the land surrounding this inlet of the lake, but she hadn't really understood what that involved until now. As far as she could see was just water and woods. The wide expanse of the cove, maybe a thousand yards, met the shore on the opposite side, which rose immediately and fairly sharply toward a ridge towering over them. The rim flowed around the inlet, creating a bowl the cove sat in. Con's house was the only one in sight, and it was fairly well camouflaged by its surroundings as well.

No wonder he swam naked.

Con's warm hand on the small of her back guided her to the edge of the green-tinted water. As the gently lapping waves met her toes, she was surprised to realize it was the perfect temperature—not warm, not cold. Perfect refreshing coolness.

"In you go."

Jess resisted his slight push on her back. "I like to ease in."

Without warning Con scooped her up, one hand under her back, one under her knees. Jess whooped. "Put me down!"

He tucked her up effortlessly, bringing her face close to his. "I think we've determined I'm not the easing-in type."

Without giving her time to protest, he forced a hard kiss to her open lips and then threw her into the air. Jess landed with a scream in the chilled water feet away, her head going under, the shock of the water's temperature zapping through her body. She came up sputtering.

Con stood in the same spot as before, laughing.

"Oh, it's on now," she declared, swiping hair out of her eyes. She jumped for him, and before she knew it, a full-blown water battle had commenced.

The tension that had held her prisoner slowly unknotted and floated away as they cavorted like kids in the late summer sun. It reminded her that life wasn't only about Brit, not even partly. It was about the people she loved and lived with and enjoyed. It was about actually living, not just going through the motions—and that's what she'd been doing for the last couple of days, just going through the motions. Letting Brit win.

Not anymore, not if she could help it.

Conlan finally collapsed in the shallows with a huff. "No more. I'm done."

She dragged herself up beside him, enjoying the warmth of the sunlight, the cool of the water beneath her, and watching the dappled shadows play across Con's muscular body. She'd never known someone so comfortable in their skin, literally. As she traced the shape of a leaf's shadow on his stomach, she asked, "You grew up here?"

"Here and in town. My grandparents bought the land cheap right after they married, just walked into the realty office with a sack full of cash and walked out with the deed. They never sold. I spent a lot of time here after my mother died, summers too, while my dad worked. Brought Jack and Lee out here."

The mention of his dead friend squeezed Jess's heart. "You miss him, don't you?"

"Lee?"

"Yeah."

Conlan didn't answer for a long while. Jess didn't look at him, just kept tracing patterns on his skin, dipping into the water and running cool drops over the hills and valleys of his sculpted muscles. When she thought he might never respond, he said, "I do." A heavy sigh caved in his ribs. "I miss him and I hate him."

"What? Why?"

"Because..." One big hand rose to cup her cheek, the chill of his water-soaked skin refreshing against hers. "Because I can finally see that what happened to Lee wasn't just Sarah's fault. Lee let her have that hold on him; he didn't have to, but he let her control him. He gave in instead of fighting. Not for her—she wasn't worth it—but for us."

"Oh." And Conlan would never give in without a fight. He certainly wouldn't want anyone controlling him the way Lee had.

"He was an idiot."

She jerked her head up to meet his eyes.

"They both called it love, but neither one of them knew what love really is; they only knew obsession."

"And..." Jess tried to discreetly clear her throat. "And you do know what love really is?"

"I do." Conlan trailed his finger down her cheekbone to her mouth, rubbing the thick tip along her bottom lip. "I definitely do."

A sudden giddiness took up residence in her belly. He wasn't saying outright that he loved her, but... She couldn't help the grin that escaped. "Good."

Conlan sat up, his grin matching hers. Water sloshed around him. "Good? What about you?"

The giddiness doubled. "I know what it really is too."

Did I really just tell him I love him? Yes, I think I did.

Conlan's mouth widened to a full-out smile. "Good."

It was ridiculous—they were both mature adults, but here they were speaking in code like kids with a decoder ring—but her cheeks hurt, she smiled so wide. She barely managed to open her mouth to speak before he had her hauled into his lap, one leg on either side of his hips, her body nestled nice and close. Even in the cool lake water, he was hot—his skin, his breath, and God, his shaft scorched her mound. When she'd thought about sex, it had been about the mechanics, the logistics, not the heat of a muscular body against hers, the heartbeat of another person running under their skin, through their most private parts. The love she felt for Conlan burst through her, multiplying the wonder of the moment until it saturated every pore, every cell. She arched against him, wishing she could absorb his very essence into her heart.

Conlan growled. One arm circled behind her, holding her steady, while the other cupped the back of her neck. Something about that touch, so primitive, so controlling, made her wet. Achy. Needy. She needed him, needed to show him, not just tell him, how much she loved him, in a way she never had before.

Bringing her face up to his, nose beside nose, gray eyes searing her with their intensity, she whispered, "Stand up."

Conlan's pupils contracted at the words. Jess watched, fascinated, holding her breath at the beauty of the man cradling her against him.

A shudder shook him, and he tightened his grip on her ribs. "Jess," he whispered, his voice agonized.

"Stand up, right here. In the water."

His dark eyes stayed locked with hers for another endless moment, searching for she knew not what, but it felt like he delved all the way to her soul. Finally a lopsided smile pulled at his lips. "You want to play with fire."

"I want to play with you."

The groan that escaped sounded torn from his very depths, full of gravel and hunger and desire. His grip on her nape tightened, dragged her forward until he fit her lips to his perfect mouth. She teased the crease with her tongue.

He opened to her, sucking her tongue inside, tangling with it as he explored her mouth in a rough kiss. His thrusting tongue took her breath, but he replaced it with his own. When he finally pulled back, they were both racing to catch their breath. "In that case…"

Jess came to her feet. Water sloshed around her as she held out a surprisingly steady hand to the man before her. He took it and stood, tall and straight and gloriously nude, a sun god gracing this lowly earth with his beauty.

He's obviously not worried about the neighbors, she thought with a light laugh. She wanted to be bare with him, wanted to hear his breath speed up at the sight of her the way hers did with him. She reached behind her and grasped the ends of the string tie to her bikini. By the time the wet top plopped on the shore a few feet away, she had her wish.

Her nipples hardened immediately in the now cool air. The heavy throb tried to distract her, but she pushed it away, focused on the demanding jut of Conlan's hard sex pointing straight at her. His shaft was flushed almost purple, sprinkled with water droplets and a thick pearl of precum right at the tip. Her mouth watered at the sight.

She went down on her knees.

Con's fingers tunneled through her hair.

His touch stripped her bare in a way taking off her top couldn't. She surrendered to it, to the pull of his hands guiding her to his erection. She didn't take him right away; she nuzzled him, rubbing the smoothness of her cheek and chin over the rigid muscle, the thin, tender skin. That drop of precum beckoned, and she smeared it across her lips before darting her tongue out to taste.

Tart. Thick. All male—and so very good.

"Conlan."

"I love that you use my full name," he said huskily.

Another drop appeared in the tiny slit, and this time she snagged it immediately, savoring it before murmuring into his skin, "It's more you, all of you."

When Conlan's hands would've guided her to take him into her mouth, she pulled them from her hair. "Let me," she said, twining their fingers together and holding them out away from his hips.

Conlan hissed. Hard, proud, aroused male waited directly before her eyes.

"Jess." The word was as hard and aroused as he was.

She chuckled at the insistence in his voice. Sinking into the moment, she ruffled her nose down the crease between his flat, rigid stomach and thigh.

"You know, I'm not even slightly tempted to laugh—not with your mouth so close to my dick."

"My mouth?" Leaning forward, she blew lightly on him, fascinated when his cock twitched in response.

"Jess." Sounding slightly crazed, Conlan bumped his hips forward, pushing his steely length closer, his fingers tensing around hers. "Get on with it," he choked out.

She wanted to. She also wanted to savor, watching this gorgeous man surrender to desire in the bright sunlight. She'd heard women say a man's penis wasn't beautiful the way a woman's body was beautiful, but Conlan was. His cock's blatant demand for her attention was all masculine beauty.

She leaned in slow, inch by inch by inch, before tentatively taking the swollen mushroom head between her lips.

"That's it, baby," he said, his rough hands disentangling her so he could grip her head and fine-tune the angle. He surged forward, forcing his way into her tight mouth, moaning in gratitude when she opened for more of him. "Take me in; suck that head."

She laid one hand on his thigh, tracing the scar that named him a warrior, and laved his erection with her tongue, suckled gently, laved again. His taste appeased her hunger even as the musky male flavor multiplied it. God, she would never get enough of him.

"Ease down; that's a good girl." His deep voice coached and cajoled. She took him in again, easing down until he touched the back of her throat. She choked.

"It's all right. Just relax," he crooned. "Open up and let me in; you can take it. Suck me."

She did. Careful of her teeth, she eased back, then forward, taking him as deep as she could. When the urge to gag hit, she followed his instructions, breathing in and swallowing. Her heart swelled at his agonized groans. Yes, that's what she wanted—to give him pleasure.

Again. She set up a rhythm, gentle thrusts, traveling the length from his tip to the fingers she'd wrapped around the base, loving the feel of his meaty stalk in her mouth, down her throat.

"Harder; that's it. God, baby."

She could feel him getting close, his flesh swelling, throbbing in her fist, even as his hands stayed tender and easy on her head, his advances careful and controlled. Needing to explore, she lightly stroked his sac with her free hand. He rewarded her by leaning into her touch, his thrusts just that little bit more desperate. When she hummed her pleasure around him, she felt his sac tighten, draw up, the silken fuzz wrinkling as he neared climax.

"Jess." His harsh tone matched his jerky movements, both pushing closer and closer to frantic. *Almost there.* She sucked harder. Once. Twice. Again. On the fourth stroke she felt him spurt, his warm cum filling the back of her throat with the taste of hot, salty male. She swallowed, continuing her rhythm, determined to get all he had to give.

The grip in her hair tightened just short of pain, holding her head steady, still. He strained, emptying into her mouth. "Ahh, baby."

Conlan sagged over her, his body trembling. Jess locked her gaze on his face, his eyes closed in pure bliss, his body protective even as he shuddered in release. The most beautiful thing she'd ever seen. Unable to resist, she ran her tongue gently over his cock, taking her time, collecting every last drop of his essence—tangy, slick—enjoying the feel of him as he softened in her mouth, the freedom to touch him. She tongued the slit at the end, sucked gently, then let him go.

He growled, leaning down to take her mouth in a hungry kiss. When he pulled back, they were both panting. His forehead met hers as he said, "Jesus, Jess, your mouth is lethal."

She couldn't decide if the words or his wrung-out tone boosted her confidence more. "I love you," she said, her voice rough with emotion and use.

"Damn, baby." Conlan jerked her out of the water, her bare, wet breasts meeting his chest with a slap. Brown eyes met gray, and the devastating emotion they shared shook her hard.

"I think I need to return that favor," Con said hoarsely. He hoisted her over his shoulder, ignoring her protest, and strode toward the house like the water was on fire. Jess caught a last glimpse of her bikini top on the shore before it was forgotten in the frantic need Conlan's hands and mouth ignited.

22

―――――

"So how's Cristina?" Conlan asked as Jess wandered into the living room. They'd been holed up at the lake all week, and though in many ways it had felt a bit like a honeymoon, Jess figured she hadn't hidden how antsy she was getting very well when Conlan suggested she give her best friend a call. Jess had showed her gratitude thoroughly—her body still tingled at the memory of just how thoroughly—before taking him up on his suggestion.

A bubble of happiness and relief welled in her chest, making her smile. "Great. No more spotting." She plopped down on the couch on the opposite end from Conlan, stretching her legs out between them. "The doctor's keeping her on bed rest for a little longer, but things are looking good. The baby's heartbeat is strong."

"Good." Grabbing her ankle—it still surprised her how comfortable he was touching her, and how comfortable she was with his touch—Conlan gave it a yank. "Lie down with me."

"That's what you said earlier. You remember what happened then."

"Yes, I do," he said, so much male satisfaction in the words they practically oozed testosterone.

Jess snuggled down next to him anyway, her feet against his chest, his feet resting on the arm of the couch behind her head. The thin T-shirt covering Conlan's torso had ridden up, revealing that silky treasure trail leading into his jeans that she just couldn't resist. She turned on her side and slid her fingers through the thin line of hair.

"Stop that!" Conlan swatted ineffectually at her hand.

She tickled him. "What? Mr. Ready and Waiting wants me to stop?"

"That's what my limp dick says."

"Conlan!" A surprised laugh escaped her. He threw a little smile toward her end of the couch as he lifted an arm, thick biceps beautifully showcased, to cover his eyes. The posture might've looked as limp as he claimed his dick was, his breathing slow and easy and even, but somehow she doubted it. He didn't drift into sleep, just lay there, and as Jess watched him, her mouth went dry.

This was too easy, too much like really living together. She shouldn't get used to it, but looking at him like this, she just couldn't help it. He was perfect. Mostly.

"Too limp for dinner?" she teased.

Conlan snorted. "Hey, I provided the orgasms. You're on your own with dinner."

Jess couldn't help cracking up. Several minutes passed before she finally managed to stop clutching her sides and gasping for air. "Seriously, though—"

Con's arm lifted, allowing his incredulous stare to meet hers. "I'm one hundred percent dead serious, baby. I'm not twenty-one anymore. I didn't know I had it in me." He dropped his arm back over his face. "There's definitely no more 'it' left. I'm wrecked."

"Really?" She sat up, intent on showing him exactly how not wrecked he was, when a hard rap echoed through the great room.

Conlan was up and on full alert before the sound died away. "Stay here."

The tinny *crunch* of a key being inserted into the lock relaxed Con's shoulders. He continued to walk across the room, but the tension that had filled him a moment ago was gone. Just as he reached the front door, it opened and Jack strolled into the house. He reached across and keyed in the code for the alarm without blinking. The two men do the bro-hug thing before returning to the living room. Jess sat where she was and waited for the heart-stopping burst of adrenaline to fade.

"What did you do, park down the road and walk just to see if I would notice?"

"You didn't, did you? Figured I'd catch you with your pants down."

Conlan sputtered. "Just for that you can get—"

"I brought dinner." Jack strode past the couch toward the kitchen, throwing a wink Jess's way, two brown paper bags hanging from one hand.

Conlan rejoined Jess on the sofa, shaking his head. "Bring me a Coke," he called after Jack, then, glancing at her with an upturned brow and receiving a nod, he added, "Two Cokes."

"Get your ass up and get in here, you whiner," Jack yelled from the kitchen. Conlan grumbled but disappeared into the other room to help his friend.

They were settled in the living room with full plates of fajitas and cold sodas in minutes. The sound of popping metal tops and sizzling fizz took over the room. Jack tilted his head back and drank, and Jess stared a bit blindly at the sexy stretch of neck and shoulders, unsurprised that, though Jack was gorgeous, she didn't react to him beyond a certain abstract appreciation. Only Conlan seemed to stir the heat within her.

"Damn, this is good," Con said around a mouthful of meat. Jess sipped her drink, then set it aside to dive in to the food.

Jack snorted. "You're just saying that because you didn't have to cook it."

"Anything he doesn't cook is good," Jess teased.

Jack huffed out a laugh at her comment. "The honeymoon is ovah!"

Con ignored them and took another bite of his food, half of a fajita disappearing into his mouth.

"You got a little...something"—Jack swiped at the corner of his own mouth—"right...there."

"Hmm?" Conlan brought a napkin to his face.

"I think it's drool," Jack said.

Conlan threw him a mean look from behind the white paper square. "Asshole."

Jess laughed. The two were definitely like brothers, that was for sure.

They were halfway through their meal when the crunch of tires on the gravel driveway was heard. Conlan jerked up from the couch.

Jack held out a calming hand. "It's Patrick. Try not to shoot him."

"He'll be lucky if I don't. He should've called."

"He texted me earlier," Jack said.

"Why didn't he text me?"

Jack's gaze drifted from Conlan to Jess, his dark lashes hiding something that made her distinctly uneasy. Whatever Gaines was here for, she had a feeling she wouldn't like it. And from the sour look on Conlan's face, she didn't think he would either.

Conlan had the front door open before Gaines could knock. "All of a sudden it's Grand Central Station around here," he said, tension grating through his voice.

Gaines didn't bother to reply, just stepped inside. He watched as Conlan closed the door and reset the alarm before turning toward the living room. "Ms. Kingston."

Jess sighed. The bite of refried beans she'd been about to take went back to her plate. "Detective Gaines."

"If I'd known dinner was on, I'd have waited to come out."

"Or come earlier," Jack suggested. Settling into an armchair, Gaines returned Jack's smirk with one of his own. That small tilt of his lips transformed the man into someone less unassuming, more real. No wonder he kept that bland-accountant look for police work. Hiding a true personality behind no personality.

"Just tell us whatever you came to say, Gaines," Conlan demanded as he returned to his seat next to Jess.

Gaines shrugged. "Dental records on our Jane Doe came back. They're a match to Rebecca Wellsley."

Well, he told us why he came. Jess shoved her plate away, her stomach roiling too much to finish. Deep inside, in a place she hadn't wanted to acknowledge, she'd known this would be the outcome. She'd hoped it wasn't, that Rebecca was somewhere out there, living a carefree, Brit-free life on her own terms.

But she wasn't. She wasn't living at all.

"What about my parents?"

Gaines shook his head grimly. Jess sucked in a shaky breath.

"We don't know. Based on the limited evidence still

available to us, we will probably never know," he said. "Off the record, I don't think the timing of their deaths and Mr. Wellsley's would be that convenient without 'help,' but we can't prove he did anything to cause it."

"Oh...God."

Conlan reached around her shoulders and drew her under his arm, nestling her close. The thump of his heart in her ear was normal, reassuring. As she listened to it, she realized hers was too. The idea that Brit was responsible for the deaths of so many people sickened her, made her grieve, but over the past week, somehow she'd accepted it, numbed herself to it. It didn't make her afraid—or maybe she was just so used to fearing Brit that it didn't register anymore.

She leaned her head into the hollow of Conlan's shoulder and waited for the rest.

"We haven't found even a trace of him," Gaines was saying. "The warrants yielded nothing. Surveillance on his parents, office, apartment came up empty. His car hasn't been touched; regular bank accounts are frozen. Our forensic accountant found evidence that he was stashing money somewhere—the numbers just don't add up—but we can't find where."

Jack stood to pace in front of the coffee table. "I've been watching for computer activity, anyone searching for info on you, the house, the business—nothing. We know he connected you to JCL and to Jess, but I don't know how. And that bothers me."

It bothered Jess too. From what Conlan had told her, Jack was pretty much unmatched as a hacker.

"What he could be searching for—or finding—now is anyone's guess," Jack told them. "I can figure it out; it'll just take time. And if he's fled the country, that will take longer to track down."

The men continued to talk around her, but Jess was stuck back on Jack's *"It'll just take time."* How much time? The thought of months, possibly years, of waiting and worrying that Brit would appear, that another attack would come, made her want to huddle up in a corner and cover her eyes. But it wouldn't make a difference. Like the bogeyman, Brit was still there, even when she couldn't see him. He wouldn't give up, not if he'd killed her parents just to have her all to himself. Time wouldn't stop him from targeting the people she loved. And the idea that she could live like this, not for days or weeks, but years, while Brit ran free, started a sizzle of rage inside her that she couldn't ignore.

She glanced up at Conlan. His gray eyes were almost black, intense, focused. He hadn't said the words, but the certainty that he loved her came through every time they touched. He would do anything he had to in order to protect her. But maybe it was time she did the protecting. The need to do something, anything but cower in a corner, bit deep. She'd come out of her corner fighting once; she could do it again.

And if she didn't make it this time?

Searching her lover's face, she knew she wasn't ready to leave him. But if she did? If Brit won?

It was a chance she had to take. She would keep Conlan safe, even if it meant giving up her life. That was loving someone, and Conlan couldn't corner the market on protecting his loved ones.

She cleared her throat, catching the men's attention. "If there's been no activity, what does that mean for me?"

Jack shook his head. "Unfortunately we have to assume you're not safe. Even if he's gone, it's most likely not for good. This level of obsession won't allow him to leave a victim behind." His gaze went distant, as if seeing something she couldn't, as he continued to pace the length of the living room.

Conlan's chin nudged the top of her head as he tracked Jack's progress. "The reality," he said quietly, "is that we have no idea how long this could go on."

Okay. That was it, then. "What about trying to draw him out?"

The words fell like a bomb in the middle of the room.

"What the hell are you talking about, Jess?" Conlan asked as he surged to his feet.

Jack froze in place, staring at her from across the room. "You mean using yourself as bait, don't you?"

Only Gaines didn't respond, and when she glanced his way, she saw in his eyes that this was what he'd been waiting for. The tiniest spark of fear shivered through her determination.

Unable to sit while Conlan and Jack loomed over her, she stood on legs that suddenly felt as strong as cooked noodles. "Yes, bait. What other choice do we have?" *Please come up with something, anything!*

"The only other choice we have is to wait him out, hope we can catch something we haven't already," Gaines said, finality in his tone.

"Which is no choice at all. I can't live in hiding forever."

A strangled laugh pulled her attention to Conlan. Fire blazed in his black eyes. His face was white, sick. "We won't risk you like that. Holbrooke is dangerous; you know he is."

She forced a calm into her voice she definitely didn't feel. "I have to; at some point I've got to get back out there and get on with my life."

"What life?" Conlan demanded. "Because when—not if —he returns, you won't have a life. Jack and I have seen situations like this enough to know that's guaranteed."

Resentment ripped through Jess, coloring her words. "Then what exactly do you suggest, Mr. Expert? I can't live for the next God knows how long, always waiting, wondering when he's going to turn up next, going to destroy something else I love, going to hurt the people I care about. I can't let him hurt you."

Her tongue faltered on the *you*. Fortunately Jack didn't wait.

"It's risky, Jess. There are no guarantees that you'll come out safe on the other side."

"Shut up, Jack. She's not doing it." Conlan's burning gaze held hers as he stalked toward her, his big hands gripping her arms to give her a little shake. "You can't seriously be considering this. It's too—"

"Dangerous?" It wasn't funny, but she laughed anyway. "Right now I can't walk across a parking lot, Conlan. I can't go home to my apartment. I can't visit my friends. I can't go to work. How do I live a normal life hoping the man who was obsessed enough to try to kill me doesn't decide to come back?"

"You'll have security—"

"For how long? Six months? A year? You can't stay with me 24-7. And then what?" How long could she argue about this before her bones shook apart? "He's not going to stop until he gets what he wants. At least this way, we have a chance of catching him and giving all of us some peace."

"No, Jess. No! You can't do this."

She reached up, cupping his cheeks in her shaky hands despite the pinch of his strong grip. Her mouth was dry, her stomach a bottomless pit of knotting anxiety, but she had to convince him. For Conlan, she would do anything to get Brit out of her life and off the streets. "It's never going to stop. This is the only way—"

"No. I won't risk you. I won't let you," he said through gritted teeth. "There's no way in hell—"

"Why not, Conlan? Why?" Her voice came out a low croak, but she forced it to work, forced herself to lay bare everything she felt. "I want a life with you. I want to love you. And yes, it would be utterly fantastic to hole up in this cabin forever and play house and forget the outside world ever existed, but we can't do that. You have a business to run. I have a job. We need groceries and to pay bills and to ride that damn fine Harley you have stashed in the garage because we can't leave the house. I can't ask you to live like that. I won't live like that."

"I would!" Con stared down at her, the desperation she felt reflected in his eyes. "I'd do it forever if it meant you were safe. *I love you*, Jess. You can't make me love you and then do something like this. You can't ask me to risk you. It will tear my heart out."

"It's our only choice."

"You know she's right, Con," Jack said quietly. Conlan rounded on him with a vengeance.

"Shut up! This isn't about the woman you love. This isn't me asking you to put her in the line of fire. You think it hurt when Lee took that bullet? You think watching him slowly disintegrate into a man we didn't know, a man whose every thought was consumed with pain because he lost the woman he loved, was hard? You didn't even have a front-row seat, but you will this time. There wouldn't be a slow descent, either. I wouldn't wait for the enemy; I'd eat my gun if something happened to her, and not think twice about it."

Jess's heart squeezed so hard she couldn't breathe. "Conlan, no."

Conlan turned back to her. "Yes. The only thing that would delay me would be taking that bastard out any way I could." Conlan brought his face down to hers, cheek against cheek, his arms gathering her close with a tenderness that was unbearable. "I'd follow you, Jess. I'd go wherever you are, baby; don't you doubt it."

Jess could feel the shudders coursing through her, through him. Racking their bodies. She rocked him quietly, holding him, wishing with all that was in her that she'd never met Brit, never brought this mess into Conlan's life. But she couldn't regret meeting Con, knowing him, loving him. She would love him through eternity. She just had to find a way to make sure they spent it together, alive. And safe.

"We don't have a choice, love," she whispered in his ear. Conlan's big body shook against hers. Lifting his head, he crushed her to him, cursing as he struggled to accept what they both knew had to be done.

"Shit. Goddamn it, Jack, just...shit."

"I agree," Jack said. His voice was almost as raw as Conlan's.

When Gaines spoke, they all startled. "We will do everything we can to keep her safe; you know that."

"No." Conlan turned, tucking her protectively behind his back. "*We* will do everything to keep her safe. You focus on Holbrooke."

"I can't allow—"

"You can't stop it," Jack told Gaines. "It's our way or nothing."

Gaines eyed the two men as if considering his chances of grabbing Jess and getting out of here alive. Jess could tell him they were nil, but he seemed to reach that conclusion on his own. "We can work something out."

Jack nodded. Conlan's grip on her hips went tight, then

relaxed. Jess laid her cheek in the furrow of his spine, her eyelids slipping closed.

He'd said it. He loved her. Despite what she knew was coming, that knowledge curled up and settled in the deepest part of her soul. This man loved her. Together they were complete.

They would defeat Brit. She wouldn't accept anything else.

That same determination filled Conlan's voice as he gathered her into his arms again. "This has to be done right. Let's get to work."

———

THE BEDROOM WAS silent when he finally entered. They'd planned long into the night, long past Jess going to bed, but he still wasn't happy with what they'd come up with. He didn't think any plan would make him happy; nonetheless... Jack had finally overruled him with a "Nothing's perfect, but we'll make it work," to which Con had responded with a raised middle finger. Jack was lucky he hadn't pulled a gun. Score one for a level head.

He brushed his teeth, shucked his jeans and shirt, and climbed slowly into the bed, trying not to wake Jess. She needed the sleep. Jack was already putting things in motion, laying the Internet seeds that would bear fruit soon. When they woke in the morning, it would be to an unsafe world. He could give Jess one night of peace.

He'd been such a damn fool. Had he really thought, such a short time ago, that he could get close to Jess, share her body and her life, and not want to keep her? Not have her become as necessary to him as breathing? Because that's what she was—and he'd be damned if he figured that out, just to lose her again. Holbrooke's days were numbered; Con guaranteed it.

Next to him, Jess jerked, a near-silent whimper leaving her lips. A nightmare. Con growled at the reminder that, even in her sleep, she wasn't safe. Holbrooke was definitely going to die.

He scooted over. Jess whimpered again. The sound broke the restraints chaining him back.

"Jess."

A sniffle broke the silence.

Then a muffled choke.

Then a soft cry.

Her pain was shredding his gut like a razor. He reached across the bed, into the darkness, and dragged her forcibly to him. Jess startled awake.

"Shh, baby. It's all right."

Her tense muscles relaxed at the sound of his voice. "I was dreaming..."

"I know." Spooning her, he tucked her hips against his crotch, tilted his head down over hers, and kissed the bare skin of her shoulder. "I know. You're okay now."

Jess shuddered. Her head settled lower in the pillow, giving him access to her neck, baring herself to him. "I'm glad you're here," she whispered.

"Me too," he said against her skin.

"I'm scared."

Those two little words ripped his guts out. He clamped his hands together over her belly, right over the spot where his child might grow, if not now then in the future, and prayed his touch would ease her. "Tell me."

Jess drew in a ragged breath. "I know...I know it has to be done, in my head, but—" Another breath. "My body remembers what he did, how much it hurt, how terrifying..." A hard tremor shook her almost out of his arms. "I don't want to go through that again."

And this was why he'd come unglued earlier. He wanted to tell her she wouldn't, but lying wasn't an option, not between them. And as much as he'd try to prevent it, he knew there was a possibility she would get hurt. That was why none of the scenarios they'd run felt acceptable. Anything could happen.

And usually did.

But he wouldn't tell her that either. He'd hope for the best even though the world had taught him not to a long time ago.

He gave her, gave them both, the only reassurance he had. "You are strong, Jess, the strongest woman I know. You can get through anything. I will do my best to protect you."

"I know you will."

He closed his eyes, absorbing the absolute certainty in her voice. "Just remember, no matter what happens, no matter what goes wrong, what he does, I'll come. No matter what."

"No matter what," she whispered. The trust in her words wound around his heart, binding him even more than his promise.

"Jess..." His heart in his throat, Con breathed deep, then placed his lips right against her ear. "I love you, baby. So much. I love you like I've never loved anyone ever before."

Jess twisted around until they were face-to-face. Her eyes glittered in the darkness, the only light he could see. "Say it again."

"I love you." His hand shook as he reached out to tuck the thick fall of her hair behind one ear. "I love you."

"Con—" The word choked off. Her arms slid around his neck, then, "Help me. Help me be strong."

Light glinted off the tears as they sneaked onto her lashes. "Don't cry, baby, please. Not about this. I'll be beside you the whole way." Except their plan meant that wouldn't always be true. Helpless to find the answers they both needed, the answers that would make everything all right, he pulled her tight to him and took her mouth.

The tears kept coming. She sobbed into his mouth, and he took her fear, her pain into his soul. He held her as tight as his muscles would allow, and still it wasn't close enough, secure enough to keep her safe, to make the tears go away. She needed to cry; he'd let her cry. He held her and kissed her and felt his heart swell with love until, as quickly as the tears had come, they stopped, and Jess lay quiet, exhausted, in his arms.

She finally tilted her head up, her breath brushing his neck as she whispered against his skin, "I love you too, Conlan James. So much. Always."

It felt a little too much like goodbye.

Con stole the last word with his kiss, and in the hours that followed, he made sure every part of her was filled completely by him, including her heart.

23

Jess stood at the door to the cabin, feet chilled in the early morning breeze, Conlan's warm arms the only thing keeping the cold at bay. She hated him leaving. It didn't matter how much she told herself he'd be back, how many guards she knew were posted around the cabin and the inlet—she hated telling him goodbye.

"I'll be back in a little bit," he said, his mouth buried at her neck so no one could read his lips. That freaked her out even more, the knowledge that Brit might be out there somewhere, close enough that he could see what Conlan was saying, because that meant he'd somehow gotten around the perimeter Gaines's men had set. He could be inside that line right now, watching them through a scope, feasting on the anticipation of the moment. She squeezed Conlan harder before he could pull away.

Three days. They'd been doing this for three days, not knowing if Brit was watching, if he had even picked up the trail Jack had left not too openly for him to follow. Not knowing if this was all for nothing. While Conlan worried about the men growing complacent, she worried about not getting kidnapped. The point was, after all, for Brit to get close enough to take her so that they could take him. What if he didn't show? What if this didn't work?

What if it did?

"You go to the library," he murmured. Jess nodded. The library contained the entrance to the tunnel, the one only Con, Jack, Gaines, and Jess knew about. The backup plan in case something went wrong and Brit got too close. Her fingers bit into the muscles of Con's shoulders at the thought.

Conlan eased back from her death-like grip. His kiss, however, was unyielding, as if he could imbue them both with confidence with just the touch of their lips. "I'll be back."

"Okay."

Mark, the bodyguard assigned to be with her inside the house, gripped her arm gently and maneuvered her through the front door. Jess had to wonder how Conlan and Jack had managed to corner the market on all the bulky security guards in Atlanta. Nicolas had been big, but Mark was built like a semi. He didn't talk much. After seeing her through the door, he set the house alarm and then watched silently as she set a countdown on her phone. Three hours. It was the only window of time that she was without Conlan each day, long enough for him to drive into town, appear to handle some "work," and drive home. And it terrified her every time.

Gaines had originally suggested that Con follow his normal workday routine, but they'd all agreed Brit would never believe Conlan would leave her alone all day. This was the compromise. Jack worked video surveillance of several points around the cove from the JCL office and kept things there running smoothly during the day. Most nights he came out to the cabin after dark, sneaking in and standing watch while she and Conlan slept. Gaines had three eight-hour shifts of on- and off-duty personnel staking out the woods surrounding the house, blending in, staying hidden so that Brit could "infiltrate" their perimeter to get to her. Though the number of bodies multiplied by half while Conlan was gone, she knew and they knew that this was the most likely time for Brit to make a try for her.

And she was stuck in the house with Mark the Mack Truck.

Two hours and fifty-five minutes.

The sound of shuffling cards came from the entry to the hallway. "Want to play?" Mark asked quietly.

She knew from experience that he could play solitaire for hours. Needing the distraction, she said, "Rummy or poker?"

"Rummy." Mark hadn't been familiar with the game until, in desperation, she'd taken the time to teach him yesterday. Maybe she'd pull out King's Corner today. She hadn't played that since she was a child, but cards seemed to be Mark's go-to distraction, and if they were going to be holed up here at the cabin for days on end, she needed the variety additional card games would provide.

"You set up the game. Coffee?" she asked, already walking toward the kitchen.

Mark shook his head, more of a gentle sway, but followed her into the kitchen instead of going on to the library without her. She poured her second cup of the morning, desperate for the caffeine after three mostly sleepless nights. When she was all played out, maybe she'd take a nap until Conlan got home. It would certainly help pass the time.

Down the hall, inside the book-lined room that

reminded her of cozy afternoons by the fire, Mark dealt the cards, and Jess sipped her steaming coffee. Two hands later, only twenty minutes had passed; she'd won once, Mark once.

She couldn't keep doing this.

"Again?" he asked.

"No thanks."

Mark followed, watching with cautious eyes as she returned her cup to the kitchen sink, then walked back into the living room. The filtered morning sunshine drew her to the back windows. What a revelation that had been, finding out the windows were bulletproof. The walls of the cabin were also reinforced and painted inside and out with a fire-resistance substance. Conlan even had a sprinkler system installed along the perimeter, not to water the nonexistent grass but to douse the woods in case someone started a fire to smoke him out. The man lived a freaky kind of life with so many precautions, except now they were coming in handy, weren't they? He and Jack had even gone to extra lengths to be sure some of those measures were visible; they wanted Brit knowing about them, knowing this wouldn't be easy for him. As Conlan had explained to her, they needed Brit to believe this setup was real.

"Come away from the glass, Ms. Kingston."

Mark's gruff words startled her. She turned, meeting dark blue eyes full of concern despite the safety glass, and didn't grumble as she walked down the hall again. Mark immediately began setting up cards on the coffee table for a game of solitaire. Jess lay down on the well-cushioned couch, feeling fatigue wash over her despite the coffee. A throw pillow in one corner beckoned, and she laid her head on it, pulling the cashmere throw off the back of the couch and cuddling into it. Mark flipped cards, shuffled, and rearranged until he finished the game and started another. He cheated, she noticed. The thought brought a smile as she let the rhythm of his movements send her into sleep.

She awoke to the press of a hard hand against her mouth, a sharp hiss of air filling her ear. Instinctively she fought, desperate to loosen the grip that cut off her breathing and kept her from moving. She clawed and tossed her head and bucked until her panic receded enough to realize it was getting her nowhere. Tilting her head up, she met the cold, hard gaze of her ex-boyfriend.

"Hello, sleepyhead."

Her first reflex was to gag. The only reason she didn't give in was the sure belief that he would make her choke on it rather than let go and risk her throwing up on him.

"Mhmm."

"What was that, little mouse?"

She fought to control the bile rising persistently in her throat, the acid burning the back of her tongue. *Focus. Think.* Where was Mark?

Straining to turn her head, she finally caught a glimpse of the big man in the nearby armchair. His head lolled to the side, eyes closed, a small dart sticking out from the side of his neck. A tranquilizer? Why hadn't Brit shot her? How the hell had he gotten inside in the first place, and where were Gaines's men?

A glance toward the opposite side of the room showed the middle section of the bookcases open, a gaping hole beyond. Brit had found the tunnel.

That answered one question.

The image of several cops lying outside, drugged, unable to report in...the thought of the complete helplessness a tranquilizer would leave her with sparked another round of adrenaline. Clawing, flailing, she gave in to the panic for long seconds. Brit raised his free arm, circling over hers and clamping both of them tight against his ribs. No matter how she moved, nothing worked. What good were Conlan's lessons if she couldn't use them?

Stop! Think! What had Con said to do?

Panic, then get over it. He won't expect you to fight back.

Focus on where he's vulnerable, targets you can reach.

Brit was talking, a low, menacing snarl battering her control. "You didn't think I was going to let you just disappear, did you? You didn't think you could just walk away, pick up some asshole off the street, and fuck him to your heart's content without consequences? You. Are. Mine." Every word was punctuated with a sharp shove of his hand over her mouth, forcing her head to ram into the arm of the couch and crushing her lips against her teeth. "Always. I don't give up what's mine. It stays mine or it dies."

Jess shook her head wildly. "Nnnn—"

She couldn't get the whole word out, but Brit understood. His once-cultured smile was now small, mean as he leaned closer. "Yes. Looks like you're going to have to learn that lesson all over again."

Jess slammed her head forward, into his smothering hand, then back sharply. Brit's grip slipped. Jess opened her mouth and bit down hard.

"Damn it—" A heavy smack hit the side of her face, breaking her grip. Stars shone in front of her eyes. When she opened her mouth to scream, a thick rubber ball took up the space.

God almighty, a ball gag. She didn't know whether to laugh or cry.

Brit had her gagged in seconds. In short order he had a zip tie around her hands. He subdued her so easily, so quickly. How did he know just what to do? How could he think when all she could do was panic?

Practice.

Even as the thought hit her, Brit settled a hand between her breasts, pressing down, a hundred-and-eighty-pound weight she couldn't shake off. He hovered over her, crushing her lungs, and stroked her face where he'd struck her moments before. The tenderness in his touch had her shuddering with fear.

"Don't make me do that again. I'll punish you when the time is right." His hand traveled to her hair, grabbing a handful in a hard, hateful grip. "You won't like it if it comes too early. Be patient."

Forcing herself to breathe through her nose, Jess concentrated on her options to block out the sound of his threats. The satisfaction in his voice as he talked about punishing her was sickening. She would do everything she could not to be taken, even if it meant dying. She'd much rather it happen here and quick than what she imagined Brit had planned for her.

Jess shot her bound arms out to one side of Brit, swinging them out and around, catching his shoulder and shoving him toward her lower body. At the same time she brought her knee up and landed a solid strike to the side of his head. He dropped like a stone. Jess was up before he hit the floor.

Lungs gasping, heart pounding, she ran toward the hall for all she was worth. There had to be a way out, a place to hide, a door she could put between her and Brit. *Go go go go!*

The bedroom loomed to her left. She darted toward it, so close she reached out her hands to grasp the doorknob, but a tackle hit her from behind, taking her to the floor and stealing her last wheeze of air in a single instant. Her head bounced off the door.

"So you learned something from your little lover, hmm?"

What felt like a knee landed hard on her spine. Jess screamed behind the gag.

"You passed our exit, little mouse. Didn't you know that?" The metallic *snick* of a knife opening sounded near her ear. Jess rethought trying to buck Brit off.

"That's right. I think you're going anywhere I say you are, little mouse. Now move."

Brit dragged her up. The library was halfway down the hall, several feet and mere moments away. Brit pulled her inside and slammed the door shut. Dread tightened her muscles until every step was barely a shuffle. She couldn't let him take her down the tunnel. No one outside but Gaines knew it was there; no one would know where to look for her. She couldn't go with him. She couldn't—

The tip of the knife dug into the muscles of her back as she resisted, each movement shooting twinges of pain around her middle, warning her to comply. The first few steps down into the dark were the hardest she'd ever taken, not just because of the threat of the knife, but because of the fear. It scurried through her brain like rats on crack. She couldn't stop remembering, couldn't stop wondering, what would Con do? Would he be able to find her in time? Would he blame himself if he didn't?

Hell no. She was not leaving him with those kinds of scars. She wasn't going to let Brit do that to either of them. She just had to find the right opportunity.

It came about ten steps into the tunnel.

Her foot hit a shallow depression. The misstep shifted her weight forward. Brit's tight grip on her pulled him off balance too. Jess went with the motion, ducking down into a tight ball, allowing Brit's momentum to trip him.

He rolled right over her back.

She was almost to the tunnel entrance when a hand grabbed the back of her shirt. Brit snatched her backward, pulling her off the ground and slamming her spine against his chest. She lifted her feet, letting him take her full weight, but instead of holding her, he spun her around, flinging her to the ground in the direction she'd just come. She kept rolling, desperate to get away.

"No you don't! Come back here, you little bitch!"

He lunged once more, his full weight pinning her to the ground and taking her breath with him. Even as she struggled, his hand came into view, a syringe in his fist, hitting the side of her neck like a cobra strike. Her panicked scream echoed in her head as darkness fell over her.

24

Conlan was halfway back to the house when his phone vibrated in his pocket. Three short buzzes. *Jack.*

"Yeah."

"Con—"

The stress in Jack's voice immediately sent Con's heartbeat into his throat. "Just tell me she's alive."

When Jack remained silent, Con swerved the car onto the shoulder of the road and slammed on the brakes.

"Tell me."

"I don't know. Gaines is looking now."

His grip on the steering wheel went vise tight. Questions tumbled through his head, but he narrowed it down to one. "What's going on?"

"I did some digging into Holbrooke Technologies' current projects. They aren't just working commercial applications; they have government contracts on the books. Top-secret contracts."

Con didn't bother asking how Jack found that out.

"One of those projects just happens to work with high-altitude drones. I just found a purchase order on the same project for ground-penetrating radar, the kind they use in archeological digs. The kind used to find buried artifacts— and tunnels."

Shit. Shit shit shit!

"Gaines has to get her out of there."

"He's doing that— Hang on." Mumbling, a shout, then Jack was back on the line. "She's gone."

"No! Jack, no."

"Yes." Jack went back to the other caller, his words muffled. Con waited, throat desert-dry, until his friend returned.

"He took her out the tunnel?" he asked.

"Yes."

Okay, they couldn't be far. It couldn't have been that long; he'd only been gone two and a half hours. It would be okay.

"Where's Mark?" Con was going to kill the big man; he swore he would.

"Mark's been drugged."

"But he's alive?"

"For now. He was luckier than the men outside the tunnel."

Con squeezed his eyes shut, not wanting to ask. "What happened to the men outside the tunnel?"

"They're dead."

Jesus Christ. "How?"

"It looks like they were drugged as well, but then he slit their throats."

Jess, her neck ringed in red. *Don't think about it. Don't. It's gonna be okay.*

"He took out the cameras too?" No way would Jack miss something this big going down.

"They were hacked and looped. We didn't notice until it was too late. If I hadn't found those files... I underestimated what he could do. After all this time, knowing what— Fuckin'..." Jack's voice faded out, and Con heard a door slam. When Jack returned, the air on the line sounded different, quieter, enclosed. An engine started. "God, Con, I'm so sorry."

It's okay. It's gonna be okay. "Has the tracker been activated?" They'd made sure a tracking bug was sewn into the lining of every bra Jess had. They would be able to track her in real time, even internationally.

Jack paused. "You need to get there as fast as you can."

"Jack, the tracker—"

"She's not wearing it!" His shout rang in Con's ear. "They found her clothes, all of them, in the tunnel."

Fucking— Jesus. He almost didn't get the door open fast enough to throw up. Images of what could be happening to Jess right now, to her vulnerable *naked* body, filled his head. He couldn't lock them away. He'd seen too much violence in his job not to know what it looked like on a human body; the thought of seeing that on Jess, on the body he'd touched and tasted and loved, sent him into another round of heaving and shuddering before he could stop it.

"Con, damn it, get your ass back to the cabin now. I'm right behind you."

He hit the gas before the door was even closed. He didn't know if Jack ended the call; he didn't care. He forced himself back under control, forced the thoughts swirling his mind like a toilet bowl back into submission. Thinking that way couldn't help him or Jess now. Nothing mattered but that she was alive when they found her. That was all. She just had to stay alive.

He wiped his mouth and pushed harder on the gas, speeding around a curve.

It's gonna be okay.

I'm coming, Jess. Hold on.

The thirty minutes it took to pull into his driveway seemed to last forever.

The lights flashing a red and blue warning outside his cabin door threatened to undo him once more. An ambulance, rear doors open, was parked behind several patrol cars. Two body bags, obviously full, lay on the ground in front of the house. As Con parked, paramedics came out the front door pushing a gurney with Mark strapped on, an IV attached and oxygen flowing through a mask. He was still out. Considering his height and weight, he had to have been hit with a major sedative. At the thought of the same stuff pumped into Jess, Con's stomach churned, but there was nothing left to come up.

Gaines's black sedan already waited in the driveway. Jack's 4x4 sprayed gravel just behind Con's car as he rushed to park. His friend was at his door, a steadying hand on his arm, as Con stepped out of the car.

They met Gaines halfway across the yard. "What happened?" Con demanded.

"The lock shows no signs of tampering. We checked the log. It lists an entry ninety minutes ago with your fingerprint."

Fuck. Why he was surprised, he didn't know. His fingerprints were on file after his military stint and forming JCL, though they weren't a matter of public record. Hacking for them seemed like just another link in the chain Hoolbrooke had forged with seeming ease. Tricking the scanner had been just as easy as everything else, for this bastard anyway.

That Con had underestimated his opponent so thoroughly—that he couldn't fathom.

"And your men?"

"Long-range ketamine darts." Gaines ran a hand through his already messy curls, the only betrayal of his emotion. "The knife wounds were clean, no hesitation."

"And totally unnecessary if he'd already darted them," Jack said grimly. "The only reason Mark is alive is probably that Holbrooke needed to reach Jess before she either fought him or got away."

Con tried to take a page from Gaines's book and keep a rein on the panic in his veins. "Any signs that she fought?" *Please say no. Please...*

"There's a blanket half off the couch. My guess is he caught her asleep. Might've drugged her before she even woke up."

God, he prayed so. "Now what?"

"What we need to know is where he might have taken her," Gaines said.

Con could already see the wheels turning in Jack's head. "He wouldn't want to go far. Too much time would cut into his plans."

Conlan didn't even want to consider what those plans might be.

An officer stepped to the front door and called Gaines, who went to get more details.

Conlan rubbed his fist, wishing he could slam it into a wall. He'd never felt so helpless, not during the hundreds of cases he'd work. Not even during the war. If they didn't find Jess soon, she was dead, and they all knew it. Rebecca Wellsley's body guaranteed it. A low growl escaped his throat.

"Easy, man," Jack said, one hand gripping his shoulder

to steady him. "We've got to keep our heads on straight and figure this out. That's the only way to save her now."

"How?" Conlan's voice was high with desperation. "Tell me how, Jack, because right now I'm lost. I love her so damn much."

Jack snorted. "That is fucking obvious, even to me. Come on; let's get your girl back. I've got an idea."

JESS STIRRED. The sandy, metallic taste in her mouth made swallowing hard. Thinking was even harder, but she knew immediately that something watched her, waiting for the first sign of awareness. The sense of evil smothered her. She forced herself to keep her eyes closed, breathing even, trying to hear the slightest move or sound that might tell her where she was.

Where Brit was.

Oh yes, she remembered him taking her.

She hurt. Everywhere. Yet no matter how hard she strained, all she heard was silence. Trying to ease the ache, she dared the slightest move. *Quiet. Quiet.* A zing of panic hit when she came up against rope. A harder pull. Nothing, no give. Her hands and feet seemed to be bound, spread-eagle. Underneath her, crisp cloth and padding told her she was on a platform, probably a bed. The realization added a sour undertone to the current tang in her throat.

A draft of cool air whispered across her skin. Forget hiding; she had to know. She struggled to lift her head, to glance down. What looked like a towel rested across her belly. If it had been tied around her, it wasn't any longer; her breasts and between her legs were bare.

A whimper scratched through her dry vocal cords. What

had he done to her? The instinct to struggle overwhelmed everything else, but no matter how hard she pulled or twisted, she succeeded in nothing but uncovering even more of herself.

Futility swam through her. She lay, listening to the frantic beat of her heart, and remembered seeing one of the *Saw* movies on TV late one night. As she'd watched, she'd wondered if she would panic, caught in a situation like the characters were forced to go through, no way out, no escape, just the inevitability looming over your head. Now here she was, caught in a spider's web with absolutely no choice but to wait and see what horrible things Brit would do to her. The realization brought a slightly hysterical laugh to her lips.

The sound of a door opening across the room had her snapping her head around. Brit. His blond hair and blue eyes looked angelic, even now. He covered the crazy so well, but she knew it was there, lurking in the background, waiting to pounce. That was the evil she sensed, and she knew she could never get rid of it.

"Awake, I see."

Dread flowed through her veins like molasses, but she tried to shut it out. *Keep him talking.* "What did you give me?" she asked hoarsely.

He smirked. "Just a little something to make it less complicated for us to get here. You refused to come along nicely." He moved closer to the bed. "Sedatives are fairly easy to get your hands on if you know where to look."

He'd had the syringe in his pocket; a syringe, not a dart like the one he'd used on Mark. "You knew I would fight."

"Of course I did. I thought you were fun when you huddled in a corner"—a flush swept his cheeks—"but this was even better."

One hand dug in his pocket, and her heart jumped as he pulled out the long black switchblade he'd used at the house, its now familiar *snick* ringing in the air as it snapped open. Silver light reflected off the sharp edge as he twirled it in his hand. "You have been a bad, bad little mouse."

"Stop calling me that." Her voice quivered as anger built. "I'm not yours, and I sure as hell am not a mouse. Not anymore."

He quirked a brow. Another twirl, slow and relaxed. "All the more fun when I beat it out of you."

Slitting her eyelids, she prayed he couldn't see her relief. She had some time—how much, she wasn't sure, but every little bit brought her closer to the possibility of escape.

"For now," he said, continuing to twirl the knife, "I think we do need to talk about your punishment. You disobeyed me, Jess." He stepped closer. The knife mesmerized her, the sight of his pleasure as he stared at her body terrified her— all the more so because it wasn't sexual in any normal sense of the word. There was hunger, yes, but like an animal, a predator, not a lover.

She knew the difference now.

"I told you to stay away from him. I told you, and what did you do? You hid from me." He stabbed the blade toward her face. "Just being seen with you was a sacrifice, all that sniveling, whining, 'oh Brit, I'm not ready,' and you repay me by giving it up for that worthless..." His lips tightened. "I think you need a reminder of exactly who I am."

"Is that what you did to Rebecca?"

A flash of surprise lit his eyes. Brit lifted the knife, bringing the blade to his mouth, and stroked the flat of it across his bottom lip. A bright red bead of blood appeared, and he licked it away. "Ah, Rebecca." Stroke. Stroke. Stroke. "Becca made the mistake of thinking she could leave me.

Hustling off to that Arizona art commune. Do you think I could let that get out, allow everyone to know she was screwing me over? That's not how this works." His voice rose as he punctuated his words with sharp stabs of the switchblade inches from her face. "I'm the one with the power. I'm the one in charge; she belonged to me. She earned everything she got, and so have you."

Brit pushed his knee onto the bedspread and bent close. Jess held her breath as the thin silver blade caressed the exposed skin of her inner arm like a deadly lover. The light of madness shone in Brit's eyes, growing brighter as he watched his toy move.

"Becca loved it when I touched her like this. The slide of the knife, so smooth, so easy."

The urge to struggle, to run flared stronger than the fear of the knife. Jess bucked and twisted, desperate to loose her bonds.

A quick, hard backhand snapped her head to the side. "Be still. You don't want to mess up my art, now do you?"

The first slice near the vulnerable bend of her elbow was a cold shock that morphed quickly into searing pain. Jess heard herself cry out, the sound loud in the hush of the room, filling her ears, mixing with the pound of her heartbeat to drown everything else out. Maybe that was the key. Wouldn't someone notice if she made enough noise? She began to shout, scream, pleading for help, hoping someone might hear and come to see what was happening.

Brit laughed. Crawling over her, he settled his weight on her stomach, adding to the tension on her arms and legs until she thought her joints would separate from their sockets. Her skin shrank away in revulsion as he leaned down and put his mouth at her ear, forcing her to hear him. Forcing her to listen. She couldn't get away.

"Go ahead and scream, little mouse. I like it." He rubbed against her, his erection showing her just how far *like* went. "There's no one but me around to hear your pretty screams."

The slow slices began, one following the other, marching a line of fire up her arm as Jess squirmed and cried. Control was impossible. Escape was impossible. The pain jarred her, sending agony squeezing through every muscle. She struggled to breathe around the tears clogging her nose and throat, the shallow breaths just enough to cry but not enough to scream. And all the while he droned on, his voice like sandpaper along the walls of her mind. "My. Fucking. Mouse. Mine."

Gathering what little courage she had left, Jess lifted her head to stare Brit in the eye. "I can guarantee one thing, you bastard. When I take my final breath, it won't be you I'm thinking about." God no. She wheezed, spoke again, defiance searing the words in her mind. "I will *never* be yours."

Brit roared into her face, striking out with his fist. The punch knocked her head back onto the bed, and she let it stay there as he took up his knife again.

When the cuts became too much and she started to fade out of consciousness, Brit switched to his hands, smearing images, words, lines on her skin. Maybe he'd gone completely over to la-la land by now. Maybe he was just trying to drag the torture out even more. Who knew.

The pain was fogging her mind. She tried to focus, tried to figure out how long she'd been under him, how long she might have left. She couldn't; everything blurred into what seemed like forever. The part of her mind that planned, that wanted to struggle, refused to work. *Have to rest, just a little bit.*

Closing her eyes, she allowed images of Conlan to play like a reel-to-reel movie across the screen of her eyelids. The sight of him as he looked at her over the sunglasses covering his eyes. The laughter when she teased him. The intensity of his desire as he worked to bring them both pleasure. That was what kept her sane. It was only the need to see him again, to touch his face once more, that kept her from giving in. Even when her heart stuttered and she knew she couldn't last any longer, the need for Conlan wouldn't let her go.

Her cries had diminished to low moans, all she could force out while her lungs struggled to function. She heard his hand grasping along the covers, knew he was seeking the knife. When she didn't flinch at the next cut, Brit grunted with frustration and threw the weapon. The clatter as it hit the wrought-iron headboard, then bounced onto the floor, startled her.

The cuts down her legs burned like fire. They were shallow. Probably didn't want her to die too soon. Nick an artery and his fun would be over real quick. At the thought, a barely audible, slightly hysterical laugh escaped.

"What's so funny, bitch?" he snarled, rage contorting his face. There he was, the true Brit. The animal, the...beast... consumed by his growing insanity.

Just like she would be if someone didn't...come... freakin'...soon.

When she just looked at him, refusing to answer, he pressed with excruciating force into the cuts on her stomach. Sizzling shock exploded along her nerve endings, and her body convulsed. Jess fought to hold on to consciousness.

"Is that what you need?"

He slapped her, a wet *splat* in the silence of the bedroom.

"Answer me!" he shouted, spit and sweat flying.

Another slap, this one catching her lip and filling her mouth with blood.

"You need to know who's boss?"

Another.

"Me, little mouse! Me."

Red-faced, veins popping at his temples, eyes wild, he didn't even seem aware of whether or not she responded anymore.

"You."

Strike.

"Are."

Strike.

"Mine."

Strike.

"Do you hear me!"

His hands clamped down on her nose and jaw, forcing them shut. He began to shake her, cutting off her air as he screamed in her face, pressing, pressing. The world narrowed to his crazed eyes.

This is it, then.

To some faint degree, Jess was aware of the pain, the scream of her lungs, the life draining out of her, the sounds of rage filling her ears. But her mind was surprisingly separate, calm. Turned inward. She focused on her love for Conlan, wrapping it around her to muffle the world even further, and found it wasn't sadness that filled her. She had given Conlan all of her, had loved him with all she had, and she knew that love was returned.

She'd seized her chance, and for a little while, she'd had Conlan in her life. In her arms, her body. Her heart.

A last faint sigh escaped as darkness closed in. She'd held on as long as she could, but there was no way to hold on anymore. She submerged herself in the sensation of Conlan's heat warming her, his hands caressing her, his body taking hers, and safe in his memory, she let herself fly free.

25

Con huddled with Jack around a laptop in Jack's crew cab, watching as his best friend worked magic in his efforts to get them a clue. His fingers flew across the keyboard, and page after page of data streamed in front of their eyes. Tax records, it looked like. Con didn't recognize any of the names, but Jack was obviously on to something, so he didn't interrupt with questions. All he could focus on were those fingers, because if he allowed himself to think about anything else, it would be how every minute, every second it took them to find Jess could be seconds she suffered. Hurt. Maybe came closer to death. Con couldn't go there. If he did, he'd break in two.

They had to find her. Soon.

"Got it!"

Jack's triumphant whoop kicked Con's heart into an even higher gear. "What did you get?"

"Land records—family land. Two can play at this game." Jack was intent on the screen, scrolling down to find what he needed. "Damn, these people are slick, but not as slick as me." A predatory gleam filled his eyes as he watched the screen. One more tap and Jack turned the laptop to face Con. "Take a look."

It was a satellite view of a rambling house. Con shot Jack a questioning look.

"A couple of generations ago, the family estate just happened to include a lake house. Great-grandpa might be dead, but his legacy lives on. Care to guess which lake it's on?"

"You're shittin' me?" Could they possibly be that lucky? "How far?" There were hundreds of miles of lakefront property in the area that Holbrooke could easily get lost in.

Jack switched to a map view. "About thirty minutes. East."

The thought of Jess alone for thirty more minutes with Brit Holbrooke made Con want to scream, but he knew it was the best they were going to get.

"And look at this." Jack clicked back on the satellite image of the estate and zoomed in, allowing them to see the surrounding landscape and even the presence of an SUV. A fancy black SUV. "The bastard's so arrogant it doesn't even look like he's changed cars."

Was that— "Is that current?" Con asked.

"Yep." Jack folded the laptop and slid into the driver's seat.

"Should we get Gaines?" His gut told him the fewer people the better, but...

"And have them go in with guns blazing? What do you think the odds are that bastard will take her with him if dying is his only option?"

So Jack agreed with Con's gut. Good to know. He slammed the door of the truck and buckled his seat belt.

While Jack drove, Con dug in the chest bolted in place of what should've been a backseat, pulling out the equipment they would need. They didn't see action on a regular basis, but they were always prepared, a fact for which Con thanked God right now. He suited up, thumping his Kevlar vest hard before strapping on a weapons belt and loading it. He loaded Jack's too, laying everything out for his friend to slip on when they arrived.

Con's cell phone rang. He looked at the screen. "Gaines."

Jack shot him a look. "About fifteen minutes behind us. Go ahead."

Con accepted the call. After Gaines finished cussing him out, Con gave him the address of the lake house. "Right, we'll sit tight and observe. Wait for you."

"I mean it, James. Don't go in there."

"Got it." Con rolled his eyes and hung up. He threw the phone onto the console as Jack took a sharp turn onto a gravel road, fishtailing as he spewed tiny rocks behind them. "We've got orders to go in quiet and observe."

"Of course. What else would we do?"

The two men shared grim smiles. They both knew they weren't waiting any longer than it took to make sure Jess was safe. By the time Gaines arrived, Con hoped to God Holbrooke was beyond anything the Atlanta police detective could do for him.

Twenty-three minutes after leaving the house, Jack parked the truck about a mile down the road from their intended destination, hiding it in a wooded area not far from the security fence that surrounded the Holbrooke family's hidden lake house. Con followed Jack as they made their way along the perimeter, eyes intent and cautious as they closed in on the gate. The lack of security cameras worked in their favor, though the alarm was definitely armed. It took Jack almost ten minutes to deactivate it—ten minutes of sweat and worry. Con reached for the calm he drew on like armor in battle, needing the distance, the ability to judge and react without thought, emotion, but it just wasn't there. Even gunned down and watching his friend die, Con hadn't felt this shattered, this anchorless. Jess was his anchor, and until he got her back safe, calm was impossible.

He'd told her he would follow her. He had, and he would. If she was already gone, the gun in his holster had two uses: one for Holbrooke, and one for Con.

The wooded drive followed the slight hills that helped hide the estate from prying eyes. Jack and Con kept low, the scrub and baby pine trees tugging at their jeans, until they came to the clearing surrounding the house. Con tucked himself into a crouch next to Jack.

"What do you think?" He breathed the words out as quietly as he could.

Extravagant landscaping softened the lines of an austere two-story house that was nothing less than palatial. It sprawled before them, hugging the shore, the front lined with deep bay windows every few feet. Matching double panes marched across the second story, all dark.

"It's quiet," Jack murmured. "No cameras. Even rich people are stupid sometimes." His mouth curled in a quick grin. "Works for me. Need to get closer."

They bent down as they ran, ducking below the windows. The ground sloped quickly around the side of the house. The sparkle of sunlight on water flashed into his eyes, the mossy tang of the lake in his nose reminding him of summer barbecues and July Fourth celebrations. After today he was afraid that smell wouldn't remind him of anything but stomach-churning terror.

They worked their way along the side of the house, cautious. No matter how hard he strained, he couldn't hear even a hint of sound from inside. His heart skipped a beat at the thought that Jess and Holbrooke might not be here after all.

Around the back, they got another stroke of luck—a second-story deck. Underneath, hidden from view of the floor above, was a set of French double doors. Just as Jack reached out to test the door handle, they heard the voice they'd been looking for.

"What's so funny, bitch?"

A sharp, feminine cry followed.

"Jack," Con urged in a harsh whisper, rocking forward on his toes.

"I'm on it." He focused in on the lock, determination in every line of his body.

"Is that what you need? Answer me! You need to know who's boss? Me, little mouse. Me!" The crack of skin against skin sent terror skittering down Con's spine. His heart's demand to get to her hammered against his ribs, became a fire in his brain.

The *click* of the lock releasing sent him surging forward. Jack stood in his way.

"Listen to me, Con." Jack's voice sliced through the blur in his mind, his friend's viselike grip on his shoulders forcing him to stillness. "We have to be careful." He gave a little shake at Con's impatient gesture. "No. Use your brain, not your heart. She needs us to get her out. We don't know what weapons he has, what he's got with him. Stay close and stay down, okay?"

He knew Jack was right, had trained for scenarios like these. *Think! You have to think.*

Con nodded; anything to get into the house. Seeming satisfied, Jack ducked inside, Con right on his heels.

That crazed voice echoed through the house as they

raced to find a staircase. Jack led the way up as quietly as possible, then down the length of the upstairs hall, and came to a hard stop outside the last door on the right—the one above the room through which they'd come into the house. Con could hear Jess whimpering, hear movement, but no more shouting.

God, he had to get in there, had to go in now.

Now.

Jack's body blocked his way. Again.

He turned back to Con quickly, smoothly raising the handgun already in his hands. He mouthed three words:

Together. On three.

Con nodded and tensed his muscles, watching Jack's fingers lift to form the numbers as if in slow motion. One finger. Two.

Another whimper from inside.

Three.

The sight that struck him as the door yielded to Jack's weight would be etched in the recesses of his mind forever. Jess, stretched to her limits on the big bed in the center of the room, her wrists and ankles tied so tight the skin shone white around the nylon ropes. The creamy comforter cushioned her body as if she floated on a cloud—a bloody cloud. Precise slices marched in parallel rows down both arms, her stomach, her legs. *Oh God.* Brit was kneeling on top of her, his hands clenched over her face, a devil intent on the destruction of an angel.

She was silent. Pale. So deathly pale. Her eyes empty. Was she even alive? But the blood still flowed, and though the seconds seemed like an eternity, his ears finally registered a wheezing breath as she fought to get air into her tortured lungs.

He headed for Holbrooke.

Jack was there ahead of him. Even as Brit yanked his head up, attention drawn to the noise, Jack was taking aim, pulling the trigger. Brit jerked in response, blood blooming high on his chest as he fell backward off the bed. The crunch of his head hitting the hardwood floor barely registered as Con rushed to Jess's side.

"Shh, baby, it's all right." He crooned to her over and over, not even sure what he was saying as he worked at the ropes, desperate to free her, desperate to stop that blank stare, to have her in his arms and safe once more.

"Knife," Jack snapped. "Cut the ropes."

Stupid. He retrieved the knife from his belt and sliced through the ropes, freeing Jess in moments.

"This bastard is out for the count."

Con should care about that; he'd thought the need to see Holbrooke suffer would be foremost in his mind. It wasn't. All he could think about was Jess. He knelt next to her on the bed, needing to touch her, but there was so much blood. The reality of what had been done to her—the cuts, the bruises... Con's eyes burned with surging anguish.

My woman. My Jess.

"Conlan!" Her voice was a hoarse whisper, her gaze locking suddenly on his, pleading. The minute he focused on her face, she rolled into his arms, mewling in agony at the contact even as she gripped him like she'd never let go. He cuddled her close, careful, still, and felt his sanity shredding apart.

"Holbrooke's secure." Jack stepped close but didn't touch them. "I texted Gaines to get an ambulance here stat. Let me see her."

He allowed Jack a quick look. His friend grunted and reached for the comforter's edge.

"Keep this wrapped around her. It will stop some of the

bleeding until they can get here." He touched Jess's face, tilting her chin toward him. "Jess, is there anything else?" When she simply stared, he repeated, "Did he hurt you anywhere else?"

Her dazed eyes closed for a single moment, and Con held his breath. Had Holbrooke raped her?

A shake of her head allowed him to breathe again, if shallowly. Jack went downstairs to wait for the ambulance. Con couldn't look anywhere but at Jess.

Jess's tongue slipped out to wet her cracked lips. She whispered his name once again.

"What, baby?"

"I knew you would come."

His tears finally spilled over, their salty taste filling his mouth as he kissed her gently. He made no move to erase them. He didn't care. All he knew was that his heart would have died with this woman, and having her alive was more of a miracle than he'd ever expected. "I love you," he choked out, his face tucked carefully into the hollow of her neck—his favorite spot—as hot droplets fell to her skin. "I love you."

"Conlan." The rasp in her voice broke his heart anew. "I love you."

Gathering Jess closer, he tensed to lift her off the bed.

The roar that echoed off the walls startled them both. Acting completely on instinct, Con dropped Jess back to the mattress and turned quickly. He had only a moment to see Holbrooke, hands bound with the same rope he had used on Jess, both fists clutching a black-handled switchblade, lunging toward them from the other side of the bed. Instinctively Con brought his arm up, blocking the downward plunge of the knife before it could reach Jess. He twisted, grabbing Brit's fists in both of his, and forced the man's hands down and around in a big circle. When knife met skin, he shoved upward—straight into the bastard's heart. A small grunt escaped Holbrooke as Con gave a second small push and twist, embedding the knife to the hilt, before a stream of blood trickled from Holbrooke's lips and he fell back to the floor.

"Shit!" Con rounded the bed, shaking with the rush of adrenaline, and placed his fingers over Holbrooke's nonexistent pulse. Not wanting to take another chance, he felt for breath, any indication that life was still present, but didn't remove the knife. Staring down at the lines of madness on the man's dead face, adrenaline turned to satisfaction and hate. Without remorse he reared back and kicked the dead man in the ribs.

Holbrooke had gotten what he deserved. Finally.

But when he turned to Jess, he knew death would never be enough. Brit Holbrooke had deserved far more punishment than that. Too bad he couldn't die more than once.

Jack hurried through the door as Con lifted Jess against his chest. "Ambulance is on its way up the drive. How is she?"

"Better than he is," Con said.

"He can wait for the second one."

"He won't need it. Let's go." He walked out of the room with the only thing that mattered held tight in his arms.

26

C on was leaning back against the wall outside Jess's hospital room when his dad returned from getting coffee. He reached for a cup and ran a weary hand down his face, trying to scrub away the last twenty-four hours.

Con watched his dad taste the dark hospital brew, then grimace. Like Con, he'd always appreciated good coffee, and neither one of them had gotten "good" since they'd arrived. Con didn't drink, just held the cup in his hand.

Ben jerked his chin toward Jess's closed door. "Everything okay?"

"Yeah. The nurse is checking her bandages now and making sure everything is still stable. She threw me out."

Ben grunted, then choked when he attempted another sip of the acrid coffee. Con pounded his back absently.

"Thanks," Ben said drily. "So that's how Jess is doing. How about you? You okay?"

Meeting his dad's gray eyes was like looking into a slightly faded mirror. Right now all the concern Con felt for Jess stared back at him.

ELLA SHERIDAN

"No." *God, no.* His mind was brittle with lack of sleep and the continuing fear that this whole thing wasn't quite over yet. "I'm not okay." He screwed his eyelids shut tight and whispered, "She's not okay. She tries to sleep, but she keeps jerking awake, crying, wheezing when there's no reason to wheeze. She's reliving it, and there's nothing I can do to stop it—again." It was as if Brit's torture returned in cycles to torment them both.

His dad stepped close, the solid warmth of his body standing shoulder to shoulder with Con giving him back some small semblance of calm.

"It's my fault, Dad. I never should have left her at the house. I never should've taken so long to admit...I love her." His muscles started a steady tremor as he breathed out his greatest shame to the only person he would ever trust to hear it. "I did this to her."

Ben reached down to set his cup on the floor. When he stood back up, he took Con's shoulders in a tight grip. "Look at me, Son."

Con wanted to, but it was impossible. His gaze weighed a thousand pounds, and he couldn't lift it off the floor. He couldn't face this man who'd raised him, who'd taught him to protect those around him, while he carried the knowledge that he had failed the one person that mattered most.

Ben's voice went hard, that drill-sergeant voice he'd learned in the military much better than Con had. "I said look at me."

Con's eyes snapped up to meet his father's.

Ben leaned in, nose to nose, eye to eye, just as he had so many times during Con's childhood when he'd wanted his son to truly hear him. "Do you blame me for what Delia did?"

He jerked in his father's hold. "Absolutely not."

"Why not? For the first few years, before you could talk, I didn't really recognize what was going on. She was bitchy, sure, but... Once you were older, part of me just didn't want to admit I could have been so wrong about someone I thought I loved. Someone who claimed to love me. I tried to protect you as best I could, but I should've walked away and taken you with me instead of upholding vows that obviously didn't mean diddly-squat to her. You got hurt, even though I tried to prevent it. Why don't you blame me?"

Conlan ran his fingers through his tangled hair in frustration. "You loved me. You did the best you could."

Ben dropped his head, still and silent for a moment before he raised it once again to meet Con's eyes. "You love her. You did the best you could." He squeezed down on Con's shoulders. "You love this woman; I see it in your eyes. You gave her the chance to stop that bastard even though you didn't want to risk her. The fact that it didn't end up the way either of you thought it would isn't on you or her; it's on Holbrooke. You did the best you could," he said again, staring Con down.

When Con opened his mouth to argue, his dad stopped him with a shake of his head. "It's the truth, Son. It will take time, but you have to decide—do you want to hang on to that guilt and let it eat you up inside, destroy everything you could have with Jess, or do you want to focus on the woman lying in that bed in there who needs you, loves you, and forgives you?"

Staring into his father's eyes, Con struggled with the choice. He didn't want to forgive himself, didn't know how Jess ever could. Then he remembered what she had said as she lay bleeding out onto that damn white comforter.

"I knew you would come."

No blame, only love. Acceptance. Peace. She was his peace. For her, he would work through anything.

"I love her so much, Dad." He was unashamed that his voice cracked on the final word.

"I know, Son. I know. And that's what's gonna get you through."

Jack showed up a few minutes later to find them side by side, a matching set of bookends squatting against the wall, sipping bitter coffee to try and stay awake. As he tipped his head back to look at Jack, Con wondered if the weariness dragging at him showed as much on him as it did on his best friend. Con wasn't sure if he wanted to hear what the cops had found. Jack had run interference, dealing with the local PD and Gaines when he'd finally arrived, straightening out the mess they had left in the bedroom, and generally making sure no one bothered them as they worked to get Jess stable. Con knew they hadn't gone easy on Jack. Having his friend guard their backs anyway meant more than Con would probably ever be able to express.

"Hey, man," he said.

"Hey, yourself." Jack jerked his chin toward the still-closed door to Jess's room. "How's she doing?"

"We're out of the woods. Doc says they'll keep her here another couple of days just to be sure. Too many stitches to count, several pints of blood to replace what she lost, concussion, broken rib..." He could go on, but Jack had seen her in that bedroom; he got the idea.

"Hm."

Jack's shoulders hunched forward, but the single syllable was all they got out of him. Con didn't know whether to be worried or grateful. He assumed there was news, and he certainly didn't want to hear they were putting his ass in jail, but he could really use a few hours with only good things coming their way. When Jack motioned for them to step over to a lounge area across the hall, he figured the scale was tipping away from his chances of getting those dreamed-of hours.

"What'd Gaines find at the lake house?"

"Nothing good. Enough to make me wish the bastard could die all over again." The brown of Jack's eyes was almost as dark as Conlan's, his anger was so fierce. "We couldn't find evidence at his apartment because it was all stashed at the family vacation spot. Pictures, journals, computer files, clothing and other stuff from Jess's apartment. Videos."

"Videos?" Ben asked.

Jack shook his head. "Apparently our boy had a penchant for filming his girlfriends—and ex-girlfriends. With and without their knowledge."

Now it was Con's turn to growl. "Jess?"

The short jerk of Jack's head confirmed his fears.

"Don't worry, Con. She never has to know—thanks to you." A malicious grin lit Jack's face. "No trial."

Ben grunted his approval.

"Anyway, it will be a while before it's all sorted out. There'll probably be a grand jury hearing into the shooting, but Gaines doesn't expect anything to come of it." He rubbed a finger over one dark brow. "Final coroner's report on Rebecca Wellsley crossed Gaines's desk. Injuries very similar to Jess's."

Con swayed, and Jack reached out to grasp his biceps, keeping him upright. "It's okay. She's safe. She'll recover."

Con prayed Jack was right.

"Conlan!"

The high, feminine voice caused Con to wince.

"Conlan James!"

He stepped reluctantly back into the hall, not wanting Cris to disturb Jess before he could get her calmed down. The little blonde dynamo almost overshot him as he came through the door, then pivoted to grasp his arms in a shaking death grip.

"Where is she?" Cris demanded.

"Hon, calm down. It's gonna be all right." Steven came to a stop next to Con and reached out to wrap his wife in a one-sided hug. "Remember the baby."

Cris growled but subsided. The fiery look she shot Con said it all.

"She's with the nurse right now," Con told her. "She's gonna be fine."

"How bad?"

Con glanced at Steven, then down to Cris's stomach. The weight of worry made his shoulders ache. When Jack and his dad stepped up to flank him on each side, the support brought profound relief.

This wasn't his problem alone. They all loved Jess, and they would all take care of her.

"How bad?" This time Cris's words verged on teary.

He sighed. "Bad enough they'll keep her a few days."

"Oh." She started to cry. Con looked to Steven in sheer panic.

Cris's husband soothed her, murmuring nonsense and rocking her back and forth until the tears finally subsided. "Hormones," he said, but his eyes were moist as well.

Cris punched her husband in the belly. Good thing she was tiny; her reach didn't allow for much momentum. But when she turned back to him, the hurt in her eyes made Con flinch.

"What the hell happened?" she asked.

Con drew the couple back into the lounge before Cris's rising voice could disturb the entire hospital. They settled onto the various mismatched couches and worn chairs around a circa-1970 plywood coffee table, and Jack diplomatically stepped in to describe the basics of what had happened, keeping the worst details out of it. Con was grateful for that; his ability to deal with the never-ending questions had dwindled to nil. His heart and mind were focused on one thing—getting back to Jess as soon as the nurse would let him.

When Jack finished, Cris turned to Con, her cheeks red from the return of tears, her eyes reflecting her pain clearly. "You said you'd keep her safe."

That hurt. But all he said was, "I know."

Cris's gaze seared him, searched for the truth, for understanding. "So you killed the bastard, huh?"

Con squared his shoulders. "Yeah."

"Good." She looked back at Steven, then turned to Con again. "When can I see her?"

Mentally kissing any time with Jess goodbye for the next little while, Con reached out to help the woman to her feet. "Let's go talk to the nurse."

Two hours later, Jess's slitted gaze watched the door close behind her friend. Con could see the glaze in her eyes, though crying, recriminations, explanations—hell, practically wailing and gnashing of teeth, not that he blamed Cris one bit—had been endured by her in a silent haze of drugged calm. Even when he gathered her hand in his, he could feel the slight shivering of pain-induced shock no medicine could completely dissipate. Still her fingers clamped down hard on his as he sat carefully on the edge of the bed.

He locked eyes with her and ducked down to her level,

inches apart—his dad's trick—before whispering, "I love you, Jess."

For a moment she didn't move, didn't react, almost as if the words hadn't registered. "What?"

"I love you."

"I know."

No change of expression, no other words. Con's heart squeezed hard. He leaned even closer until his lips rubbed against hers. "I love you, Jess. Wanna hear it again?" he asked, tilting his mouth into a smile. "Me too. I love you. I do."

"I do to—"

A soft kiss silenced her. When her mouth relaxed and let him in, he stroked inside gently, careful of her split lip, letting his actions do the talking. Wet warmth greeted him, a soft moan caressed his tongue, and Con reveled in the knowledge that his woman was here, safe, in his arms. He loved her. All the rest was in the past—only the two of them counted. The two of them and their future.

Pulling back, Jess stared up at him. Dark purple shadows underlined her eyes, and a faint pink streak of blood marred her temple. Reaching out to wipe away the offending reminder, he said the only words that mattered right now, maybe ever. "Come home with me, baby."

Two white lines appeared between her brows as she frowned. "For now?"

He shook his head, smiled, and whispered against her mouth before kissing her once more, "For always."

27

The shadows lengthened on the deck as Jess sat, journal in hand, trying to decide what she needed to say tonight. Cicadas raised a chorus that blended with the wind over the lake, the rustle of leaves, and the distant hoot of an owl. The night's song soaked into her bones, relaxing her muscles, emptying the day's tension onto the wooden slats of the deck's floor. She imagined it seeping down, through the cracks, to disappear into the healing soil. This place, this life had become hers in a way she'd never imagined it could be a few short weeks ago. For that she was ever grateful.

This ritual with pen and paper and nature's song was her nightly solace. And it helped. Her therapist had said it would, and Jess found that excavating her soul cleansed her in a way nothing else could. Four weeks she'd been home from the hospital, and still she woke with sweat-soaked gasps on a regular basis, clutching her throat, feeling the cold pain of metal sliding through her skin—but no longer every night, several times a night, like she had when she first came home.

Home. She smiled into the twilight and thought about that word, about what she'd finally found here. But it wasn't really the lake house itself that was her home; it was the man who lived here.

Light filtered through the French doors behind her, passing over one shoulder, setting the heart-shaped diamond on her left hand into flame. Her period had come and gone, confirming the hospital's negative results, and yet last night, right here on this deck, Conlan had dropped down on one knee, a suspicious sheen in his eyes, and officially asked her to marry him. To share his life, be his happiness. It was all she'd ever wanted. All she could have hoped for. A small, late-summer wedding by the water, just family and friends, and a future as bright as the sun that would shine down on their special day.

There was only one thing marring that happiness, holding her back on her road to recovery.

He hadn't made love to her.

And whose fault is that, Jess?

Night after night, cuddled into his warm body, her thin T-shirts and his flimsy cotton boxer briefs no barrier at all to the erotic swelling of his shaft against the small of her back. His body fairly vibrated with the need to take her, but he held back.

He knew she wasn't ready. And he was right.

It tore her apart inside, this feeling of being frozen in time, caught between the horror of the past and the freedom of the future. Limbo was hell, and it was wearing on her very last nerve. She was tired of it, tired of letting Brit control a part of her he'd never had to begin with. A part that was and always had been Conlan's alone: her body.

Her therapist's words from their session this morning filtered through her mind. *"You know in your head you're safe, that your attacker is dead and gone, but it may take time for your body to truly believe it."*

For the first couple of weeks, Conlan had treated her as if she were fine porcelain, touch her and she might break. It wasn't until she'd thrown a pillow at him in frustration that he'd gotten the picture. She hadn't wanted to be treated like porcelain then, and she didn't want to be treated that way now. So why was she allowing herself to hold back?

If she was honest, she knew why: because she was afraid. She was afraid to lose what she now had. She feared having Conlan on top of her and being able to see nothing but Brit. Having his hands caress her and feel nothing but the knife and fists. Having him whisper words of love and hear nothing but the dying roar of hate.

Oh yes, she was afraid.

What if...what if...what if... It was a revolving door blending her brain into a froth of foaming panic that would never stop until she made it stop, until she took control away from Brit's dead hands and put it back where it belonged—into hers and Conlan's. Life was never easy, and it sure as hell was never guaranteed. Things would go wrong, she would be afraid, but with Conlan by her side, she could face anything. They'd done it before, four long weeks ago, and now they would do it again.

Jess timed it just right, waiting until she sensed Conlan behind her, making one of his frequent trips to the door to check that she was still okay. Deliberately she slid to her feet to stretch, careful not to look back at him. She stood for a moment staring into the dark beyond the railing, trying to breathe through the racing of her heart. It wasn't working.

Just hurry up and get it over with.

Gathering her courage and the hem of her oversize sleeping T-shirt, she drew them both up, slow and sure, until courage steadied her and her shirttail rested just under her breasts. Conlan's gasp reached her clearly as her bare bottom came into view. It was the husky sound of that choked air that helped her over the last hurdle, and she pulled the shirt the rest of the way off, dropping it to the deck at her feet as she turned, head down, and gave him his first full glimpse of her body in a month.

She was shaking apart. Everything inside her screamed to grab her shirt, cover her scars. She couldn't bear to look at them except in the privacy of the bathroom behind a securely locked door, and every time they made her cry. Con deserved better. He deserved someone whole. He—

She couldn't do this. She reached for the cloth.

The *squeak* of the doorknob turning froze her. Light spilled out onto the deck. She closed her eyes, sick, knowing Con could see every faint, raised scar across her limbs, her stomach, the hot wash of tears from the fear she couldn't shake, no matter how much she wanted to. No matter how much her heart told her he didn't care. He loved her.

But what if—

And then he was there, right in front of her. Jess's mouth went desert dry. She watched, fists clenched, as Con's gaze traveled over her face, her neck, down her body, her stomach. He traced her limbs with a careful look that missed nothing—and what she saw reflected back at her wasn't disgust or revulsion. It was heat. Desire. Love.

His love gave her back her confidence.

His gaze gave her back her strength.

His kiss, when it came, gave her everything inside him, nothing held back, and demanded the same from her. Jess could do nothing but comply. Brit couldn't have her anymore. Con deserved every last part of her, and he was going to get it. Now.

Con ravaged her mouth. He licked and probed and suckled, he nipped and thrust, and the moans that filled the air —both his and hers—blended with the song of the night perfectly. He didn't touch her anywhere else; he didn't have to. Her body quickened for him, and when he finally released her, she moaned for more.

He didn't wait. Placing his hands on the railing on either side of her hips, he bent slightly, aligning himself with her breasts, and sucked one taut nipple into the warm cavern of his mouth. Pressure built on the hardening tip, matching the pressure building between her legs. His hunger overwhelmed her; his need soothed her. It was as if he'd been waiting on that single indication of her readiness to let loose the restraints holding back the explosive desire that had existed between them from that first mutual spark in the coffee shop, and finally that time was here.

A soft *pop* sounded as Conlan released her, allowing the heavy globe to bounce gently under his devouring stare. He took the other, sucking and sucking until her breath roared like a freight train and she could barely hold back the need to climb his body and demand what she so desperately missed. She twisted, writhing, begging without words for more, but his hands stayed on the railing and his mouth refused to stop.

"Conlan, please."

He broke the suction with a grin. "That's what I wanted." He returned to her breasts, nipping the sensitized tips, and Jess surged up onto her toes, her body and words begging in unison. Conlan chuckled, the sound deep and satisfied.

But he made no move to take her. Instead he shifted, turning his gaze to the silky white, ravaged skin of her arm. He slid his tongue across each line he encountered, starting at the delicate ridge of her wrist and working his way up. The tenderness in each touch buckled her knees.

Hard hands grasped her bottom, lifting, supporting, holding her immobile for his attention. "You're not going anywhere, baby. Now be still and let me work."

He didn't stop. The slight muscle of her biceps received his attention, the curve of her shoulder. The firm ridge of her collarbone. Every lick soothed and excited, and frightened and thrilled her. She wanted him to stop, wanted to hide the signs of the past from his eyes, his touch. But she also wanted it to continue, to have Conlan brand her flesh with a power stronger than any knife could ever wield, to mark her flesh and her heart in a way that was only possible with him—because she loved him. When he bent to her opposite wrist and started the journey all over again, she knew he would succeed. Her body belonged to him just as his belonged to her, two parts of a whole, and the past and the pain and the scars could never erase that. She tilted her head back, closed her eyes, and reveled in the pleasure of his touch.

With a final suck on the sensitive flesh of her neck, a suck she was certain left a visible mark, Con slid his hands from the railing, down her body, and knelt at her feet. His tongue worked its magic over every inch of her scar-striped legs, replacing fear with so much hunger she couldn't help but shake. Sweat trickled from the nape of her neck as heat enveloped her. Pleasure built. Moisture pooled at the apex of her thighs. Her nipples throbbed with the need for attention, and still Con worked. He didn't pause, didn't hurry. And Jess didn't flinch.

Until he lifted his mouth to the soft curve of her stomach.

The feel of his tongue against the deeper scars etched

into her skin, the cuts Brit hadn't held back on, was more than she could handle. A whimper escaped and echoed through the trees. She didn't want to be ugly to him.

"Shh," Conlan whispered, voice dark and knowing and determined. "You're mine."

She hunched, feeling like she'd taken a punch to the stomach. Those words, the hated words Brit had shouted at her, the ownership he'd taken, rang in her ears. She heard them, felt the blows, the slimy sense of evil. "No!"

"Yes." Conlan stood, his steady hands coming up to cup her face. "You are mine, Jess."

Her breath hitched on a sob. "I can't— I..."

Conlan kissed the tears from one cheek, then the other. "You are mine. Hear me; hear my voice. Feel my love in every fiber of your being."

"I-I... Conlan..."

"You are mine." He whispered the words along her skin, trailing them down the long line of her neck, washing the scars with his breath. "You are mine," he murmured against the underside of one full breast, then the other. "These are mine." He sucked each softening nipple, bringing them back to rigid life. "And this is mine," he said with a soft kiss over her pounding heart.

"You're mine, Jess. Now say it."

His mouth returned to her breast, tugging the desire from deep inside her. She wanted to comply, wanted to give him as much as he was giving her, but her tongue tangled around the words, a heady cry escaping instead.

A sharp tug on her nipple. "Say it."

His mouth slid down to her belly, her scars. She tried, even opening her mouth to obey, but her revulsion was too strong, slowly stealing the red-hot passion from her body and leaving her ice-cold in its wake. The words stuck in her mind, overpowered by pain and shame. She wanted to run, to hide, to never have started this in the first place.

The opposite nipple received its punishment for her disobedience.

"Jess." Conlan unleashed was a force of nature, commanding, conquering. This was the man who had ridden into view on a gleaming black Harley and changed her simple life into something far richer. This was the man who had taught her about a world of heat and need she'd never known existed, who had earned her trust, her love. Her name in his deep voice ruled her, crowding out everything else. All she could think of was pleasing him.

Another stinging bite. She moaned.

"Say. It."

He slicked his tongue across the deepest scar, just under her left breast, not once, but over and over again. His nose nudged her nipple. Tingles of pleasure shot through her, and just when she thought she couldn't take any more, two long fingers snaked between her legs and speared her wet channel, driving deep.

She sucked in a breath. She knew what he was doing. Until she destroyed that sense of ownership that lingered on her skin, on her soul, she couldn't be free. And in order to do that, she had to say it out loud.

She'd never belonged to Brit, no matter what games his words had played with her mind. She belonged to herself, and she chose to give herself to Conlan. Only him.

"I'm..."

Another lick, another thrust, another demand. She swayed beneath his touch.

"I'm...yours."

"Whose?"

"Yours."

His fingers pushed forward, rubbing rigid circles along her G-spot. Jess bore down on them as something in her soul snapped free. "I'm yours, Conlan. Only yours." She shook, this time in pleasure, riding his fingers and the thumb that pressed hard on her clit. "I'm yours." She drove her hands into his thick black hair and gave herself up to the heat he created. "Yours. Yours!"

Her reward was as effective as her punishment. Conlan dropped back to his knees, and before she could guess his intentions, his mouth had replaced his thumb and he was pushing her over the edge into climax.

Her entire body convulsed, shuddering with satisfaction. "I'm yours, Conlan. And you're mine. Always."

His lips came back to hers, hot and needy, carrying the essence of her satisfaction, and she savored it, savored him.

Always.

————

Did you enjoy *TEACH ME*? If so, you can leave a review at your favorite retailer to tell other readers about the book. And thank you!

For news on Ella's new releases, free book opportunities, and more, sign up for her monthly newsletter at ellasheridanauthor.com.

Before you go...

Jack has seen love in Con and Jess. Now he wants a woman of his own. Don't miss his story:

TRUST ME

Southern Nights 2

VENGEANCE CONSUMES HER LIFE. Love would risk it all.

Maddie Baker has spent years seeking vengeance against the abuser who destroyed her life. When her search leads her to a small town outside Atlanta, she learns of another missing teenager. Nothing will stand in the way of her mission, including a jackass of an ex-soldier who reawakens emotions best left to die.

Jack Quinn learned to recognize trouble in the Marines, and he sees it in Maddie the minute he lays eyes on the pretty, sexy bartender. Her secrets may be hidden deep, but secrets are his specialty, and peeling away her barriers only makes him want her more. He'll do whatever it takes for her to trust him, with her body and her heart.

Staying hidden kept Maddie safe, but the search for justice brings her into the open and face-to-face with her treacherous past. Risking her life is one thing, but risking her heart is another. In both, she must trust Jack to lead her —and pray they both come out alive.

Buy your copy of TRUST ME at your favorite retailer today!

Continue to the next page to read the first chapter!

CHAPTER 1

Jack Quinn hit the heavy wooden doors that led into the Halftime Bar like a runaway train on the downside of a mountain. Even the hard slam didn't help his frustration. His muscles swelled with it, his skin so tight it could burst. He wished it would so he could finally get rid of the feeling that he wasn't at home in his own body.

He didn't recognize himself anymore, and deciding what to do about it was a drive pushing him closer and closer to the edge. Tonight might just tip him over.

The crash of music against his senses as he crossed the uneven planks of the floor into the darkened interior of the country bar was a welcome reprieve. The beat pounded in his head, his body, matching the adrenaline-laced rhythm of his heart and telling him he wasn't alone in his need to pound something. Preferably his best friend, Con.

The minefield of dancing couples was lighter than usual tonight. Jack didn't swerve; he made his own path straight to the bar. Anyone in his way could take one look at his face and see they needed to be the one to move aside. They moved. He saved a civil nod for Taylor, the tall blonde wait-ress who so often served him, as she wove her way through the tables on the far side of the dance floor. Most of them were empty, save a few clustered around the three high-defi-nition TVs hanging along one wall.

Ignoring everyone else, Jack zeroed in on his favorite barstool, the one that should have the shape of his ass tattooed on its surface considering how much time he'd spent on it lately. The stool was the only one positioned where the long mahogany bar top took a sharp turn into the wall. The short span on that end and the wall at his back meant no one shared his space while allowing him to see everyone and everything around him. His guard could stand down and he could relax for just a little while.

Maybe. If—and that was a big-ass *if*—he could stop wanting to punch Con just one time. But then Jess would complain about her pretty-boy husband's black eye, and Jack wouldn't hear the end of it for a while.

He sighed as he sat on his stool. Probably wasn't worth it after all.

"You're early, Jack. Run out of asses to kick? People to intimidate?"

Jack grunted at the big bruiser of a man making his way down the bar toward him. John, Halftime's regular bartender, had the shoulders of a defensive lineman, foot-ball pads and all. Except he wasn't wearing any. Jack some-times held his breath as he watched the man maneuver behind the bar, waiting for one wrong turn to throw John against a shelf and send bottles of liquor and glasses crashing to the floor. Tonight he flicked a bird in John's general direction as payment for the sarcasm and pretended interest in a couple of women preening at one corner of the dance floor.

Yeah, he was in a pissy mood. That wasn't unusual lately. Didn't mean Con had the right to send him home like a little kid. Time off wasn't going to help.

John laughed as he stopped in front of Jack. "If you're needing to relieve a bit of tension, they're probably up for it," he said, nodding toward the two women. "Pickings are otherwise slim tonight."

"I bet." Shirts a bit too tight, a bit too small, makeup a bit too heavy for the eyelashes batting his way. Not out of their early twenties, he'd guess. Way too young for him, especially tonight. Even at their age, he hadn't felt as young and innocent as they looked; he sure as hell didn't feel it now, at thirty-four.

Besides, quick and dirty and meaningless wasn't what his gut churned for. He'd seen the real thing now, every time Con and Jess were together—hell, every time the man said something about his wife or even thought about her, it seemed—and Jack had a bad feeling that meaningless wasn't going to do it for him anymore. If he had a sweet something waiting at home for him like Con did, Jack wouldn't have to be told to go home; he'd rush there voluntarily. But he didn't. Work was all he had, and if he wanted to put in extra hours to avoid the silence his house practically throbbed with? That was his choice, not his best friend's, business partner or not.

The best friend who was currently at home, probably curled around—or inside—his wife's warm body, while Jack was stuck with the occasional one-night stand or a not so satisfying handjob. Jack was damn jealous, not of Jess but of Jess and Con's relationship. No wonder he was spending so much damn time at the neighborhood bar.

He needed a life. A hobby. A dog.

Jesus, he was losing it.

His expression must've given his answer, because John snickered. "Didn't think so. What'll ya have?"

"The usual."

John nodded. Twisting to look over his shoulder, he yelled, "Maddie, Sam Adams."

"Who's Maddie?"

John turned sideways, showing what his bulk had hidden up till now. Jack glanced down the long service area behind the bar and almost swallowed his tongue.

A woman. A blonde woman, but not the same kind of blonde as the waitress, Taylor. This woman had a straw-colored mane, thick enough it almost didn't fit in the claw clip holding it in a graceful twist at the back of her head. Spikes stuck from the top of the clip to fall along the sides, pointing to the creamy curve of her ear as she bent her head to focus on the frosted glass she was filling at the tap. A slender neck led to a body encased in a tight white T-shirt and short black vest. The clothes silhouetted her tucked-in waist and a sexy strip of bare skin above Levi's he would swear were painted on. And boots; God, he had such a thing for boots on a woman. And this woman wore them with the ease of longtime use, confirmation that balancing on them was second nature. One look at those boots and his dick shot straight up and strained in her direction as if she were true north and he was a compass.

Damn.

"Roll your tongue back in your head," John told him, laughter tangling with the words.

Jack glanced at the bartender, over at the woman, back to John. Swallowed. "Right."

John shrugged, and his easy smile widened. "I had the same reaction. Heck, every red-blooded male that's walked through the door since she was hired Monday has had that reaction. She is something."

"Damn straight."

The towel resting on the new bartender's shoulder slid off, landing with a *plop* on the ground. She bent to grab it.

Both men groaned.

The woman glanced over her shoulder.

John startled, actually blushing. Jack kept looking, appreciating the view from the front as much as the back when the new bartender stood to face them. She had a sweet body with curves in all the right, mouthwatering places.

"Can I help you gentlemen?" she asked, interrupting his reconnaissance. Jack met her eyes, a brown so dark he couldn't tell iris from pupil, though the narrowing of her eyelids might've had something to do with it too. Her lips were tight, pressing together in a way that made him want to tug them apart with his teeth.

The brittle edge to her expression had him narrowing his eyes too. His mama had taught him manners, even if she hadn't insisted on them for herself, but it wasn't like he was leering. He believed in appreciating what was before him; nothing crude or ugly about that. Most women he knew basked in the attention.

And maybe you're getting a bit too arrogant, dickhead.

He answered her look with a wry smile of his own.

The dish towel got a toss into the nearby hamper as the new bartender made her way toward them, Jack's lager in hand. John tucked himself against the back wall so she could make her delivery.

"Maddie, this is Jack."

"Nice to meet you." Jack extended his hand to shake, the

anticipation of touching her forcing his erection harder against his zipper.

Down, boy.

Maddie shoved his beer into his hand. "You too."

Her voice was feminine, husky, arousing. Which was a ridiculous thought, because she didn't sound like it was nice to meet him. John sniggered. Jack ignored him, bringing the cold glass mug to his lips.

The deep, earthy bark of hops settled in his nose as he took his first drink, but his eyes stayed on Maddie's. She didn't back down, didn't blush, just raised a brow and stared right back. Why in hell did that make him so hot?

When he set the beer on the bar, Maddie nodded toward it. "All right?"

"Absolutely, darlin'," he said, the endearment slipping out automatically.

The eyebrow got higher. "Good."

He kept staring as Maddie returned to her end of the bar. The spikes of hair sticking up from her clip bounced with every step. Jack imagined his fingers fisting the long length, holding her still for him. Taming the shrew, so to speak. He had not a single doubt that she'd be feisty as hell. Yeah, he'd definitely like to get his hands in that hair.

John's laugh sliced through his sexual haze. He shot the bartender a sharp look. "Shut the hell up."

John laughed harder.

Jack opened his mouth—to say what, he didn't know—but an angry bellow cut him off. The trailing cry followed, high-pitched and feminine, had every muscle in Jack's body tightening. His beer hit the counter and he was off his seat long before the motion registered.

Maddie was faster, and she was closer to the chaos than he was.

Jack watched in slow-motion fascination as the small bundle of angry woman hit the hinged half door marking the end of the bar at a full-out run. She didn't even pause at the impact, just kept on going, across the uneven floor in those heeled boots, through the tabled area to the edge of the dance floor. He gained on her as the fight came into view.

One of the waitresses, Elena, struggled in the grip of a burly, obviously angry drunk, tears on her pale cheeks. She whimpered in his hold as her skin whitened around the fist enclosing her fragile wrist.

"I told you I want another. Now go get it, you little slut!"

Jack heard the waitress's muffled gasp in response as she shook her head no.

"Yes," the man shouted, shaking her in his grip.

Maddie closed the last three feet of distance between herself and the drunk with no hesitation, stepping right into his space. Jack's heart leaped into his throat, a warning rising to just behind his teeth...

Maddie gripped the drunk's thumb where it rested atop Elena's arm, one finger on the bottom joint and one sliding right up underneath—perfect positioning—and shoved back hard. The move forced the man to release his hold or have his thumb broken. He chose release.

"Ow! Damn bitch," the man growled, reaching with his other hand to make a grab for Maddie now.

"Bitch is right," she muttered, her voice rough with menace and a thread of satisfaction that had all of Jack's senses screaming to alert. She twisted to the side, slipping the drunk's hold easily. On the back swing, she clasped her hands together in a firm grip and used them as a brace to shove her elbow up toward the drunk's face. The three-inch heels on her boots allowed her to hit him square in the nose, which promptly gave way. Blood spurted in a crazy arc.

The whole thing took seconds. Jack watched, stunned, as the man's head fell back, as droplets of blood landed on the smooth expanse of Maddie's face. For a single moment the image of an equally beautiful blonde, long hair bloody and tangled as she cowered in a corner, hit him in the gut. And then the moment was gone and he was in arm's reach of Maddie and her drunk opponent.

"That's it." With a growl of his own, Jack grabbed the bartender around the waist and moved her bodily away from the attack, subduing her kicks and struggles easily with his six feet four inches of military-trained muscle. Maddie bucked in his arms, her head hitting his collarbone. Pain shot across his shoulder, and the hold on his temper, the one he usually kept with barely any effort at all, snapped in two.

"Stop!" Planting her firmly on the ground out of the way, Jack whipped her to face him. Wild eyes latched on to his, her face going red with impotent anger. He gripped her biceps before she could explode into violence. Maddie twisted her arms, trying to slip his grip the same as she had the drunk's, but he was ready for her and clamped down tighter, giving her a little shake. "Maddie, stop."

Her name seemed to register, but the anger was still there. One side of those full lips lifted in a snarl. Jack allowed every ounce of command he possessed to shine from his eyes, using attitude as much as strength to subdue her. Only when Maddie sank back on her heels did he let go.

"Stay!" His pointed finger told her where, though the way her mouth dropped open and the stunned look on her face assured him he only had moments to work before her surprise wore off and she came after him again.

Moving quickly toward the bellowing drunk now holding his bloody nose, Jack gripped the man's thick neck and pushed him onto the dance floor. The man pulled away with a loud grunt, swinging a shaky fist in the general direction of Jack's chest. Batting the hand away like a pesky fly, Jack twisted one burly arm behind the man's back, using it as a lever to frog-march him across the room.

"Don't," he warned as the man struggled in his grip. "I've got no problem fucking you up, asshole, and trust me, you won't enjoy it."

A carrot-topped head appeared through the crowd of onlookers. Troy, Halftime's bouncer, forced his way over. "Jack, no beatin' up the clientele. I told you that before."

Snorting at the man's sarcasm, Jack gave his prisoner another shove. "Not me. Blondie." He jerked his head in the direction where he'd left the new bartender. "This guy's drunk, and I'm pretty sure his nose is broken."

"She's got good aim," Troy said, eyeing the injured man. "Guess that'll teach you, huh, Bernie?"

"Dat bitch broke my node!"

"Yeah, yeah." Troy grimaced before taking Jack's place behind Bernie's back. "I might break something else if you don't come quietly, so come quietly."

"But—"

Troy gave the man's wrist a slight twist, forcing him up on his toes. "Quietly, I said."

Jack stayed where he was a moment, watching the pair exit the heavy double doors out front, trying to calm the fire of adrenaline racing through his veins, to get ahold of the fear that had threatened to choke him when Maddie grabbed Bernie's hand. To get the hot desire that had flooded him as her firm ass pressed against his cock under control. He inhaled, held the air for a count of ten, then let it out. Did it again. When he got the emotion down to a hard simmer, he turned back to the little troublemaker.

Maddie's position as she bent over to examine Elena's bruised wrist showcased her mouthwatering backside in a way that did absolutely nothing to calm him down. He circled the pair. "What the hell were you thinking?"

Her head jerked up, innocent eyes meeting his squarely. *Innocent, my ass.* "What?"

"You heard me," he gritted out through his teeth.

"Yeah, I did." She straightened, only to turn her stiff back on him, murmuring to the waitress once more.

"You didn't answer me."

"I don't answer dumb questions," she threw over her shoulder. Draping an arm around Elena's slender shoulders, Maddie urged her toward the kitchen. Halftime's owner, Tommy Ray, came rushing to meet them, his face a mix of displeasure and concern.

"What happened, girl?"

"Bernie," Elena said. She cradled her wrist in her opposite hand.

"Damn."

"Yeah, and now his nose is broken," Jack said sourly. "Troy's handling him."

Bushy black eyebrows rose in unison above Tommy Ray's dark gaze. "How did his nose get broken?" He eyed Elena's tiny stature uncertainly.

"Her." Jack nodded toward Maddie. "You got yourself a bundle of surprises behind your bar, Tommy Ray."

Tommy Ray looked to Maddie this time, surprise and a hint of amusement mixing with the concern. "Maddie?"

Jack clenched his fists, his entire body tense.

Maddie shrugged. "I saw Elena needed help, and I helped."

"You were reckless and damned lucky, you mean. I just don't get what you were thinking." The chaos in Jack's mind roughened the words to a rumble.

"What were you thinking? You were right behind me, jackass."

Jackass. Clever. He glared. "I'm trained for this. Most people at least hesitate."

She scoffed. "Not likely. No one's getting hurt on my watch if I can help it."

"Look—"

"Jack," Tommy Ray warned.

That cocky blonde eyebrow lifted in his direction. Again. "Who the hell are you, anyway?" Maddie asked. "My keeper?"

"It looks like you need one." He was not going to yell. He would not lose it that far. No matter how fast he felt his control slipping through his fingers. No matter how calm, cool, and condescending she looked. No matter how damn good she'd felt against him, and how much his body raged to jerk her against him again and take all this aggression out on her full lips and generous curves.

Not gonna happen.

Maddie leaned forward, mere inches separating him from her sweet breath. "You wish."

"Damn it!" Jack snarled.

Elena's shoulders began to shake with laughter. Tommy Ray rolled his eyes. "Now, children..."

Maddie squared off with Jack, the heels of her boots barely bringing her height to his shoulder. Her eyes blazed. "You can take your opinion and shove it up your—"

"Enough." Tommy Ray stepped between them, or at

least his rounded belly did. He pointed a finger at Maddie. "You've got drinks to make. Get back behind the bar. And next time"—he lowered those caterpillar brows at her —"call Troy. That's what he's here for."

Jack rocked on his heels and watched her stalk back to her station. He waited, ignoring the sweat trickling between his shoulder blades, while Tommy Ray sent Elena to the kitchen for an ice pack before turning back to him.

Jack shifted to keep Maddie and the bar in his sight. "Who is she, Tommy Ray?"

"New girl. John's needin' more time for his classes; she needed a job. It seemed like a good trade. She knows her stuff behind the bar."

"And in front of it too, looks like. Or thinks she does." He could still feel her glare burning through him. "Where's she from?"

"Don't know. Doesn't matter." The stubborn look on his friend's face said that was all he would share. It could be all the man knew. It wouldn't be the first time Tommy Ray had taken in a stray puppy with no paperwork. Jack's friend didn't care as long as she could do the job. So why did Jack care?

"I'd keep an eye on her. She's a firecracker waiting to go off, and you know what kind of damage that can do."

The other man laughed. "Yeah, I sure do. Too hot to handle, at least for an old guy like me." He patted his burly chest and turned serious. "I'll have Troy keep an eye on her, but if she can handle Bernie, she'll do fine."

"Tommy Ray—"

The man held up one huge paw. "You know I don't allow any trouble around here, Jack. I run a clean bar; otherwise you and a bunch of others wouldn't come here. But I'll keep an eye out."

Jack watched his friend head back to the kitchen instead of letting his gaze turn back to the bar. *Me too.*

Grab TRUST ME at your favorite retailer today!

———

"Ms. Sheridan writes suspense that grabs you and won't let go."
~ Tea and Book

ABOUT THE AUTHOR

Born and raised in the Deep South, Ella Sheridan spent years telling herself stories before finally writing her own. Romantic suspense, paranormal romance, sexy contemporaries—she can't seem to stick to just one. Her goal in life is to finish every series she begins (if only she'd stop adding new series so that would be possible!).

Now Ella calls North Alabama home. Spending time cuddling with her sweet tabby, Oliver, is her number one priority, followed closely by writing, working, and writing some more. You can find her online at her website, ellasheridanauthor.com, or the social media sites below.

For news on Ella's new releases, free book opportunities, and more, sign up for Ella's newsletter at ellasheridanauthor.com. Or join Ella's Escape Room on Facebook for daily fun, games, and first dibs on all the news!

Made in the USA
Columbia, SC
29 April 2024